FURTHERMORE

A TERRIBLY BRAVE AND DANGEROUS DECISION

"What's it like?" she whispered. "Furthermore?"

Oliver looked away, but not before Alice saw a flash of nervousness flit in and out of his eyes. "There's a reason we don't talk about it," was all he said.

Alice gasped, finally understanding.

"Oh, Oliver," she said. "Is it dangerous? Has Father gotten himself into trouble?"

Oliver turned to face her, determined now. He nodded at the box between them. "Are you willing to find out?"

Alice looked into the box and the tiny door it held. She thought of fear and she thought of courage; she thought of home and hope and the chance for adventure.

She thought of Mother.

Mother, who wouldn't miss her; three brothers, who never knew her; and Father, who always loved her.

Alice had nothing left to lose and an entire father to find.

There it was: For the very second time, she knew what she was meant to do. So she reached inside and turned the knob.

ALSO BY TAHEREH MAFI

Shatter Me

Unravel Me

Ignite Me

Whichwood

FURTHERMORE

FURTHERMORE

TAHEREH MAFI

PUFFIN BOOKS

PUFFIN BOOKS
An imprint of Penguin Random House LLC
375 Hudson Street
New York, New York 10014

First published in the United States of America by Dutton Children's Books,
an imprint of Penguin Random House LLC, 2016
Published by Puffin Books, an imprint of Penguin Random House LLC, 2017

THE LIBRARY OF CONGRESS HAS CATALOGED THE DUTTON CHILDREN'S BOOKS EDITION AS FOLLOWS:
Names: Mafi, Tahereh, author.
Title: Furthermore : a novel / by Tahereh Mafi.
Description: New York, NY : Dutton Children's Books, an imprint of Penguin Random House, [2016] | Summary: "Twelve-year-old Alice Queensmeadow, with the help of her friend Oliver, travels through the dangerous, magical land of Furthermore in order to rescue her missing father and prove her own magical abilities"—Provided by publisher.
Identifiers: LCCN 2015044898 | ISBN 9781101994764 (hardback)
Subjects: | CYAC: Fantasy. | Magic—Fiction. | Missing persons—Fiction. | Adventure and adventurers—Fiction. | BISAC: JUVENILE FICTION / Fantasy & Magic. | JUVENILE FICTION / Social Issues / Friendship. | JUVENILE FICTION / Family / General (see also headings under Social Issues).
Classification: LCC PZ7.M2695 Fu 2016 | DDC [Fic]—dc23 LC record available at https://lccn.loc.gov/2015044898

Puffin Books ISBN 9781101994771

Printed in the United States of America

1 3 5 7 9 10 8 6 4 2

Edited by Julie Strauss-Gabel
Design by Theresa Evangelista

For Ransom, forever

Once upon a time, a girl was born.

It was rather uneventful.

Her parents were happy enough, the mother glad to be done carrying it, and the father glad to be done with the mystery of it all. But then one day they realized that their baby, the one they'd named Alice, had no pigment at all. Her hair and skin were white as milk; her heart and soul as soft as silk. Her eyes alone had been spared a spot of color: only just clinging to the faintest shade of honey. It was the kind of child her world could not appreciate.

Ferenwood had been built on color. Bursts of it, swaths of it, depths and breadths of it. Its people were known to be the brightest—modeled after the planets, they'd said—and young Alice was deemed simply too dim, even though she knew she was not. Once upon a time, a girl was forgot.

AND SO IT BEGINS

The sun was raining again.

Soft and bright, rainlight fell through the sky, each drop tearing a neat hole in the season. Winter had been steady and predictable, but it was quite poked through now, and spring was peeking out from underneath it. The world was ready for a change. The people of Ferenwood were excited for spring, but this was to be expected; they had always been fond of predictable, reliable sorts of changes, like night turning into day and rain turning into snow. They didn't much care for night turning into cake or rain turning into shoelaces, because that wouldn't make sense, and making sense was terribly important to these people who'd built their lives around magic. And squint as they might, it was very difficult for them to make any sense of Alice.

Alice was a young girl and, naturally, she was all the things you'd expect a young girl to be: smart and lively and passionate about any number of critical issues. But Alice was also lacking a great deal of something important, and it was this—her lack of something important—that made her so interesting, and so very unusual. More on that soon.

◆

The afternoon our story begins, the quiet parts of being alive were the busiest: wind unlocking windows; rainlight nudging curtains apart; fresh-cut grass tickling unsocked feet. Days like this made Alice want to set off on a great adventure, and—at almost twelve years old—she'd very nearly figured out how to fashion one together. The annual Surrender was only a single pair of days away, and Alice—who was determined to win—knew it was her chance to set sail for something new.

She was on her way home now, occasionally peeking over her shoulder at the glittering town in the distance. The village square was undergoing no small transformation in honor of the upcoming festivities, and the clamor of instruction and construction rang out across the hills. Alice jumped from flagstone to flagstone, her face caught in the rainlight glow, her hands grasping for a touch of gold. The town's excitement was contagious, and the air was so thick with promise Alice could almost bite into it. She smiled, cheeks appled in delight, and stared up at the sky. The light was beginning to spark and fade, and the clouds were still hard at work weaving together, breaking and building as they had been all week. One more day of this, Alice thought, and everything would change.

She couldn't wait.

She'd moved on to the main road now, a dirt path flanked by green. She held tight to her basket as neighbors passed, nodding hello and waving good-bye, happy to have remembered her clothes today. Mother was always bothering her about that.

Alice plucked a tulip from her pocket and bit off the top. She felt the petals pressing against her tongue; she could taste the velvet, the magenta of it all. She closed her eyes and licked her lips before biting into the stem. Not quite green but brighter, more vibrant; there was a song in that color and she could feel it singing inside of her. She bent down to greet a blade of grass and whispered, *Hello, me too, me too, we're still alive.*

Alice was an odd girl, even for Ferenwood, where the sun occasionally rained and the colors were brighter than usual and magic was as common as a frowning parent. Her oddness was evident even in the simplest things she did, though most especially in her inability to walk home in a straight line. She stopped too many times, wandering off the main path, catching deep breaths and holding them, too selfish to let them go. She spun until her skirts circled around her, smiling so wide she thought her face would break and blossom. She hopped around on tiptoe, and only when she could stand it no longer would she exhale what wasn't hers to keep.

Alice would grow up to be a wildflower, Father once said to

her. A wildflower in flowing skirts, braided hair dancing from head to knee. She'd always hoped that he was right, that maybe Mother had gotten it wrong, that Alice was never meant to be such a complicated thing with all these limbs and needs. She often wanted to plant herself back into the earth to see if she'd grow into something better this time, maybe a dandelion or an oak tree or a walnut no one could crack. But Mother insisted (the way she often did) that Alice must be a girl, and so she was.

Alice didn't like Mother very much. She found her a bit old and confusing, and didn't like the way Mother worried about walls and doors and the money that put them there. But Alice loved Mother, too, in the way that children did. Mother was soft and warm, and Mother's smiles came easily when she looked at Alice. Anger and tears, too, but those Alice never cared for.

Alice gripped her basket tighter and danced down the road to a song she found in her ear; her toes warmed the earth, and her hair, too heavy for her head, tried to keep up. Her bangles mimicked the rain, simple melodies colliding in the space between elbows and wrists. She closed her eyes. She knew this dance the way she knew her own name; its syllables found her, rolled off her hips with an intimacy that could not be taught.

This was her skill, her talent, her great gift to Ferenwood. It was her ticket to greatness. She'd been practicing for years and years and was determined that it would not be for nothing.

It would not b—

"Hey there! What are you doing?"

Alice startled. Something tripped and fell, and she looked around in dismay to realize it had been her. Crumpled skirts and silent bangles, the rainlight gone from the sky. She was late. Mother would be upset again.

"Hey!" The same voice as before. "What are you—"

Alice gathered her skirts and fumbled in the dark for her basket, reaching blindly as panic set in. Don't talk to strangers, Mother had always said—especially strange men. *Being afraid meant it was okay to forget your manners. If you're afraid, you never have to be nice. Do you understand?*

Alice had nodded.

And now Mother was not here and she could not explain why, exactly, but Alice was afraid. So she did not feel the need to be nice.

The stranger wasn't much of a man at all, it turned out. More like a boy. Alice wanted to tell him very firmly to go away, but she'd somehow gotten it into her head that being quiet meant being invisible and so she prayed that her silence would somehow make him blind, instead of louder.

Unfortunately, her wish seemed to work on both of them.

The sun had folded itself away and the moon was in no hurry to replace it. Darkness engulfed her. Alice's basket was nowhere to be felt or found.

She was very worried.

Suddenly Alice understood all about being worried and she promised herself she would never judge Mother for being worried all the time. Suddenly she understood that it is a very hard thing, to be afraid of things, and that it takes up so much time. Suddenly she understood why Mother rarely got around to doing the dishes.

"Does this belong to you?"

Alice turned just a bit and found a chest in her face. There was a chest in her face and a heart in that chest and it was beating quite hard. She could hear the pitters, the patters—the blood rushing around in ebbs and flows. *Don't be distracted*, she told herself, begged herself. *Think of Mother.*

But, oh.

What a heart.

What a symphony inside that body.

Alice gasped.

He'd touched her arm, so, really, she had no choice but to punch him. Her bangles were helpful in this regard. She punched and kicked and screamed a little and she wrenched her basket from his hands and she ran all the way home, out of breath and a little excited, so glad the moon had finally decided to join her.

Alice never did get to tell Mother her story.

Mother was so upset Alice was late that she nearly bit off her daughter's hands. She didn't give Alice a chance to explain *why* her skirts were dirty or *why* the basket had broken (only a little bit, really) or *why* her hair was so full of grass. Mother made a terrible face and pointed to a chair at the table and told Alice that if she was late one more time she would knot her fingers together. Again.

Oh, Mother was always threatening her.

Threatening made Mother feel better but made Alice feel bored. Alice usually ignored Mother's threats (*If you don't eat your breakfast I will whisk you into an elephant*, she once said to her, and Alice half hoped she really would), but then one time Alice took her clothes off at the dinner table and Mother threatened to turn her into a *boy*, and that scared her so dizzy that Alice kept on her outerthings for a whole week after that. Since then, Alice had often wondered whether her brothers had been boys to begin with, or whether they'd just been naughty enough to deserve being tricked into it.

❖

Mother was unpacking Alice's basket very carefully, paying far more attention to its contents than to any of her four children sitting at the worn kitchen table. Alice ran her hands along its weathered top, the bare boards rubbed smooth from years of use. Father had made this table himself, and Alice often pretended she could remember the day he built it. That was silly of course; Father had built it long before she was born.

She glanced toward his place at the table. His chair was empty—as it had grown accustomed to being—and Alice dropped her head, because sadness had left hinges in her bones. With some effort she managed to look up again, and when she did, she found her brothers, whose small forms took up the three remaining chairs, staring at her expectantly, as though she might turn their tunics into turnips. On any other occasion she would've liked to, had she been so inclined, but Mother was already quite mad and Alice did not want to sleep with the pigs tonight.

Alice was beginning to realize that while she didn't much like Mother, Mother didn't much like her, either. Mother didn't care for the oddness of Alice; she wasn't a parent who was predisposed to liking her children. She didn't find their quirks endearing. She thought Alice was a perfectly functional, occasionally absurd child, but on an honest afternoon Mother would tell you that she didn't care for children, never had, not really, but here they were. (There were plenty of nice things Mother had said about Alice, too, but Mother was never very good at making sure she said those things out loud.)

Alice picked out a blossom from her dinner and dropped it on her tongue, rolling the taste of it around in her mouth. She loved blossoms; one bite and she felt refreshed, ready to begin again. Mother liked dipping them in honey, but Alice preferred the unmasked taste. Alice liked truth: on her lips and in her mouth.

The kitchen was warm and cozy, but only halfheartedly. Alice and Mother did their best in the wake of Father's absence, but some evenings all the unspoken hurts piled high on their plates and they ate sorrow with their syrup without saying a word about it. Tonight wasn't so bad. Tonight the stove glowed lavender as Mother stoked the flames and tossed in some of the berries Alice had collected. Soon the whole house smelled of warm figs and peppermints and Alice was certain that if she tried, she could lick the air right out of the room. Mother was smiling, finally content. Ferenberries always succeeded in reminding Mother of happier times with Father, of days long ago when all was safe and all was good. The berries were a rare treat for those lucky enough to find them (they were a fruit especially difficult to procure), but in Father's absence Mother had become obsessed. The trouble was, she needed *Alice* to find the ferenberries (I'll explain why later), and Alice always did, because life at home had been so much better since the berries. Alice had been late and she'd been lazy, messy and argumentative, but she had never not come home with the berries.

She almost hadn't tonight.

Alice always felt Mother was using her for the berries; she knew they were the only medicine that helped Mother's heart in Father's absence. Alice knew Mother needed her, but she did not feel appreciated; and though she felt sad for Mother, she felt more sorry than sad. She wanted Mother to grow up—or maybe grow down—into the mother she and her brothers really needed. But Mother could not unbecome herself, so Alice was resigned to loving and disliking her just as she was, for as long as she could bear it. Soon, Alice thought, very soon, she would be on her way to something better. Something bigger. The seasons were changing in Ferenwood, and Alice had waited long enough.

She would win the Surrender and she would show Mother she could make her own way in the world and she would never need a pair of stockings again. She would be an explorer! An inventor! No—a painter! She would capture the world with a few broad strokes! Her hand moved of its own accord, making shapes in her honey-laden plate. Her arm flew up in a moment of triumph and her paintbrush fork flew from her hands only to land, quite elegantly, in her brother's hair.

Alice ducked down in her chair, the future forgotten, as Mother came at her with a ladle.

Oh, she would be sleeping with the pigs tonight.

MORE

CHAPTERS

THIS WAY

The pigs weren't so bad. They were warm and shared their straw and made little pig noises that helped Alice relax. She pulled her only two finks from her pocket and snapped one in half, saving the other, and suddenly the pigs smelled of fresh lemons and glass apples and soon there was nothing at all to be bothered by. The night was warm and fragrant, the sky sneaking through a few broken boards in the roof. The twinkles looked merry enough, but the planets were the true stars tonight: bright spots of color seducing the sky. Six hundred and thirty-two planets dotted Alice's upside-down vision, spinning their bangles just as she spun hers.

Her two arms were bangles and bangles from elbow to wrist, her ankles similarly adorned. She'd collected these bangles from all over, from most every market in every neighborhill she'd ever climbed into. She'd traveled the whole of Ferenwood after Father left, knocking on door after door, asking anyone and everyone where he might've gone.

Anyone and everyone had a different answer.

All anyone knew was that Father took nothing but a ruler when he left, so some said he'd gone to measure the sea. Others said the sky. The moon. Maybe he'd learned to fly and had forgotten how to come back down. She never said this to Mother, but Alice often wondered whether he hadn't planted himself back into the ground to see if maybe he'd sprout taller this time.

She touched her circlets of gold and silver and stone. Mother gave her three finks every month and she always spent one on a bangle. They weren't worth much to anyone but her, and that made them even more precious; Father had been the one to give her the first bangle—just before he left—and for every month he stayed gone, Alice added another to her collection.

This week, she would have thirty-eight altogether.

Maybe, she thought, her eyes heavy with sleep, her bangles would help Father find her. Maybe he would hear her looking for him. She was sure that if he listened closely, he would hear her dancing for him to come home.

And then she rolled over, and began to dream.

Now, while our young Alice is sleeping, let us make quick work of important details.

First: The magic of Ferenwood required no wands or potions you might recognize; no incantations, not really. Ferenwood was, simply stated, a land rich in natural resources, chief among them: color and magic. It was a very small, very old village in the countryside of Fennelskein, and as no one ever went to Fennelskein (a shame, really; it's quite lovely in the summers), the people of Ferenwood had always kept to themselves, harvesting color and magic from the air and earth and building an entire system of currency around it. There's quite a lot to say on the history and geography of Ferenwood, but I shouldn't like to tell you more than this, lest I spoil our story too soon.

Second: Every citizen of Ferenwood was born with a bit of magical talent, but anything more than that cost money, and Alice's family had little extra. Alice herself had never had more than a few finks, and she'd always stared longingly at other children, pockets full of stoppicks, choosing from an array of treats in shop windows.

Tonight, Alice was dreaming of the dillypop she would purchase the following day. (To be clear, Alice had no idea she'd be purchasing a dillypop the following day, but we have ways of knowing these things.) Dillypops were a favorite—little cheekfuls of grass and honeycomb—and just this once she wouldn't care that they'd cost her the remainder of her savings.

It was there, nestled up with the pigs, dreaming of sugar, skirts up to her ears and bangled ankles resting on a nearby stool, that Alice heard the voice of the boy with the chest.

He said something like "hello" or "how do you do" (I can't quite remember), and Alice was too irritated by the interruption to remember to be afraid. She sighed loudly, face still turned up at the planets, and pinched her eyes shut. "I would not like to punch and kick you again," she said, "so if you would please carry on your way, I'd be much obliged."

"I can see your underwear," he said. Rudely.

Alice jumped up, beet-red and mortified. She nearly kicked a pig on her way up and when she finally managed to gather herself, she tripped on a slop bucket and fell backward against the wall.

"Who are you?" she demanded, all the while trying to remember where she'd left the shovel.

Alice heard a pair of fingers snap and soon the shed was full of light, glowing as if caught in a halo. She spotted the shovel immediately, but just as she was crafting a plan to grab it, the boy offered it to her of his own accord.

She took it from him.

His face was oddly familiar. Alice squinted at him in the light and held the sharp end of the shovel up to his chin.

"Who are you?" she asked again angrily. Then, "And can you teach me how you did that just now? I've been trying to snaplight for years and it's never worked for m—"

"Alice." He cut her off with a laugh. Shook his head. "It's me."

She blinked, then gaped at him.

"Father?" she gasped.

Alice looked him up and down, dropping the shovel in the

process. "Oh but Father you've gotten so much younger since you left—I'm not sure Mother will be pleased—"

"Alice!" The perhaps-stranger laughed again and grabbed Alice's arms, fixing her with a straight stare. His skin was a warm brown and his eyes were an alarming shade of blue, almost violet. He had a very straight nose and a very nice mouth and very nice eyebrows and very excellent cheekbones and hair the color of silver herring and he looked nothing at all like Father.

She grabbed her shovel again.

"Impostor!" Alice cried. She lifted the shovel above her head, ready to break it over his skull, when he caught her arms again. He was a bit (a lot) taller than her, which made it easy for him to intimidate her, but she wasn't yet ready to admit defeat.

So she bit his arm.

Quite hard, I'm afraid.

He yelped, stumbling backward. When he looked up, Alice hit him in the legs with the shovel and he fell hard on his knees. She stood over him, shovel hovering above his head.

"Goodness, Alice, what are you doing?" he cried, shielding his face with his arms, anticipating the final blow. "It's me, Oliver!"

Alice lowered her shovel, just a little, but she wasn't quite ready to be ashamed of herself. "Who?"

He looked up slowly. "Oliver Newbanks. Don't you remember me?"

"No," she wanted to say, because she'd been very much looking forward to hitting him on the head and dragging his limp body inside for Mother to see (*I've protected the family from an intruder!* she'd say) but Oliver looked so very scared that it wasn't long before her excitement gave way to sympathy, and soon she was putting down the shovel and looking at Oliver Newbanks like he was someone she should remember.

"Really, Alice—we were in middlecare together!"

Alice considered him closely. Oliver Newbanks was a name that sounded familiar to her, but she felt certain she didn't know him until she noticed a scar above his left ear.

She gasped, this time louder than before.

Oh, she knew him alright.

Alice grabbed her shovel and hit him in the legs so hard his snaplight broke and the shed went dark. The pigs were squealing and Oliver was squealing and she chased him out of the shed and into the night and was busy telling him to never come back or she'd have her brothers eat him for breaksnack when Mother came into the yard and announced she was going to cook *her* for breaksnack and then *Alice* was squealing and by the time Mother caught up to her, Oliver was long gone.

Alice's bottom hurt for a whole week after that.

Alice's evening had left her in a foul temper.

She'd woken up this morning with the smell of pig fresh in the air, straw sticking to her hair and poking at her toes. She was angry with Mother and angry with Oliver and one of the pigs had licked her face from chin to eyeball and, good-grief-and-peanut-pie, she very desperately needed a bath.

Alice shook out her skirts (stupid skirts) as best she could and set off for the pond. She was so preoccupied with the sorts of thoughts that preoccupied an almost twelve-year-old that even a perfect morning full of rainlight couldn't soothe her.

Stupid Oliver Newbanks—she kicked a clump of dirt—had the gooseberries to talk to her—she kicked another clump—no good ferenbleeding skyhole! She scooped up a handful of dirt and threw it at nothing in particular.

Alice hadn't seen Oliver Newbanks since he told the entire class that she was the ugliest girl in all of Ferenwood. He went on and on about how she had a very big nose and very small eyes and very thin lips and hair the color of old milk and she thought she might cry when he said it. He was wrong, she'd insisted. Her nose was a nice nose and her eyes were quite lovely and her lips were perfectly full and her hair looked more like cotton flowers but he wouldn't listen.

No one would.

It was bad enough that Father had left, bad enough that Mother had become a prune of a person, bad enough that their life savings consisted of only twenty-five stoppicks and ten tintons. Alice had been having a rough year and she couldn't take much more. Everyone had laughed and laughed as she stomped a bangled ankle, furious and blinking back tears. She'd decided that perhaps she'd leave more of an impression on Oliver if she spent all her finks pulling off his ear and making him eat it in front of everyone. *That will teach him to listen to me*, she thought. But then Alice was kicked out of school because apparently what *she* did was worse than what *he* said, which seemed awful-cruel because mean words tasted so much worse than his stupid ears and anyway, Mother has had to home-teach her ever since.

Alice was starting to understand why Mother might not like her very much.

Alice sighed and gave up on her skirts, untying the ties and letting them fall to the grass. Clothes exhausted her. She hated pants even more than she hated skirts, so on they stayed, as long as Mother was around. It was indecent, Mother had said to her, to walk around in her underthings, so Alice decided right then that one day she would grow a pair of wings and fly away. Were it up to Alice, she would've walked around in her underthings forever, barefoot and bangled, vanilla hair braided down to her knees.

She pulled off her blouse and tossed that to the ground, too, closing her eyes as she lifted her head toward the sun. Rainlight drenched the air, bathing everything in an unearthly glow. She opened her mouth to taste it, but no matter how desperately she'd tried, she never could. Rainlight did not touch the people, because it was made only for the land. Rainlight was what put the magic in their world; it filtered through the air and into the soil; it grew their plants and trees and added dimension and vibrance to the explosion of colors they lived in. Red was ruby, green was fluorescent, yellow was simply incandescent. Color was life. Color was *everything.*

Color, you see, was the universal sign of magic.

❖

The people of Ferenwood were all born with their own small spark of magic, and the food of the land nurtured that gentle flame of their being. They each had one gift. One great magical talent. And they would perform this magical talent—a *Surrender*, it was called—in exchange for the ultimate task. It was tradition.

❖

Alice opened her eyes. Today the clouds seemed puffed into existence, exhalations from the mouth of a greater being. Soon the clouds, too, would rain, and Alice's life would thunder into something new.

Purpose.

She would be twelve years old. This was the year.

Tomorrow, she thought. *Tomorrow.*

She let herself breathe, casting off the Oliver Newbankses of the world, casting off the pain Mother had caused her, casting off the pain Father had caused them, casting off the uselessness of three entire brothers who were far too small to be of any help when help was needed most. So what if she wasn't as colorful as everyone else in Ferenwood? Alice was just as magical, and she'd finally have the chance to prove it.

She picked up a fallen twig and tied its bendy body around her neck, pinching it together with her thumb and index finger as she hummed a familiar song. Eyes closed, feet dancing their way toward the pond, she was her own music, her body her favorite thing she'd ever owned.

Oh, life had been a lonely one, but she knew how to pass the time.

❖

The warm pond was the color of green amethyst. It smelled of sweet nectar but tasted like nothing at all. Alice untied her underthings and left them in the grass, pausing only to unweave her braid before jumping in.

She sank right to the bottom. She sat there awhile, letting her limbs relax. Soon, she felt the familiar tickles of kissingfish and opened her eyes long enough to see them nibbling at her skin. She smiled and swam up, the fish following her every move. They wriggled alongside her, nudging her elbows and knees in an attempt to get closer.

Alice swam until she was so clean she practically shined, and then the warm air dried her hair and skin so quickly she had time left to wander before her ferenberry picking for the day.

Alice was always trying to find her own adventures while the other kids were in school. Mother was supposed to be home-teaching her, but she rarely did. Two years ago, when Mother was still freshly angry with Alice for getting kicked out of school (and for what she'd done to Oliver Newbanks), she'd left a stack of books on the kitchen table and told Alice to study them, warning her that if she didn't, she'd grow up to be the silliest girl in all of Ferenwood, never mind the ugliest.

Sometimes Alice wanted to say unkind things to Mother.

Still, Alice loved her mother. Really, she did. Alice had made peace with her parental lot in life long ago. But let us put this plainly: Alice had always preferred Father and she had no trouble saying so. Father was more than a parent to Alice; he was her friend and confidant. Life with Father had made all hard things bearable; he'd seen to it that his daughter was so thoroughly loved that she'd never known the depth of her own insecurities. In fact, he took up so much room in her heart that she'd seldom noticed she had no other friends to name.

It was only when Father disappeared that Alice began to see and feel the things she'd been long protected from. The shock of loss unlatched her armor, and soon cold winds and whispers of fear snuck through the cracks in her skin; she wept until the whites of her eyes dried up and the lids rusted open, refusing to close long enough to let her sleep.

Grief was a tangible weight Alice's small body slowly learned to carry. She was just nine years old when Father left, but even tiny Alice would wake up scraping the bottom of her heart in search of him, and each time she came up raw, hollow, and aching.

Dear reader: You should know that Alice, a decidedly proud girl, wouldn't approve of my sharing this personal information with you. I recognize that the details of her grief are private. But it is imperative, in my humble opinion, that you know just how deeply she loved Father. Losing him had unzipped her from top to bottom, and yet, her love for him had solidified her spirit. She was broken and unbroken all at once, and the longer she stayed in Ferenwood without him, the lonelier she became.

For Alice Alexis Queensmeadow, some things were very simple: If Father had gone, so too would she, because Alice had never wanted anything more than to follow his lead.

Succeeding in the Surrender, you see, was her only way out.

Mother was waiting in the yard when Alice got back. Her amber eyes were bright against her brown skin and narrowed in Alice's direction. She had one hand on her hip and one hand holding a basket. Mother wore skirts, just as Alice did, but Mother liked hers clean and simple, solid colors and layers; long-sleeved blouses tucked into her skirts and folded up to the elbows. Alice's skirts were cumbersome, weighted down with beads and jewels and sequins, intricate patterns embroidered into the cloth.

Plain fabric gave Alice headaches.

Alice watched Mother closely—her hay-green curls had sprung all about her face—and Alice thought she was growing finer and lovelier every day. Sometimes looking at Mother made Alice miss Father even more. If he'd had any idea how much beauty was waiting for him at home, Alice thought, surely he would have returned.

Mother's eyes softened their stare as Alice approached. She

shifted her weight and let the basket gentle onto the grass, holding her now-empty hand out to her daughter.

Alice took it.

They walked in silence toward the four-room cottage that was their home, its honeyed-stone exterior a familiar sight. A room for eating, a room for sitting, a room for Mother, and a room for Alice and the triplets. It wasn't enough, but somehow it was.

The clay shingles were suffocated by climbing ivy that had braided itself across the roof so tightly it was nearly impossible to remove. A few tendrils had escaped down the sides of the house, and Mother pushed stray vines out of the way as they walked through the open front door.

The house was still. Her brothers were still at school.

Mother pointed to an empty chair. Alice stared at it.

Alice took her seat, and Mother sat down beside her and set her with a look so fierce that Alice hadn't even realized she was in trouble until just then. Her heart, poor thing, had grown feet and was kicking her from the inside. She clasped her hands together and, despite a sudden moment of panic, wondered what she should eat for noonlunch.

Mother sighed. "I had a visit from Mrs. Newbanks this morning."

Stupid Mrs. Newbanks, Alice nearly said out loud.

"She says Oliver has been trying to get in touch with you. You remember Oliver, of course."

More silence from Alice.

"Alice," Mother said softly, looking at the wall now. "Oliver was Surrendered last year. He's thirteen now."

Alice knew this already.

Alice knew Oliver was a year older than she was, that he was never supposed to be in her middlecare class. But she also knew he'd taken a year off to tend to Mr. Newbanks when Mr. Newbanks had come down with the fluke, so Oliver had to stay back a year and ended up in her class. Stupid, sick Mr. Newbanks ruining her entire stupid life. Stupid Mrs. Newbanks having such a stupid kid. Stupid Newbankses being stupid all over the place.

Alice didn't care if Oliver had already Surrendered. Who cared? She didn't. She didn't care about him. She cared about *her*.

Tomorrow was the day her whole life would change.

She was sure of it.

Alice crossed her arms. Uncrossed them. "I don't know why we're having this conversation," she finally said. "I don't care a knuckle for Oliver Newbanks. Oliver Newbanks can choke on a toad."

Mother tried not to smile. She stood up to stir a pot on the stove. "You are not curious," Mother asked, her back to Alice, "to know what his Surrender tasked him to do?"

"No." Alice got up to leave, shoving her chair back in the process, wood screeching against wood.

"Sit down, Alice." Mother's voice was no longer gentle.

Alice hesitated in the doorway, fists clenched. "No," she said again.

"Alice Alexis Queensmeadow, you will sit back down this instant."

"No."

"*Alice—*"

She tore off running.

Out the door and down the path and through the meadow and into the field, past the pond and across the bridge and over the hill and up and up and up the tallest tree in all of Ferenwood. There she sat, heart bumping into bone, and decided she would not leave this tree until she died.

Or until she got bored.

Whichever came first.

No one had come to find her.

Alice doubted anyone would. Not Mother, certainly, and not her triplet ten-year-old brothers, who were more interested in turning their socks into slingshots than wondering where their sister had gone for the day.

She was bitter, it was true.

Alice had half hoped a search party would come looking for her. Maybe the village would've come together in a show of support for the ugliest girl in Ferenwood.

She'd half hoped Mother would worry.

But Alice had so often slept in trees and woods and fields and sheds that Mother already knew she'd be just fine; in fact, Mother was probably relieved she wouldn't have to deal with her daughter until later. In any case, Alice hadn't collected any new ferenberries today, but she'd collected enough yesterday, so she figured she had plenty of time to throw a fit and dispense with any practicalities planned for the afternoon.

She sighed.

Being alive, she realized, was very tiresome.

Alice let her legs dangle from a branch and leaned forward to listen, to see, to take in her world. She could see all of Ferenwood from here: the rolling hills, the endless explosion of color cascading down and across the lush landscape. Reds and blues; maroons and ceruleans. Greens and pinks; shamrocks and peaches. Yellow and tangerine and violet and aquamarine. Every hue held a flavor, a heartbeat, a life. She took a deep breath and drew it all in.

There were rows upon rows of little homes, windows glowing gold in the fading rainlight. Chimneys puffed and birds fell in love and blooms let their scents sweeten the sky. The rainlight was almost gone, and with it, the sun. Sundance was nearly done for the year, and that meant no rainlight for another twelve months. A part of Alice mourned the loss of Sundance; the weeklong showers of rainlight, the way the glow gave dignity to everything it touched. But she couldn't be too sad; not this year.

Tomorrow was her day. The first day of spring.

In the wake of Father's leaving, the Surrender was all she'd ever looked forward to, and now the day was nearly upon her. Tomorrow the clouds would break open with a promise and a purpose. Tomorrow she would dance her way to fame. To a future that needed her, expected her, required her. Winning the

Surrender would mean she'd finally proven herself as a true Ferenwood citizen—and it would be her one chance to escape the life that no longer included Father.

Her heart nearly burst in anticipation of it all.

She got to her feet, carefully balancing herself on a branch, and jumped, catching more branches to slow her fall on the way down. Her bare feet touched the grass and she tumbled into a seated position, out of breath and exhilarated. There were only a couple of hours of rainlight left, and now that she'd had enough time to sulk, Alice felt ready to be optimistic again.

She was hungry, she realized.

Alice plucked flowers as she went, pocketing them gently. Flowers were just about her favorite things to snack on. She liked some nuts, some berries, and some plants (they tasted best when cooked into a soup), but flowers—oh, flowers were her favorite.

Alice bit down on petals and stems, savoring the flavors but stuffing herself all the same. She found a brook and took a deep drink, stopping just long enough to dip her toes in, and once all was said and done, she felt refreshed and ready to finish the day. She should've headed home then. Apologized to Mother. Heard what Mother had wanted to tell her. *I should be mature*, Alice scolded herself.

Still, she hesitated.

Alice had no room of her own at home. No place, no real sense of belonging. She needed to belong somewhere. But a girl like her—a daughter who looked nothing like her mother, a sister who looked nothing like her brothers—was low on options. She felt most comfortable in nature, where things weren't required to look like the other in order to live together peacefully.

Anyway, it wasn't that she *needed* anyone to like her.

It was just that she already liked herself so much and found herself so very interesting (and smart and creative and nice and funny and friendly and genuine) that she really couldn't understand why it wasn't easier for her to fit in.

And besides, Alice thought she was very pretty.

Her hair didn't have any color or shape to it, but there wasn't anything *wrong* with it. It didn't talk or spit on people or accidentally kick small children in the toes.

And her skin had no color or luster to it, but it covered all her inside parts, and it wasn't foul or sticky or covered in fur.

And maybe her eyes weren't spectacularly brown—maybe they only had a tiny bit of color—but they were bright and big and, well, perhaps they hadn't always worked perfectly, but Father had made sure Alice got her vision fixed, and *anyway*, she was extremely good at pretending she didn't give a cat's bottom what anyone thought of her.

Things would be just fine.

In fact, things had just started being fine again—she was

practicing her dance for the hundredth time when—wouldn't you know it—Oliver Newbanks decided to ruin everything for the third time in two days.

Alice really wished she had her shovel.

"Your mother told me I might find you here," was the first thing he said to her.

Alice counted beats in her head, her feet falling and hips swaying and arms rising and skirts spinning in all the right places. Her bangles moved in perfect harmony with her steps; she felt like she was a part of it all—a part of the world itself.

Music gave her access to the earth.

Her feet had grown roots, planting her into the ground with each footfall. She could feel the reverberations rising through her, beyond her. She never wanted to stop. She never wanted to forget this feeling.

"Alice, I'm sorry," he said.

She kept spinning.

"I'm so sorry. Please, give me a chance to explain—"

Alice stopped. Her skirts swung all about her, momentum whipping them against her legs. She was out of breath and out of patience and she did not care for this conversation, not one whit.

She stepped right up to Oliver Newbanks and grabbed a fistful of his shirt. Yanked him down to meet her eye to eye. (He was so unaccountably tall; it was only fair.)

"What do you want?" she demanded.

Oliver was startled but he hid it well. She could hear his heart again and she was immediately thrown by the beauty of it. The songs of his soul; the harmony within him: It was incredible. She'd heard this symphony when she first ran into his chest, too distracted then to understand what it might mean.

She dropped his shirt and her jaw and took a few steps back. She didn't want to get near him again.

"Please," he said, holding his hands together in supplication. "That was so long ago, Alice. I was a stupid kid. I didn't mean it."

Alice stared at him for what felt like an abominably long time.

Then, "Okay."

And she turned and left.

She was halfway down the meadow when he caught up to her, breathing hard. "What do you mean, 'okay'?" he asked.

Alice rolled her eyes but he couldn't see.

"Does that mean we can be friends?"

"Definitely not," she said.

"Why not?"

"Because I will never be able to trust you."

"Aw, c'mon, Alice—I didn't mean it—"

Alice turned on him. Narrowed her eyes. "You don't think I'm the ugliest girl in Ferenwood?"

"No! Of course n—"

"Then why did you say it?"

He had no answer.

"You're a cruel, silly boy," she said, walking again. "And I do not like you. So go away, and please stop talking to me."

There. Now he would leave.

"I can't."

Alice stopped. "What?"

"I can't," he said again, this time with a sigh. He looked into his hands, looked away.

So this was what Mother was smiling about. This was it. She thought it was funny. She probably thought this was hilarious.

"*Alice*," Oliver whispered.

"Don't say it."

"Alice—"

She covered her ears and hummed.

"Alice!" Oliver pulled her arms down, gripped her hands. "Alice, I've been tasked . . . to you."

"Oh, Oliver." She looked up at the sky. She wanted to kick him very hard. "You terrible liar."

"I'm in love with you."

"Good grief." She kept walking.

Oliver was stunned. He blinked a few times. "But, Alice—"

"You were tasked to me? When? A year ago? And it's taken you this long to gather the gooseberries to tell me?"

"I—I was nervous," he stammered. "I didn't expect it. I took the year to think about it—to understand—"

"You are as much in love with me as I am in love with this tree stump over here," Alice said, pointing to the tree stump. "Now, I'll be on my way, thank you very much. It was awful talking to you."

"But—"

"Go away, Oliver." She kept walking.

"Fine," he said, catching up to her. He was frustrated now. Frustrated and impatient. "Fine—I'm sorry." He clenched his jaw. Fixed a look at her. "I lied, okay? I lied."

She stared back. "What do you want from me?"

He shook his head, confused. "How did you know? No one can ever tell when I'm lying—it's the only thing I'm any good at—"

"What do you want?" she said again.

"Alice." He stepped in front of her. "I need your help."

Alice took a flower out of her pocket. Bit off the top. "Of course you do," she said, mouth full of petals. She shook her head. "Typical."

TURN THE PAGE
FOR MORE CHAPTERS

Alice found a nice patch of grass and sat down in it, spreading her skirts about her. She leaned back on both hands, legs crossed at the ankles, the stem of an unfinished daisy sticking out of her mouth.

"Go on, then," she said, squinting up at Oliver in the rain-light. He was a pretty kind of person, she supposed, but she thought he'd look much prettier if he traded in his personality for something better.

Oliver ran a hand through his silver hair, and a few strands fell across his eyes, contrasting sharply against the brown of his skin. His hair was definitely the color of silver herring, and Alice wondered for a moment if he'd ever eaten fish as a child. She stifled a shudder.

He leaned against a nearby tree, arms crossed against his chest. He leveled her with a glare. She glared back.

"This is going to be much more complicated than I thought," he muttered.

"Oh?" She chewed on her daisy stem.

"How can you be so unaffected by persuasion?"

Alice shrugged. "How can you be such an awful person?"

"I'm not an awful person." He frowned.

"You still think I'm the ugliest girl in Ferenwood, don't you?"

He considered her. Hesitated.

"You should know," Alice said to him, "that I won't help you worth a twig unless you are always honest with me." She reached into her pocket for a tulip and offered it to him. He cringed, shook his head and looked away.

"I don't know how you eat that stuff," she heard him say.

Alice made a face and shoved the whole tulip in her mouth at once.

"So?" she said, still chewing. "You think I'm hideous."

Oliver looked her over. Shook his head.

Alice froze.

"No?" She'd practically whispered the word, heart thumping hard. She hadn't realized how much she'd hoped he'd changed his mind. She didn't want to be ugly. She so very desperately didn't want to be ugly. "You don't think I'm hideous?" she asked him.

Oliver shrugged. "I think you look like nothing."

"Oh."

Alice ducked her head. His words stung, neat little slaps for each syllable against her face.

Nothing was so much worse than ugly.

Alice's cheeks had bloomed, reds and pinks warming her face. Oliver noticed.

"Hey," he said gently. "I was just being honest, just like you told me to—"

"Good." She spoke too loudly, blinking fast. She did not want his sympathy. She looked him right in the eye then, all red cheeks and racing heart, and told herself it did not matter what Oliver Newbanks thought of her, even though somehow it did. "So be honest about what you want," she said to him. "Why are you here?"

Oliver sighed. Looked into his hands and then up at her. Then back into his hands, and then finally, firmly, back at her. "I know what you can do."

A half-chewed petal fell out of her open mouth. "I'm sure I'm not sure I have any idea what you're talking about."

"You're not the only one who knows truths, Alice."

"What?" Her eyes went wide. "Is that how you know?" she whispered. "Can you . . . read minds?"

"No." Oliver laughed. "I have the talent of persuasion. With the added benefit of knowing one thing about each person I meet."

"Oh?"

He nodded.

"And what's that?" Alice asked.

"Their most private secret of all."

If she hadn't been sitting down, Alice would've needed to then.

It made perfect sense. His heart and bones—the beauty she'd heard before. She understood then, right then, that it was because he'd been collecting the secret songs and whispers of every soul he'd met. For thirteen years.

It was incredible.

"So," he said, more at ease now. "I've been honest with you. In exchange, I'll need your help."

"Sit down," she told him. And pointed to a place beside her.

He obliged.

"How long have you known?" she asked.

"Known what?"

"About my . . . you know . . ." Alice made a gesture that meant exactly nothing.

Oliver seemed to understand anyway. "Since the day I met you," he said.

"And why now? Why tell me this now?"

"Because." He sighed. "It's been an entire year since my Surrender, and I haven't been able to complete my task. It's been nearly impossible."

"But using me—that would be cheating, wouldn't it?"

"No one would have to know."

"They would if I told them," she pointed out.

"You're not going to tell them."

Alice stood up at once. "Oliver Newbanks," she said, astounded. "I've only told three lies in my entire life and I certainly will not tell a fourth one for you. And if you think you can bully me into using magic I don't even believe in, you've left your head and your horse behind."

"Well no one's *asked* you to do any magic, have they?" he said, scrambling to his feet as well.

Alice glared.

Oliver shrugged. "In any case, I think you would change your mind about helping me if you heard what I had to say."

"I wouldn't."

"You would," he said. "Because I can offer you something in return for your cooperation."

"There is nothing you could offer me that I would want, you overgrown pineapple."

Oliver hesitated. Looked at her carefully. "Alice," he said. "I know where your father is."

"Oh."

Alice felt oddly disconnected as she floated down to the ground. She looked around like she didn't know where she was. "Oh my."

Oliver crouched in front of her. "You help me," he said, "and I help you. It's that simple."

Alice had never been able to prove it, but she'd always known that Father was still alive. She'd mourned his absence, yes, but she'd never mourned his death, because she'd been sure—absolutely sure—that one day, somehow, she would find him again. Father was out there. Somewhere. He had to be!

Though she really ought to make sure.

"*What if you're lying?*" she whispered, eyes the size of sunflowers.

"You would know, wouldn't you?" He looked unhappy about that.

But it was true. She would.

The week after Father left, Alice had made the biggest purchase of her life. At the time, her savings were a total of seven finks—just one fink short of a stoppick—and she used them to make an ever-binding promise: For as long as a single lie never left her lips, she could never be fooled by one. It was the only way she could be sure she'd find Father one day. To never be led astray.

(A gentle aside: While it is very common practice in Ferenwood to spend finks and stoppicks on any number of impermanent tricks and promises, it is my personal belief that Alice's gesture, while exceedingly romantic, was altogether impractical. A waste of seven finks, for certain, but then, we cannot fault the girl for wanting to exercise some control over the situation, can we? But I digress.)

"Oh Oliver where is he?" Alice asked suddenly, heart racing and hopes soaring and hands shaking. "Where did he go?"

"Not so fast," Oliver said, holding up a hand. "First we solve my task, and then we get your father."

"But that doesn't seem fair—"

"It's the only deal I'll offer."

"We both have something to lose," she protested. "If you don't finish your task—"

"I know," he said, cutting her off with an unkind look. "I already know what will happen to me if I don't finish my task. You don't have to say it out loud."

Alice was about to say it out loud anyway when she remembered something awful. She fell back against the tree, gasping "Oh no, oh no" over and over again.

"What?" Oliver tried not to look concerned. "What is it?"

She looked up. "Tomorrow," she said. "Tomorrow is the first day of spring."

"So?"

"So," she insisted, irritated now. "Tomorrow I will be getting a task of my own!"

"You're twelve already?" Oliver gaped at her, running both hands through his hair. "I thought you were nine."

Alice chose to ignore that last bit.

Instead, she said, "What if I have to catch a dragon like Fenny Birdfinsk? Or if I'm sent to the stars like Sellie Sodcryer or, oh, if I have to spend a year mending a cow with nothing but a silver penny!"

"Don't be ridiculous," Oliver said. "No one has ever had to mend a cow with a silver penny. They'll let you use a gold nickel, at the very least—"

"Oh kick the cow, Oliver, it will be impossible for me to help you!"

"Right," he said, dragging a hand across his face. "Yes, right."

Alice's hopes had been dashed. They fell into a neat pile beside her feet.

"Unless," Oliver said suddenly.

She looked up.

"Unless—" he said again, then hesitated.

"Go on."

He looked at her out of the corner of his eye. "Unless you waive your Surrender."

Alice gasped.

Waiving her Surrender was an option that had never been an option. Her Surrender was a ticket to something new—a task that would set her life in motion. Every child in Ferenwood grew up aching to be tasked—awaiting adventure and the thrill of a challenge.

Alice had been dreaming of this day her entire life.

Different though she may have looked, her heart was a Ferenwood heart, and she had the right to her task just like everyone else. She'd clung to this all through kindercare and middlecare and hometeaching with Mother—this hope, this truth—that one day, no matter her differences, she would be just like everyone else in this small way.

Losing it would break her heart.

Just as losing Father had broken her heart.

Picnicsticks, she didn't know what to do.

Alice wandered toward town in a daze. She wasn't entirely sure why she was headed this way, but today had been a strange day, and she couldn't face going home just yet. Still, she seldom traveled this far out, because going into town was a painful treat. There was so much she wanted to explore (and purchase!) but with just one fink in her pocket, Alice could only do so much.

She ambled down familiar grassy lanes toward the stone-paved streets of town with none of her usual excitement; she kept tripping over roots and sleeping birds and had to pause occasionally to rest her head against a tree trunk. There was so much on her mind she hardly had room for things like balance and hand-eye coordination. Alice sighed and prepared to set off again, but then she heard a rustle of paper and soon spotted the culprit: the town newspaper caught in a tree, clutched in a fist of branches. She managed to tug the paper free, scanning the front page with little interest. Boiled potatoes were five finks a sackful. The town square would be under construction in preparation for the Surrender, please excuse the mess. Had anyone seen Mr. Perciful's pygmy goat? Zeynab Tinkser was selling a lemon canoe for fifteen tintons.

Alice's eyes went wide at that last line.

Fifteen tintons was more magic than she'd ever seen. She couldn't even imagine what she'd do with it all. (Though that was nonsense, wasn't it? Of course she could. She'd use it all to find Father.) Not for the first time, Alice wished she was old enough to earn a few stoppicks of her own and not have to rely on Mother's unreliable ways.

Alice tucked the newspaper under her arm.

Ferenwood never had much news to tell; things were always predictably lovely. The most recent trouble their little town had encountered was losing a few pigs to a particularly strong gust of wind, but that was a few days ago. The *worst* thing that had ever happened in Ferenwood was losing Father, of course. That had been the strangest thing of all, because leaving Ferenwood was something no one ever did. Not really.

Alice had certainly never left Ferenwood. None of the other children had, either. Being tasked was the one great exception—it was an adventure on which every Ferenwood citizen was expected to embark—but everyone always came home in the end. Besides, they were surrounded by sea on every side but one, and to get out to the great unknown they had to pass through Fennelskein, which, as I mentioned earlier, no one ever visited, for obvious reasons. (I should note here that these reasons were not readily obvious to *me*, an outsider, but try as I might, I couldn't get anyone to explain why, exactly, they never visited the town of Fennelskein. I think the unexciting answer was that they found the town unbearably dull, but we may never know for certain.)

But the simple reason no one ever left Ferenwood for very long was that Ferenwood folk needed magic to survive. Father had been gone for more than three years, a length of time that was considered unsurvivable. The children of Ferenwood were taught—from the moment they could talk—that leaving for long would never do. Magic was what they ate and breathed; it was the essence of all they were. Their relationship with the land was entirely symbiotic: They lived peacefully among the plants and trees, and in return, the land helped them thrive. The seed of magic inside all people of Ferenwood was nurtured and sustained by the land they tilled and harvested.

Without that, they'd be lost.

And this was the real problem, the real heart of the hurt, the truth that made Father's loss so much more painful: that there was no magic outside of Ferenwood. Certainly not anywhere anyone had heard of. There had been rumors, of course, of other distant, magical lands, but there were always rumors, weren't there? Rumors bred of boredom and nonsense born of recklessness. And everyone in Ferenwood knew better than to believe nonsense. Ferenwood didn't hold with nonsense. At least, Alice didn't *think* they did, but she was never really sure. Losing Father to the great unknown had made Alice a believer in all kinds of nonsense, and she didn't mind that it made her odd. Maybe Father had found a bit of magic elsewhere, and maybe he was holding on. Maybe, she thought, he was still trying to find his way home.

Alice lived in a time before proper maps, before street signs and numbered homes. She lived in a time when leaving home meant saying good-bye and hoping you'd be able to find your way back.

Hope, you see, was all she had, and she would hold on to it, come hills or high water.

The center of town was always a bit of a shock for Alice no matter how many times she'd wandered through, and I can't say I blame the girl. It *was* a bit of a shock at first glance. The endless sequence of bold buildings appeared to be shoved together in what was, apparently, a fine show of geometry well studied. Curves shook up and into straight lines, tops capped by triangle or dome or dollop of roof (depending on the storefront) while walls were textured by octagonal, triangular, and starlike tile work. Chimneys were spirals of brick charging into the sky, doors were tall as walls and nearly as wide, and—as you might have already imagined—colors were sharp and bright and endless. (Indeed, one might occasionally be pressed to wonder whether the aesthetic of Ferenwood wasn't a direct answer to the question, *How many colors might we fit in one place?*) It was a string of streets woven together in no particular fashion and for no particular reason other than to accommodate the buildings that appeared to have sprouted straight from the ground.

Alice's family was one of the very few that lived so far from town, and though it was sometimes hard to be high up in the hills and far from the heart of things, she was also seldom bothered with the business of seeing old schoolmates or nosy grown-ups who thrived on the buzz and babble of crowds. For the most part, Alice relished her occasional ambles into the middle of the middle; but though she was eager for a peek at the excitement, she was always swiftly reminded of her place within it.

Alice stood at the very edge of it all and let herself be swallowed up by the sounds and scents of city life. Rainlight ensured that the day was warm and the flowers fresh, and bells rang out while friends called to one another. Fathers clasped hands with mothers who called for children to *please be still* while shopkeepers stood on stoops and waved their wares. Alice felt the weight of the single fink in her pocket as she stared and wished, as always, that Father were there to hold her hand.

But no matter.

Alice held her own hand, one clenched tightly in the other, and pushed her way through the throng. She wasn't tall enough to see very far ahead, but she was certainly short enough to be knocked into by strangers and occasionally snapped in the cheek by a windblown skirt. The air had been tousled by the hands of careful spicekeepers, and Alice tasted mint silk and snips of coconut and nearly everything she touched left her smelling like saffron.

A gaggle of children had crowded around Asal Masal & Chai, eagerly testing samples of a tea that guaranteed they'd grow a full inch by morning. Teenagers were digging through ornate tubs of temporary enchantments—

FIVE FINKS TO FALL IN LOVE
SEVEN FINKS TO GROW YOUR HAIR
A STOPPICK TO DISAPPEAR

—while the older crowd was found relaxing at a series of tables and chairs pressed with intricate patterns of colorful glass. The ladies and gentlemen old enough to indulge puffed on curlicued gold pipes and smiled, blue and red and purple smoke escaping their lips as they laughed. Alice snuck a sniff as she tiptoed past and felt her head go sideways with the weight of it. She smiled despite herself and, not for the first time, found herself wishing she were old enough to do more interesting things.

Alice pressed forward, determined, toward Shirini Firini, the absolute best sweets shop in town. She scrambled over gentle mountains of handwoven rugs, each dense with color and detail. She slowed only to stare in awe at a stall stacked with warm, freshly baked discs of bread, all golden-brown and haphazardly kneaded. Poor Alice was so distracted by the aroma of baked goods she nearly collided with a crowd of men singing in the street; she managed to dart away just in time to avoid the sight of Danyal Rubin, who'd been crossing the road to join the crooners. Alice fought back a scowl.

Oh, there was always someone to be envied, wasn't there?

For Alice-of-little-color, Danyal Rubin was a nightmare. He was the most radiant twelve-year-old she knew, with his rich black hair and ink-like eyes. His skin was the color of dusk: auburn and magenta and cinnamon all at once. He had color and he wore it well, framing his already-luminous eyes in kohl that served only to make Alice feel worse. She'd heard the whispers; she knew the rumors. The town was betting on Danyal to win the Surrender this year, because someone so colorful was undoubtedly the most magical. In the hearts of Ferenwood folk, Alice didn't stand a chance.

But she would prove them wrong.

Alice clenched her fists and pushed forward through the crowd with such force that she nearly knocked into a group of girls tinting their nails with henna. For just a moment Alice froze, overcome by a great longing to join them, but quickly shook it off, keeping her head down as she passed, ever mindful of the limitations of her pocket. When she finally reached Shirini Firini, Alice was out of breath and exhausted.

Coming into town was always a trek, but she should've known better than to have ventured out today, on the eve of the Surrender. All of Ferenwood was out to celebrate, and the festivities would likely last all week. Alice checked the sun as she stepped inside the store and noted she had very little time to get home before dark.

❖

The moment she stepped over the threshold, Alice was overpowered by a heady perfume of sugar. By second three, she was in a happy daze, her every thought sweeter, her very heart lighter, and her hands happily grabbing for everything in sight. Alice knew better than to let the sugar dust get the better of her, but she was happy to rest for just a moment longer before she found the strength to fight again. As soon as she shook off the daze, she found herself sifting through candies with a more stable mind. One fink wouldn't afford her many options, but she liked to look around all the same.

Glass apples were hung from the ceiling, honey-canes gift wrapped in packs of three; figcherry jams were stacked in windows and honeysuckle taffies were spilling out of wooden barrels stacked in each corner. There were walls of iced plums and pomegranates, bushels of baskets weighed down by gold-chocolate leaves and tens of jars of apricot honey that fizzed in your mouth. Alice looked and looked and never tired of the splendor, but she very nearly gasped herself silly when she saw the trays of *zulzuls*. A zulzul was a spiral of fried dough soaked in honey and covered in sugared rose petals; and on any given day, Alice would tell you that zulzuls were her favorite pastry. (Note that this confession would be entirely ridiculous, as Alice had never tasted a zulzul in her life. But she could *imagine* herself loving zulzuls, and somehow, that was enough.)

Finally, reluctantly, Alice selected a single dillypop from a small plastic bin and promised herself that one day, someday, she would return with a pocketful of finks and choose as many sweets as she liked.

One day.

Her single task now accomplished, Alice was in a hurry to get home. There was very little light left, and if Alice was late one more time, she didn't know what Mother would do.

She hurried down sidewalks and tore through spice stalls and slipped between racks of skirts. She spun around shopkeepers and nearly tripped passersby and only glanced up once or thrice to sneak looks at her most favorite storefronts as she rushed home. Knot & Tug was selling self-sewing needles for only three finks apiece, and Alice tucked the information away. Sabzi, the local grocer, was selling lemon blossom twists, two finks a pound, and Alice took note for Mother. But The Danger & The Granger—the best bookshop in town—had new books on display in the window, and Alice was thrown off course. She stopped so suddenly she nearly fell over and, despite her better judgment, she snuck closer to press her nose against the glass. Once near enough to the window, the first thing Alice noticed was a small crowd of people buzzing animatedly around a man sporting a very trim beard. He wore several spectacles and an oversized tunic and Alice realized then that he was an author, ostensibly there for a reading of his book. She squinted to scan the title of the tome in his hands—

The Birth of the Stoppick: Inside the Mind of Fenjoon Heartweather and Salda Millerdon, the Greatest Harvesters of Magic in Ferenwood History

—and sighed, disappointed. Alice didn't much care for the history of harvesting. She found the business terribly boring and, if she were being honest, she might even tell you she resented the whole of it simply because she feared it would be her fate one day. Alice had worried all her young life that she'd end up good for nothing but tilling the fields. Tilling was honorable but it was an exceptionally unglamorous job, and Alice preferred to be on the other side of things: taking raw magic and transforming it into usable matter.

Anyhow, she was about to push on when she remembered the very reason she'd stopped. There were two books on display in the shop window.

The Surrender, The Task, and the Long Way Back: How to Cope When Your Child Leaves Home

and just beside it

Champions of Recent Past: Remembering our Ferenwood Heroes

Alice's eyes nearly split in four as she shoved herself through the shop doors and ran for the books in the window. Limbs trembling, heart racing, Alice picked up a copy of *Champions of Recent Past* and ran her hand over the cover. There, with a small selection of other town heroes, was a picture of Father, aged twelve and glorious, the winner of his own Surrender just thirty years prior.

Alice had always known Father was a Champion. Father won the title for his dexterity of mind and for his ability to retain and re-create images at will; his task was to travel the land and work with the Town Elders to become the first true cartographer of Ferenwood. He and the Elders had been working together to create maps so precise and so easily navigable that one day all Ferenwood residents would have a copy of their own, enabling them to travel from one neighborhill to another without complication or confusion. In fact, his work had been so remarkable that he'd been asked to stay on with the Town Elders ever after. This kind of treatment was fairly customary for Champions, who were considered the single most talented citizens of their year; but Father had been more than just a Champion. Father was a friend to Ferenwood. He was loved by all. In fact, it was often whispered that one day Father would be named a Town Elder, too. Instead, Father had left, and not a soul knew why.

Mother was making tea when Alice finally made it home—just before dark. Alice pushed open the front door with a secret weighing down her skirts: Inside her pocket was the one dillypop, carefully wrapped, to be saved for a special occasion. Alice would have to wait weeks to get her hands on another fink but she'd made peace with the loss of the last of her money. The triplets were eating appleberry jam straight from the jar, small purple fingers sticking to their faces. Mother was humming a tune as she moved about the kitchen and, even though Alice stood before her, Mother wiped her just-washed hands on her apron and didn't seem to notice her daughter at all.

Oh, it didn't matter.

Alice was tired, she was torn, and she took a seat, dropping her chin in her hands. What a day today had been. Nothing would shake the weight of the world from her shoulders tonight, not even a cheekful of candy. Alice wished the world would shed a few pounds. She desperately wanted to find Father, but she also desperately wanted to have a task; and so she'd come to no conclusion at all, leaving Oliver in a twist of his own.

Finding Father meant trusting Oliver. It meant sacrificing her own future to help him with *his*, and even then there was no guarantee of anything. Besides, just because she could see through a lie did not mean she had any reason to trust Oliver Newbanks.

Alice pushed away from the table and slipped into her bedroom, grateful for the chance to be alone while her brothers were busy in the kitchen. There was one small section of this room that was hers and hers alone, and it was hidden under the floorboards.

Alice had hidden her life underneath this room. Books and trinkets, clothes and flowers: the only precious things she owned.

She carefully removed a few planks of wood and unearthed her outfit for tomorrow. She'd been working on it for two years, carefully stitching it together, piece by piece. Four skirts, a half-sleeved blouse, a vest, and a cropped, sleeveless jacket all to be worn together. The final bit was the headpiece, crocheted by hand, trimmed with a train of yellow tulle and strung with hammered tin coins. Alice had spent months dyeing the fabrics and adorning the plain cloth, embroidering flowers, sewing beads and sequins into intricate patterns, and adding tiny mirrors to the hem to make the skirt glitter with every step. It was an explosion of colors, heavy with the weight of all the work she'd done. She even knew exactly which flowers she'd weave into her braid.

Alice knew she would be incredible.

She would so thoroughly impress the Town Elders that they'd have no choice but to give her the best task—the grandest task. She'd go on to be a town hero, just like Father, and she would make her family proud. She'd had it all figured out.

Children in Ferenwood prepared their whole lives for their Surrender. Each child was born with a singular magical talent, and it was the job of parents and teachers to recognize and nurture that talent and, ultimately, develop their Surrender performance. The performance was crucial because it was a presentation of untapped potential; it was critical to show just how useful your magical talent could be because the best talents would go on to receive the best tasks. The best adventures.

This was what Alice had dreamed of.

But Alice hadn't needed any of that extra help, because she'd figured it out on her own. Father had told her, many moons ago, what she needed to do. Maybe he hadn't realized it then, but she had.

"Do you hear that?" he asked her one night. They were standing under the night sky.

"Hear what?" Alice asked.

"The music."

"Which music?"

Father closed his eyes and smiled at the moon. "Oh, Alice," he whispered. "Unfold your heart. Sharpen your ears. And never say no to the world when it asks you to dance."

They slept in the grass that night, she and Father, not saying another word. Alice listened to the earth come alive: the wind singing, the grass swaying, the lakes swimming laps. Trees stretched their branches, flowers yawned themselves to sleep, the stars blinking fast as they dozed off. She witnessed it all, listening closely the whole time. She had never felt more real in all her life.

And every night after that, when Father asked her if she could hear the music, Alice knew exactly what he meant. And when the world asked her to dance, she never said no.

Alice looked up and found Mother standing in the doorway. Mother didn't look upset, but she had her arms crossed against her chest all the same. She nodded to the skirts Alice was holding in her lap.

"Are you ready?" Mother asked.

"I think so," Alice said quietly, wondering what Mother would say if she knew how selfish her daughter was. Selfish enough to consider getting tasked over finding Father.

Mother would never forgive her.

"What if I have to leave Ferenwood?" Alice said, feeling unexpectedly emotional. "Will you be alright without me? How will you get by?"

"Oh, we'll find a way to manage," Mother said, staring at her hands as she smoothed out her apron. "I've been stowing away the berries for some time now."

Alice wondered whether Mother would ever realize how deeply those words hurt her that night. Mother had answered a question Alice did not ask. Alice wanted Mother to tell her she'd be missed, that she'd be sorry to see her go. Alice wasn't asking about the ferenberries at all.

It was only then that Alice saw how little Mother needed her.

Alice did not belong in this small home where no room was her own, where her few possessions had to be buried beneath it. She knew now that no one would miss her so long as Mother had her medicine berries, and it made her feel terribly lonely. Father had already left her, and now, in her own way, Mother had, too. Alice was on her own and she knew then, in that moment, that no matter what happened, she would forever regret a decision to waive her Surrender. She would never forgive herself for not forging a path of her own.

So, it was decided. She would dance tomorrow.

(And Oliver Newbanks could step on a porcupine. Alice would find Father by herself.)

I HAVEN'T ANY IDEA HOW MANY CHAPTERS ARE IN THIS BOOK

The morning arrived the way Alice imagined a whisper would: in tendrils of gray and threads of gold, quietly, quietly. The sky was illuminated with great care and deliberation, and she leaned back to watch it bloom.

Alice was sitting atop a very high hill, the whole of Ferenwood snoozing just below. Sleeping homes exhaled quietly, smoking chimneys gently puffing, unlit windows glinting golden in the dawn. Dew had touched the earth and the earth touched back: Blades of grass shivered awake as they reached for the sky, freshly showered and slightly damp. Bees were lounging, bread was baking, birds were chirping to the trees. Everything smelled like warm velvet tea and a freshly scrubbed face and something very, very sweet. Alice smiled, clutching her arms in the breeze.

The air was cold in places, but warm where the sun touched it, so she shifted to catch a spotlight. Her skirts glimmered in the glow as she adjusted her legs, and feeling a slight quiver in her stomach, Alice plucked a nearby dandelion and popped it in her mouth.

This was it.

Today she would be competing with every twelve-year-old in the village. All eighty-six of them would stand before the Town Elders and surrender their greatest talents. In exchange, they hoped to be recognized and set with a task that would change history.

In truth, simply being tasked at all was a great accomplishment. Ferenwood never talked of the children who were rejected outright, dismissed on account of being so thoroughly incapable that they could not possibly live up to a challenge. Instead, the conversation was always about the greatest task and which child it would go to. This auspicious day was a grand celebration of magic; and for Alice, who desperately longed to be more than *nothing*, the Surrender meant everything.

It meant redemption.

Alice stood up and smoothed the creases in her skirts. She was so proud of this outfit and all the work she'd put into it. In fact, it was the only time she was happy to be wearing clothes.

Not that there was anyone around to see them.

She'd slipped out of the house while Mother and the triplets were still fast asleep. No hellos, no good-byes, just Alice moving into a new moment. This quiet morning might have been her last for a long time, and she wanted it all to herself.

Happy Birthday to me, she thought. Alice was now officially twelve years old.

She skipped a ways down the path toward the town square, skirts bunched in her hands, bangled ankles and wrists making a merry tune of their own. The path to the square was one of her favorites.

Green stood sentinel on both sides of her.

Celery trees and apple bushes and lime stalks all as tall as she, swaying to a rhythm she recognized. The dirt was soft and welcome under her bare feet, and when it felt right she stopped, digging her toes into the ground as she turned her face up to the sky. Alice could see the entire square from here, and the sight of it stopped her still, the way it always did.

Ferenwood had many tall trees, but only a few tall places, and the square was the tallest place in town. And even though the trees (Ink trees and Night trees, Sink trees and Climb trees; Berry trees and Nut trees and Red trees and Wild trees) were rich in color (corn colored and raspberry stained and even a deep dark blue), and extremely varied (some grew pink stones and others dripped orange in the night), the square was tall and colorful and varied in ways the trees were not.

The buildings in town seemed (understandably) magicked together, strokes of a paintbrush licking them into being. Swirls and swirls of color had been swept together by a careful artist. Colors melted up walls and rushed down doors, orange and lavender swirling into a plump onion of a roof that sat snugly upon a structure painted gold; this was the health house. Green and yellow tangled with sapphire and silver to create a colorful dollop of a dome atop the schoolhouse. Strokes of flaming blue and rosy white were slicked together like an upside-down ice-cream cone: this, the roof of the mint-colored courthouse.

In this light, Ferenwood looked delicious.

Alice closed her eyes and drew in a deep breath. Father had taught her to love this town, and she couldn't help but want to make her people proud.

The sky was in fine form this morning, ready for its big moment. The clouds would burst open just as soon as the ceremony was over, showering the village in felicitations from the sky. Rain meant renewal, and the people of Ferenwood welcomed it. It was what their souls were made of.

When their world was built it was so breathtakingly beautiful—so rich and colorful—the sky wept for a hundred years. Tears of great joy and grief flooded the earth, fissuring it apart and, in the process, creating rivers and lakes and oceans that still exist today. There was joy for the beauty, but great sadness, too—sadness that no one was around to appreciate the majesty of it all. And so, as the story goes, Ferenwood folk were born from the tears that watered the earth and grew them into being.

The Surrender was how they gave thanks.

At twelve they surrendered themselves and their gifts and, in return, took on a task—the purpose of which was always to help someone or someplace in need. They gave back to the world and, in the process, they grew up.

This was when their lives truly began.

I hadn't wanted to mention this earlier, but Oliver Newbanks had been standing just to the left of our Alice for over fourteen minutes before he finally stepped forward and pulled on her braid. I also feel compelled to mention that Alice responded by pinching him very, very hard.

Oliver yelped and teetered, nearly losing his balance. He tugged up his shirt to inspect the damage and offered Alice a ripe word or two to express his feelings on the matter. Alice turned away, very purposely avoiding the sight of his bare torso and the sound of his still-babbling voice.

"Would you hush?" she finally said to him. "You are ruining a perfectly good moment." She nodded to the sun inching its way up the sky.

"Alice," he said impatiently, "you need to give me an answer. You promised you'd let me know before the Surrender this morning, and now the moment is nearly upon us."

Alice squinted into the distance, still avoiding eye contact with him. She wasn't sure why she cared, but, for just a second, a very tiny part of her was almost sorry to disappoint him. She pushed it away.

"I'm afraid I cannot help you," she said quietly. "This day is too important, Oliver. I know Father would understand my decision."

Oliver seemed genuinely surprised. In fact, his wide eyes and high brows and open mouth came together to express their collective shock, all without saying a word. "*You can't be serious*," he whispered. "Alice, please—you can't really be serious—"

"Quite serious, I'm afraid."

"But your father—"

"I will find him on my own, don't you worry about him."

"But I already know where he is!" Oliver nearly shouted. "I could get to him right now if I wanted to!"

Alice shot him a dirty look. "Then why don't you?"

Oliver gaped.

"You are a rotten person," she said. "That you would dangle my father in front of me as though he were a bit of candy. It's not enough for you to simply bring him back to his family with no expectation of anything in return—"

"Hey now—"

"We have no deal, Oliver." She cut him off. "If you have even half a heart, you may tell me where my father is. Otherwise, I have a life to attend to."

"You are unbelievable!" he sputtered.

"Good day, Oliver Newbanks. And good luck with your task."

And with that, she ran down the hill toward the village square.

Oliver Newbanks was close behind.

Alice's stomach felt stuffed with twigs, each nervous tap of her toes snapping one in half. The morning was brisk and buttery and sent a sudden shiver down her spine. She was standing in line with her peers, keeping very much to herself. Some were dressed in costume, others in plain clothes. Some looked nervous, others looked pompous. There was no way of knowing what any of it meant. The twelve-year-olds had already signed in and each been assigned a number; now all that was left to do was wait, and it was proving nearly impossible. Alice had the sudden, unfortunate need to make use of the ladies' toilets and though she tried, she could not mute the din of voices around her.

The people of Ferenwood were dressed in their Ferenwood finest. Gowns made of spider silk and hats carved from cottonwood, colors clashing and sounds smashing and cheers erupting for no reason at all. The audience was beginning to take their seats, wide-eyed and excited with the smell of spring fresh in the air.

The stage looked lovely every year, but this year it looked especially fantastic. Today it was made to look just like a stretch of ocean, the plum-blue water lapping at the feet of its contestants and cascading to the ground. Just below it was an expanse of green, set with a smattering of tables and chairs carved from the arms and legs of fallen trees. Vines had knitted themselves across the backs of every chair and the tables were set with gold baskets of glass apples and honey-canes and chocolate-covered sizzle sticks and pitchers of fire-cider and candied-ice. An orchestra readied their instruments; the sky thundered in appreciation; flowers were blossoming in hundreds of glass orbs suspended in midair; and the sun set fire to the sky, streaking the backdrop with an explosion of blush and tangerine and honeyblue.

It was all rather breathtaking.

Quite.

Whoever's job it was to decorate had put a little too much sugar in the air and it was making Alice want to sneeze. She tried to stifle the impulse and coughed instead, startling the girl standing just to the left of her. Alice rocked back and forth on her heels and clasped her hands, smiling a shaky smile as the girl glanced her way. The girl smiled back and seemed to regret it. Alice stared down at her feet.

Of the eighty-six of them, Alice was fourth in line. And she would be lying if she said she hadn't felt like upending the contents of her stomach, just a little bit.

Alice spotted Mother and the triplets as they searched for their seats, and she couldn't help but feel a spot of warmth settle inside her, soothing her nerves. She had hoped they would come but, really, she wasn't sure. She never could be certain with Mother, if only because Mother had proven herself to be rather fickle these past few years. But despite their strange and often uncomfortable relationship, Alice couldn't help but want to make her mother proud.

She'd hoped to make her proud today.

In fact, the bitterness Alice felt toward Mother was just about to be forgotten until she saw Mother take a seat next to the Newbankses. Oliver caught her eye and glared (Alice glared back) as Mother laughed and shook hands and shared fruit with the family of the boy who'd been so cruel to her. Mother didn't seem to spare a single thought for her feelings.

Alice didn't want to think about it then, but the truth was staring her straight in the face and she could no longer deny it: Mother never seemed to be on her side.

Alice hung her head and drew in a deep breath, determined to keep moving, no matter what. One day, she said to herself, she would return home with Father in hand, and Mother would finally appreciate her.

Just then came the sound of trumpets and a sudden explosion of color that fell and hung neatly in the sky.

It was the official announcement. The beginning of the rest of her life.

Mr. Lottingale stepped onto the stage.

A hush fell over the crowd, and the eighty-six of them—hovering just to the side—were so collectively nervous Alice could almost hear their hearts racing in unison.

Mr. Lottingale was one of the Town Elders and he had come to make a speech. It was the obvious thing to do, to make a speech before the main event, but Alice could never take Mr. Lottingale seriously. He looked a bit like a pistachio. He was round and beige, cracked open only at the top, his head turtling out, and his brown-green hair flopped around in the breeze. She knew it wasn't fair of her to focus only on Mr. Lottingale's looks, as he was certainly a nice-enough person, but every time she looked at him she couldn't help but think of the time she saw him lick a caterpillar off his upper lip.

"Friends of Ferenwood," he boomed, caterpillar voice creeping out of his caterpillar lips. "I congratulate you all on the first day of spring."

The crowd cheered and stomped and raised their glasses of cider.

"Today is a most auspicious occasion," Lottingale went on.

And on, and on and on.

He spent the next ten minutes giving a speech about the great day that is the day of their Surrender, and I can't be bothered to remember it all (it went on for nine minutes too long, if you ask me), but suffice it to say that it was a heart-warming speech that excited the crowd and sent jitters up Alice's skirts; and anyway, I hope you don't mind but I'd like to skip ahead to the part where things actually happen.

❖

They would all perform. All eighty-six of them.

Only after all of the twelve-year-olds had surrendered their gifts would they be allowed to take seats with their families, where they'd attempt to eat a meal while the Elders took a break to deliberate. Once the decisions were final, an envelope would appear on their plates, their tasks carefully tucked inside.

Of the group, only one task would be announced to all of Ferenwood; only one child would be celebrated.

Only the best.

Alice held tight to this reminder as she watched Valentina Milly take the stage. She was the first of them, and Alice admired her for it. Valentina stood in the middle of the square with a great, quiet sort of dignity, never once letting it show that she'd been crying in the bushes just a moment before.

And then she sang.

She had the voice of a featherlily, effortlessly charming the lot of them. Valentina sang a song Alice had never heard before, and the words wrapped around their bodies, sending shivers up tree trunks and hushing the birds into a stillness Alice had never seen. The song was so lovely that Alice was blinking back tears by the end of it, certain that something strange and frightening was coming to life inside of her.

Alice knew then that Valentina Milly had no ordinary voice, and though Alice was terribly jealous, her hands found themselves clapping for her competitor all the same.

Next came Haider Zanotti, a boy with the bluest hair Alice had ever seen. Electric, violent blue, thick and rich and so gorgeous she was sorely tempted to run her hands through it. Haider stepped into the very center of the square, took a bow, and then jumped. Up. High. Straight into the sky. His hands caught something Alice could not see, and he was suspended in midair, fists clenched around what seemed to be an invisible ladder. He hoisted himself up and climbed until he was standing taller than the tallest trees, a speck in the distance held up by nothing at all.

The crowd gasped and some got to their feet, shielding their eyes against the sun as they tried to get a better look at where he'd gone.

Then, Haider jumped.

He fell fast toward the ground and a few people screamed, but Haider was prepared. He held both arms out as he came down and, with just a few feet to fall, latched on to the air, his fists curling around some impossible bit of sky. He hung there for just a moment longer before dropping to one knee.

When he finally stood up, Ferenwood had, too. They were so excited and so impressed that Mr. Lottingale had to beg them to stop cheering so the proceedings could move forward.

Haider rejoined the line looking very pleased with himself. Alice knew she should've been happy for him, but she felt the knot in her stomach tighten and so she bit her lip, hugging herself against the sudden chill creeping down her neck.

Olympia Choo was up next.

Olympia was a big girl, tall and rotund, her hair pulled back so severely she looked much older than twelve. She walked onto the stage with not an ounce of nonsense about her. And when she looked out over the crowd, they seemed almost afraid to look back.

Olympia clapped.

And everything broke.

Chairs, tables, glasses, pitchers, plates, and even one poor man's trousers. Everything came crashing to the floor, and the citizens of Ferenwood with it. But just as they were about to start shouting out in disapproval, Olympia whistled, and all wrongs righted themselves. The tables repaired, chairs reupholstered, glasses pieced back together, and torn trousers were suddenly good as new.

Alice looked down at herself; a loose thread in her skirts had sewn itself back into place. A smudge on her knee, wiped away. Even her braid was suddenly smooth, not a single hair out of place.

Alice couldn't help but be astounded.

Olympia was just about to clap again when the crowd shouted *NO!* and ducked down in fear. Mr. Lottingale ran up to shuffle Olympia offstage.

That meant Alice was next.

And oh, she was terrified.

Only three others had gone before her, and already Alice knew she had made a great mistake. No one had been around to prepare her for today, not Mother who didn't seem to care at all, and not the teachers she no longer had. Alice thought Father had given her this gift before he left—instilling in her this need to dance. She thought it was her talent. The gift she would surrender.

Alice was only now realizing that this was a true talent show, and she—well, she was no talent at all. She could not sing awake the soul, could not climb air, could not right every wrong. She could only offer a dance—and she knew then that it would not be enough.

Alice wanted to cry. But no, that wouldn't do.

Mr. Lottingale was calling her name and it was too late to give up now. Too late to tell Oliver she'd made a mistake, that she should've chosen Father over this moment of humiliation.

Suddenly Alice was sorry.

She was standing onstage, all alone, staring out at some ten thousand faces, and she could not make herself look at Mother.

So she closed her eyes.

The music found her the way it always did, and she let herself lean into it. She met the rhythm in her bones and moved the way she had a hundred times before.

Alice danced the way she breathed: instinctually.

It was an in-built reflex, something her body needed in order to survive. Her arms and legs knew the rules, knew how to bend and twist and dip and switch. She spun and twirled, hips swaying, moving to a melody only she could hear. The moves came faster, quicker, more elegant and grand. Her feet pounded against the earth, drumming the ground into a clamor that roared through her. Alice's arms were above her now, bangled arms cheering her on, and she threw her head back, face up to the sky. Faster, faster, elbows unlocking, knees bending, bangles raining music down her neck. She moved like she'd never moved before, soft and slow, sharp and fast, heels hitting and ankles flicking and fingers swimming through the air. Her skirts were a blur of color, her whole body seized by a need to know the elements, and when she was finally done, she fell to the floor.

Head bowed.

Hands folded in her lap.

Skirts billowing out around her.

Alice was a fallen flower, and she hoped she looked beautiful.

❖

She slowly lifted her head.

The audience was looking on, only politely engaged, still waiting for her to finish. Still waiting for her talent. Alice got to her feet and felt the sun explode in her cheeks.

"Are you quite finished, dear?" This, from Mr. Lottingale.

She nodded.

"Ah," he said, his slack jaw quickly firming into a smile. "Of course. Please rejoin the line, Ms. Queensmeadow."

There was a halted smattering of applause, the guests looking around at one another for a cue on how to react. Alice swallowed hard against the lump in her throat and walked back to her place in line, staring firmly at her feet and hardly daring to breathe.

Eighty-two others performed after she did, and Alice wouldn't remember any of them. There were a great many talents on display that day, and hers, as it turned out, was the strength to keep from bursting into tears in front of everyone.

Alice could not make herself sit with Mother.

After the ceremony she found a quiet branch in a very tall tree and tried desperately to stay calm. She was inhaling and exhaling in tiny gasps and she scolded herself for it, rationalizing all the reasons why she was being ridiculous. Surely, she considered, she was just being hard on herself. She was intimidated by her peers, this was normal. Besides, she'd not expected such great talent, so she was taken by surprise. And anyway, everyone was probably feeling the same insecurities she was. Most importantly, she hadn't been paying attention to the other performances; certainly someone else could've done worse.

This went on for a while.

Alice pulled her knees up to her chest and hugged them tight. She would not cry, she'd decided. There was no need. So maybe (probably) (well, definitely) she wouldn't get the best task—that was okay! Perhaps if her hopes hadn't been so high, her disappointment wouldn't have been so great, but she would learn from this and be better for it, and whichever task she did get would be just fine. She'd be grateful for it. Maybe it wouldn't be a coveted task—maybe she wouldn't even get to leave Ferenwood—but still, it would be a task, and she would be happy to finally have a purpose. It would be the start of something new.

It would be okay.

She'd finally calmed her nerves long enough to make it down the tree. There she stood, half collapsed against the trunk, and promised herself, over and over again, that everything would be okay. She had done her best, and she couldn't have asked for more of herself.

She had done her best.

Finally, the Elders reappeared. They were all smiling (a good sign!) and this gave Alice great hope. Her shoulders sagged in relief and she managed to peek out from behind the tree.

Mr. Lottingale was the first of the ten Town Elders to speak, and each of them took a moment to say something encouraging and inspiring. They spoke with such sincerity that for a minute Alice felt silly for having reacted as she did. They were looking out at the crowd with great pride; surely she'd done better than she thought.

She inched forward a bit more, no longer hidden from view. But just as Alice was considering joining Mother's table, the atmosphere changed. A trumpet blared and there was glitter in the air and thick, shimmery, plum-colored envelopes appeared on breakfast plates before her peers. The excitement was palpable. Everyone knew that an envelope contained a card of a specific color; each color represented a different score. There were five categories altogether, and Alice had them memorized for as long as she could count.

Score 5 || Green = ***Spectacularly Done***

Score 4 || Blue = ***A Very Fine Job***

Score 3 || Red = ***Perfectly Adequate***

Score 2 || Yellow = ***Good Enough***

Score 1 || White = ***Rather Unfortunate***

Children were tearing their envelopes open—some with great confidence, others with great trepidation—while Alice was still straining to see if anything had arrived for her at Mother's table.

It had, indeed.

Alice's heart would not sit still.

She couldn't read Mother's face from here, but she could see Mother holding the envelope in her hand like she wasn't quite sure what to do with it; and though she looked around the square just once, Mother didn't seem to mind that Alice wasn't around to pick it up. Mother often said that she could never be bothered to understand why Alice did the things she did, and now, more than ever, Alice thought never being bothered was a very lazy way to love someone.

Oliver's back was to her, so Alice couldn't see his face, but Mother was smiling at him, so he must have been speaking. He was likely using his gift of persuasion to ruin her life. Sure enough, after only a few seconds, Mother handed him her envelope. Just handed it over. Her entire life folded into a piece of paper and Mother just gave it away to a boy Alice wanted to kick in the teeth.

Alice nearly stomped over there and did just that.

But the truth was, Alice was still scared. She wanted to walk back into a crowd of Ferenwood folk knowing she was one of them. It was bad enough she'd been born with hardly any color, that her skin was the color of snow and her hair the color of sugar and her eyelashes the color of milk. She never liked to admit it, but the truth was true enough: By Ferenwood standards she really *was* the ugliest. Her world thrived on color, and she had none.

But a task did not care about color. It did not depend on anything but magical talent, and talent was something Alice thought she had; Ferenwood hearts were born with it. She, Alice Alexis Queensmeadow, had been born with a Ferenwood heart, and her talent needed a task.

She could not walk into that crowd without it.

Alice didn't want to look at Oliver as he headed her way. She didn't care for his pompousness and she certainly didn't want to hear him tell her how terrible her talent was. She didn't know what Oliver had surrendered, but Alice felt certain it was something stupid.

Oliver cleared his throat. She noticed he'd slung a well-worn bag across his body. He must've been on his way somewhere, and Alice hoped that meant he'd finally leave her alone.

"Hello Oliver," Alicc said curtly, plucking the envelope from his outstretched hand.

"Alice." He nodded.

"You may go now." She narrowed her eyes at him.

Oliver crossed his arms and leaned against the tree trunk. "Open it," he said.

"I do not wish to open it in front of you," she sniffed.

He rolled his eyes. "Don't be so stiff. Just because you won't be getting the best task doesn't mean—"

"And how do you know I won't?" Alice snapped, petulant in an instant. "There's no saying I can't still—"

"Because Kate Zuhair already did," he said with a sigh. "Really, Alice, calm yourself. No one is judging you."

"Oh," she said, blinking fast. It was a small consolation, but Alice was relieved to hear that at least Danyal Rubin hadn't been the one to best her. Still, her pride would not let her be calm. Certainly not in front of Oliver.

"I got a three, you know."

Alice looked up. "You got a three?"

Oliver nodded. "And it's still the hardest thing I've ever had to do. I'm not sure you'd want a five even if you'd earned it."

Alice swallowed hard. She'd never admit this to anyone, but after that performance, she was actually hoping for a 2. Anything but a 1.

1 would be humiliating.

"Go on, then." Oliver tapped the envelope in her hand. "All will be right as rainlight as soon as you open it."

"Alright," she whispered, wondering all the while why Oliver was being so nice to her. Probably he was still hoping she'd ditch her task in order to help him with his.

Which would never happen.

Her hands shook as she broke the seal on the envelope, and it was there—as fate would have it—right there, in front of Oliver Newbanks, the boy who'd crowned her the ugliest girl in all of Ferenwood, that Alice was faced with the worst reality of all.

In her envelope was no card she'd ever seen before. It wasn't yellow or even white. It was black. A simple rectangle cut from thick, heavy paper.

Oliver gasped.

Alice flipped it over.

SCORE 0

The clouds chose that exact moment to come to life. The sky broke open and rain fell so hard and fast it nearly hurt, showering them all in what were supposed to be tears of happiness. Alice felt the cold and she felt the wet, and she felt her bones breaking inside of her, and finally she lost the strength to be brave and gained instead the heart of a coward.

So she ran away.

She ran until her chest cracked, until her lungs burned, until she stumbled and tore her skirts and the tears could no longer be held.

She couldn't tell who was crying harder: herself or the sky.

By the time Oliver found her, Alice was nearly at the edge of Ferenwood, right on the border of Fennelskein, hiding under a penny bush. Alice hiccuped a sob and the pennies shook, silver chimes mocking her pain. She sniffled and choked back the last of her tears and turned her face to the clouds. The rain had stopped and the sun was bright in the sky and hundreds of rainbows had arched over everything, lending an ethereal glow to the world. Alice found the beauty unexpectedly cruel.

She did not know what happened to children who were not tasked. There had only been three children to fail their Surrender in all the hundreds of years it had gone on, and Alice had assumed they simply evaporated back into the ground. Returning to Ferenwood life certainly seemed impossible.

Maybe she would follow in the footsteps of Father and just disappear.

"Go away, Oliver," Alice said quietly. She didn't want to be mean to him, as he'd done nothing in the last hour to deserve it, but she also wanted to be left alone.

He crouched down beside her. "Come out from under there, Alice. I can see right up your skirts."

"Go away," she said again, making no effort to cross her ankles.

Neither one of them spoke for a little while.

"You really were splendid today," Oliver finally said.

"Yes, very."

"Oh come off it, Alice. I mean it."

"If you'll please excuse me," she said stiffly, "I have a great many things to do."

Oliver grabbed her ankles and tugged so hard Alice nearly fell into the brook nearby. She had just gotten her mouth full of terrible things to say to him when he plucked the envelope out of her clenched fist and held her black card up to the sky.

"You're supposed to unlock it, you know."

"You only unlock it if you're tasked," she said to him, jumping to grab the card out of his outstretched hand. "There is nothing to unlock in a zero."

"And how would you know?" Oliver shot her a look.

"It is my very firm belief."

"Oh yes," he said. "I daresay you have many firm beliefs."

Alice turned away and crossed her arms.

"What will you do now?" he asked.

"I will get my card back from you, thank you very much," and she caught his arm just long enough to snatch it back.

"And now?" He stood there staring at her.

"Now I will dig a very deep hole and live in it."

Oliver laughed and it lit up his face. Softened the hardness in his eyes. "You will do no such thing."

"What do you care? I can live in a hole if I please."

"Alice, I don't care what the Elders say. I know what you can do. Just because you chose the wrong talent to surrender—"

"I did not choose the wrong talent!"

"Certainly you did," he said, one eyebrow raised. "I can't even comprehend it. I thought for sure you would've—"

"You hush your mouth, Oliver Newbanks!"

"What? Why?"

"That is not a talent," Alice said firmly.

"*Not a talent!*" Oliver balked. "Do you know what I would give to be able to do what you do?"

"Everyone is born with color," Alice said carefully. "Mine is simply contained on the inside. That is not talent, it is biology."

"That is a biology the rest of us don't have," Oliver pointed out.

"I dance," she said to him. "That is what I do. That is my gift. I feel it, Oliver. I feel it in my heart. It's what I'm meant to do."

"I disagree."

"It's not your place to have an opinion."

"Well, clearly your opinion did not work in your favor—"

She kicked him in the shin.

"Good grief, Alice!" Oliver yelped, grabbing at his leg. "What is the matter with you? I'm only trying to help."

Alice bit her lip and looked away. "I *am* sorry," she whispered. "I don't mean to be cruel. It's just that my heart is so thoroughly broken I fear I am beyond repair."

Oliver seemed slightly mollified. He sighed. "You don't have to be so dramatic," he said. "Besides, if you're looking for adventure, my offer still stands. I still need your help."

"I don't want to help you."

"Why?" he said, exasperated. "Why on earth not? Would it really be so terrible?"

"Probably, yes."

"But for your father?" he said desperately. "Would it be so terrible to also find your father?"

"I still don't understand why you won't just bring him home," Alice said, fists clenching. "If you know where he is—"

Oliver let out a frustrated cry and threw his hands up. "You don't understand!" he said. "It's not that simple—I can't just bring him back, not without you!"

"And why not?" she demanded. "Maybe if you first brought

him back I would actually want to help you! Did you never think of that? That maybe kindness would work better than cruelty? Did you ever consider that maybe—"

"Alice, please!"

Oliver grabbed her arms and set her with a look so strong she couldn't remember enough words to speak.

"Alice," he said again. "Bringing your father home *is* my task."

Alice's body was goose bumps from hair to heel. A shiver climbed into her clothes and warmed itself against her skin. Her heart was racing and her hands were clenching and she closed her eyes and drew in the deepest breath.

Oh my very dear, she thought.

She knew Oliver Newbanks was telling the truth.

She made a sound just then, a sound that might've been a word but was mostly just a sound, and backed away from Oliver, teetering sideways and frontways until she spun and fell in her skirts, a heap of color swallowing her whole.

Finally, Alice looked up.

Oliver had his arms crossed against his chest, his eyebrows drawn tight and low. His eyes were focused on a piece of bark peeling off a nearby tree.

"Oliver," said Alice.

"What?" said he, still glaring at the tree.

"Are you angry?" she asked.

"Yes, quite." He crossed his arms more tightly.

"Don't be angry."

He harrumphed. "You are insufferable."

"Well," she said, crossing her arms, too. "So are you."

Finally, he turned to face her. "And that is all you have to say? After all I've shared with you? You still refuse to—"

"No," said Alice, scrambling to her feet. "No, I did not refuse."

Oliver's arms unthawed. They hung at his sides, limp as his bottom lip. "What?"

"I said," said Alice loudly, "that I did not refuse."

"Then you *agree*—"

"Absolutely not."

Oliver's mouth had frozen open mid-sentence, but now his jaw snapped shut. He narrowed his eyes. "You are the most confounding girl I've ever encountered—"

Alice smiled. "Well thank you—"

"Don't you dare!" Oliver cut her off, horrified. "I did not intend that as a compliment!"

Alice's eyes flashed. She was in a delicate state, and Oliver had just made himself the most convenient target for her anguish.

"Of all the things to dislike," said Alice angrily, "I fear I dislike you the most!"

"Consider the feeling mutual," Oliver snapped.

They stood there awhile, the two of them, chests heaving as they glared at each other. Each was fighting a difficult personal battle, and both were too proud to share aloud their pain.

Finally, Alice grew tired of being angry (it was an exhausting occupation) and collapsed onto the ground, biting lip and cheek and knuckle to keep from bursting into tears once more.

This, Oliver seemed to understand.

Carefully, cautiously, he sat down beside her, and a beat later, they spoke at the same time.

He said, "Do you truly dislike me more than anything else?"

And she said, "Oh, Oliver, I've lost everything, haven't I?"

And Oliver blinked, stunned. His heart, so hard just moments ago, softened as he realized that, for today at least, Alice's battles were greater than his own. He spoke gently when he said, "Of course you haven't."

Alice looked up at him, round eyes full to the brim and shining. She managed a small smile. "You're a terrible liar."

"Well then," he said, failing to suppress a smile of his own. "Come with me. Come and find what you've lost."

"But how will I ever be able to trust you?" She sniffed and wiped at her eyes, determined to pull herself together. "I haven't the slightest inclination to run off any place with any persons who tell more lies than truths."

At this, Oliver raised an eyebrow and smiled. It was perplexing, yes, but the boy appeared to be *flattered*, and we won't bother wondering why. Either way, he was now digging around in his messenger bag for something or other, and Alice was caught, deeply curious. Not a moment later Oliver reemerged, clutching no fewer than five scrolls in his fist, his smile triumphant.

"I have *maps*," was all he said.

Alice gasped appropriately.

(Dear reader: For you and I, the acquiring of maps is an altogether unimpressive feat, as maps are, generally speaking, abundant and available to any persons desiring such things. But we must remind ourselves that in Ferenwood, maps were a rare commodity; and for Alice, they were a fierce reminder of Father. Making maps, you will remember, was his lifelong work.)

Oliver, of course, understood this.

Alice made an odd, startled sort of noise, and he nodded. "Yes," he said. "They are indeed your father's maps. The Elders gave them to me before I set off for my task."

Alice appeared unable to speak, so Oliver plowed on.

"They've been searching for him since he left, you know."

Oliver paused, again allowing Alice an opportunity to respond. When she didn't, he said, "But they couldn't find the right person for the job until last year, at my Surrender. That's when they knew my skills would be just the ticket." Oliver grinned. "Impressive, no?"

"What else do you have in that bag?" Alice finally said, eyes narrowing.

"Nothing you need to be bothered with," he said quickly.

Alice opened her mouth to protest when Oliver interrupted her, hastily shoving the maps away. "Absolutely not," he said. "I shan't share a detail more unless you agree to help."

At this, Alice took a long and deep and careful breath.

Finally, she relented. "Alright," she said, and exhaled. "I'll go with you. I'll help."

Oliver, to his credit, looked so surprised Alice thought he might weep. But Alice hadn't meant to do Oliver any favors; her decision was motivated entirely by self-interest. The way she saw it, she had only two choices now: find Father with Oliver, or stay in Ferenwood and live forever in shame.

So she nodded. "I give you my word."

"Oh, Alice," Oliver said, reaching out. "Thank you—"

"Don't thank me yet," she said, swatting at his hand as she got to her feet, eager to put some distance between them. She didn't want Oliver to think she was thrilled about the situation. "You are certain you know where Father is?"

"Yes," he said, clambering to his feet as well. "Yes, yes. But—don't you see? Knowing means nothing when there's doing to be done. It's the *getting* to your father that I can't do."

Alice clasped her hands and considered the sky, pressing her lips together as she did. She looked Oliver square in the eye, all the while digging the toes of her right foot into the grass. "And can you be *sure* you know where he is?"

Oliver looked like he might fall dead of exasperation. "Have you been hearing nothing I've been saying? Of course I know where your father is, but that doesn't—"

"Yes, yes," Alice said, waving a hand. "I heard all your etceteras. But just because I know you're not lying doesn't make it any easier for me to believe you."

Oliver studied her carefully. He reached into his bag and pulled out yet another scroll of parchment that he then unrolled in the palm of his hand. The paper lay flat as a board for something that had been so tightly wound, but when Oliver next touched it, it shuddered to life. Slowly it grew, the rectangle of paper shivering into a three-dimensional box taller than Oliver was wide. He touched the top with three fingers for three seconds, and the top disappeared.

"Come then," he said to her, motioning with his free hand. "Come have a look at where your father has gone."

Alice was horrified.

"Father is in that box?" she gasped, clasping a hand to her chest. "Has he been trapped? Or broken? Do we have to put him back together? Oh, *Oliver*, I don't know a lick about fixitation—"

"He's not broken," Oliver said, shaking his head at the clouds. "Just come here and look," he said. "For heaven's sake."

"Oh, alright," she said, cheeks stinging. It was hard for Alice to like Oliver—on account of she didn't like him very much—but she wanted to find Father much more than she didn't like Oliver, so she'd have to put up with him. And so she wandered closer, close enough to peer into his box.

Inside, was a door.

Alice gasped again.

"Yes, it's very clever, isn't it?" Oliver said. "But the journey will cost us a great deal—"

"Oh I haven't any money," Alice said. "I spent my last fink on a dillypop."

"—of time."

"Right, yes, *time*." Alice cleared her throat.

"Once we step through," Oliver said, "it will be very difficult to come back. We might be gone for very long."

"As long as a caterpillar?" she asked, one eyebrow arched as she pinched the sky. "Or as long as an ocean?" She threw her arms wide.

"I don't know," he said. "Last time I was gone for a year."

"A whole year?" Alice said, dropping her arms. "That's where you've been all this time? Trying to find Father?"

He nodded.

Alice sat down.

She reached for a daisy without looking, plucking it from the ground only to stuff it in her mouth. "So where does it lead?" she asked, staring into the distance as she chewed. "The door?"

Oliver sighed.

Alice squinted up at him, shading her eyes against the rainbows. Finally, he placed the box on the ground and sat down beside her. "It goes to Furthermore."

Alice laughed, mouth half full of daisy. "Oh, go on," she said. "Really. Tell me where it goes."

"It goes to Furthermore," he said firmly.

"But—" Alice faltered.

Oliver raised an eyebrow.

"But, no," Alice said slowly, quietly. "I thought—everyone thought—" She hesitated. "Oliver, Furthermore isn't *real*."

"Your father thought it was. He was tasked to Furthermore when he was your age, didn't you know? He wasn't just mapping Ferenwood, Alice. He was making maps of *all* magical places. He was doing work far more important than anyone in Ferenwood's ever done." Oliver tapped his bag twice. "Your father's maps saved my life countless times."

Alice's eyes had gone round as plates. Alice hadn't known any of this. (Had Mother known about this?) Father, the town, and the Elders—they'd kept these truths from her. And even though she'd always hoped, always wanted to believe there was something more out there—another magical place in the world—now that the actual possibility was staring her in the face, she wasn't sure how to believe it. (Still—and perhaps unfortunately—Alice knew that Oliver spoke the truth, which made it inconvenient for her to incline toward disbelief.)

"What's it like?" she whispered. "Furthermore?"

Oliver looked away, but not before Alice saw a flash of nervousness flit in and out of his eyes. "There's a reason we don't talk about it," was all he said.

Alice gasped, finally understanding.

"Oh, Oliver," she said. "Is it dangerous? Has Father gotten himself into trouble?"

Oliver turned to face her, determined now. He nodded at the box between them. "Are you willing to find out?"

Alice looked into the box and the tiny door it held. She thought of fear and she thought of courage; she thought of home and hope and the chance for adventure.

She thought of Mother.

Mother, who wouldn't miss her; three brothers, who never knew her; and Father, who always loved her.

Alice had nothing left to lose and an entire father to find.

There it was: For the very second time, she knew what she was meant to do. So she reached inside and turned the knob.

Alice peered into the open doorway and saw nothing at all.

"There doesn't appear to be anything inside," she told Oliver, rattling the box a little. "I think maybe you've got the wrong door."

"There is nothing the matter with my door." Oliver snatched the box away from her, setting it down a few feet away. "You must step inside a world to see it honestly. A passing glance won't do."

She wanted to say something unkind to Oliver, but decided instead to study him awhile, curiouser and curiouser about this boy with the mouth of a liar and hair the color of silver herring. She noticed then that he wore a quiet tunic with no adornments. It was not very stylish. In fact, it had little to recommend it but its hue. It was the color of an unripe eggplant.

Oliver noticed her staring and began to fidget. "Well?" he said.

"Are you certain the door is the only way to get in?" Alice asked. "Perhaps there's a window, something that would give us a quick peek—"

"Are you going to question everything I say?" Oliver asked, his arms flailing about. "Is this how it'll be the entire time?" He caught a passing butterfly and whispered in its ear. "I should snip my head off right now, shouldn't I?"

Alice stifled a laugh.

"Oh very well," she said, and clambered to her feet. "Go on, then. Make me small enough so I might fit inside."

"There's no need for that," Oliver said, releasing the butterfly. It flew in circles around him only to land in his hair, where it promptly fell asleep. "There's plenty of space to fit the both of us. So do be quick about it," he said, gently plucking the butterfly from his head. "It's rude to keep the door waiting."

Alice peered into the door before glancing back at Oliver one last time. He was fighting a losing battle with the butterfly, which had very obviously fallen in love with him. It was a silly thing to do, talking to butterflies. Falling in love was their favorite way to pass the time.

Alice stepped one foot into the box and nearly screamed.

"Why on earth is it *wet*?" she shouted, panicking. She tried to pull her foot free but it was now stuck inside the door. "Why didn't you tell me it would be *wet*—?"

Alice didn't have a chance to protest before Oliver grabbed her by the waist and hoisted her up. He said, "It's wet because it's *water*, you silly girl," and dropped her in.

THIS MIGHT BE MY FAVORITE PART

Alice fell very far.

She fell back for a bit and then slightly to the left, and then up for a very long while until she finally fell down with a *plop*, soaking wet and sinking fast.

She tried to scream but spoke only in bubbles, blinking around at the sea she was drowning in. She was scared and she was mad, but mostly she was mad. Oliver had not told her she'd have to swim in these heavy clothes, and now she would die and it would be all his fault and she wouldn't even be able to tell him so, and that made her even madder and so she kicked and kicked at the water, her delicate headpiece and ankle bracelets slipping off in the process. Horrified, she finally accepted that she could only survive if she untied her cumbersome skirts—and, oh, how it broke her heart to watch them go—but it was then, just as she was thinking of how best to kill Oliver Newbanks, that he was tugging on her arm.

As soon as her head broke the surface, she could hear what he was saying.

"What in heavens are you doing?" he shouted, red in the face and shaking. "Why didn't you come out of the water? Were you trying to kill yourself?"

"What?" She spat water out of her mouth and pushed her hair out of her eyes. "Me? Kill myself? What are you talking about? I was only *drowning*, no thanks to—"

"Drowning?" he said, flabbergasted. "Alice, the water is only knee-deep!"

Ah.

That would explain how she was currently standing.

Alice looked down and around herself and spotted her skirts floating only a few feet away. She cleared her throat and said, "If you'll please excuse me," before making her way toward the clothes.

The water was clear and the color of turquoise. It wasn't cold and it wasn't hot but it was very wet and Alice was looking forward to being out of it. Once she'd secured her skirts and made her way back to Oliver, he gave her a very round look and seemed to think it best not to comment any further.

"Well?" she said, head held high as she shivered in the breeze. "Where from here?"

"Straight ahead," he said, nodding toward the shore.

Land was just a faint line in the distance, but she could see it, so she told him so. She followed Oliver as he went and asked no additional questions outside of the five questions she did ask, and paused only to sneeze when her nose required it.

She was just in the middle of a sneeze, in fact, when she noticed the wet carpet under her feet. They were very close to the shore now, and she could see straight to the end: There were tens of dozens of ancient rugs laid out along and up the sand, cutting a vertical line to land. Each rug was a rich red, but woven with threads of gold and violet and sea-foam green into intricate, abstract, faded floral patterns.

It all felt very proper.

Furthermore was welcoming them, and suddenly Alice was glad to have arrived. Suddenly she wasn't cold or wet at all. In fact, suddenly she was warm and her skirts were toasty and her hair was dry and her bare feet were walking on the thick, plush Persian rugs that had been laid straight across the beach. They were heading nowhere as far as she could tell, but she didn't mind. The sky was very pink and the clouds were very blue and the air was sweet as lemonpearl and she felt very cozy and very lazy and very this and very that and very—

"Alice!"

Oliver tugged on her arm and she heard it snap. Not her arm, no. But something. Something snapped. Suddenly they were on the sand and not the beautiful rugs and she felt very cold and very worried and very hungry and very—

Oliver was snapping his fingers in front of her face. "Alice? Alice. *Alice.*"

"What?" she said, frowning. "What is it? What is the matter?"

"You musn't stay on the rugs for long," he said urgently. "Furthermore can be tricky when you're not paying attention." He pulled her to her feet. Only then did she realize she'd sat down.

"Where are we?" she asked, looking around. Oliver had nudged them back onto the beach, but that didn't change what she saw. It was a barren landscape, nothing but sand and sea, not a person in sight.

"We are at the beginning," he said, and that was all.

They stood in the sun and said nothing more, and Alice was so confused she couldn't even remember how to say so. Besides, she was distracted. Oliver was holding her hand now and, though she tried to shake him off, he wouldn't let her.

"You need to be careful," he said to her. "We are currently at the entry of Slumber, which is just one of the sixty-eight villages we must travel through, and each village has its own very specific rules. We cannot break a single one if we are to find your father."

"Not a single rule!" she said. "In sixty-eight villages!"

"Not a single rule," he said. "In sixty-eight villages."

"But how will we know all the rules?" she asked.

"I will teach them to you as we go. I lived in Furthermore for an entire year," Oliver said, "so this is all very common to me now, but I imagine it must be very strange for you."

"Yes," she said, sneaking a look at him. "Very strange, indeed."

Oliver was looking around carefully, his eyes darting every which way. It was as though he was seeing something she could not, something he was afraid of.

"And now?" she asked. "Where do we go now?"

"We don't go anywhere," he said. "We wait for the sun to sleep."

Alice wanted to believe Oliver was joking, but she couldn't suss out the humor in his words. "Oh?"

Oliver nodded. "Though we won't wait too long, I hope." He squinted at something in the distance. "The sun in Slumber is terribly lazy and always forgetting the time. It naps so frequently that its people have stopped waiting for sunshine. Their village only appears in the dark."

"Oliver," said Alice, "are you being deliberately absurd?"

It was odd, but for a girl born and bred in magic, Alice could be disappointingly unimaginative. But then I suppose there was good reason for her reaction. After all, the people of Ferenwood had always used magic in the same steady, reliable ways, and Alice had never known magic to be manipulated frivolously; she'd no idea what a little recklessness could do. The magic of Furthermore was entirely foreign to her.

But Oliver still hadn't offered an answer to her question. He was rifling through his bag again, and this time Alice heard the unmistakable clink of coins.

She narrowed her eyes and poked him in the shoulder. "What else have you got in there?"

Instead of responding, he unhooked their hands and folded himself into a seated position, settling in for a wait. Alice very cautiously followed suit, and she was just about to ask another question when Oliver tugged something out of his bag. It was a small notebook.

"Right," he said, perusing its pages. "I nearly forgot."

"What is it?" Alice asked. "What's the matter?"

"Nothing's the matter yet," said Oliver. "I'm just checking things. Making certain and so forth."

"Making certain of what?"

"Oh, just sun cycles and such." Oliver was reading with great focus, following a few scribbled sentences with his finger. "Mmm," he said. "We should only have to wait here a few moments longer." He looked up. "What sensational luck. If we'd arrived any later, we'd have had to wait at least a good hour for the sun to sleep, and it would've been *the* most anticlimactic introduction." He turned back to his notebook. "This first bit of the journey can be terribly boring, you know."

Alice frowned. "Oliver, what—"

"Oh, ho!" Oliver jumped up with a start, squinting up at the sky. "There we are."

"What?" Alice asked, scrambling to her feet and looking around. "What's happening?"

Oliver nodded at the sun. "There. He's just about to take his nap."

"But—"

"Now give us a second, Alice," Oliver said impatiently. "It takes him a moment to roll over."

Alice blinked, and the world went black.

Alice had never in her life seen such darkness. Back home they had moons and planets and so many stars that the nighttime was never really night. Not like this. This was something she could not adequately describe. They had been plunged into a sky where everything had been snuffed out. She blinked and blinked and the blindness sent a chill through her heart she could not shake. A fear of the unknown, of the unseen, of what could be waiting for them here in this new world—it would not leave her.

"Oliver," she whispered.

"Yes?"

"Why didn't we pass through when the sun was *awake*? Wouldn't that have been safer?"

Oliver shook his head. "Slumber is the entry point into all of Furthermore, and as such, the security measures are severe. Any visitors foolish enough to enter at sunlight are seen and snatched up in an instant."

"But why?" Alice asked. "Snatched up for what?"

"Snatched up for *what*? Are you quite serious?"

"Oh, and you're surprised, are you?" Alice crossed her arms, irritated. "Surprised I know not a single thing about this land I learned existed only a moment ago?"

Oliver was slightly mollified. "Right," he said, and sighed. "My apologies. It's just that it seems so obvious to me."

"Well when will it be obvious to *me*?"

He squeezed her hand. "Soon, I'm sure."

"But how soon?"

"Patience, Alice. Best to introduce yourself to patience now, so that it might find you when you call upon it later."

"But I have so many questions," she said, tapping his shoulder very hard. "Why would they want to snatch up visitors? Is that what happened to Father?"

Oliver smiled at her in the dark. "Not exactly, no. Your father is ten steps smarter than all that."

"But—"

"While I'd like to answer all your questions," he said lightly, "we've little time to spare and many appetites to avoid. I won't be the reason you end up in someone's stew tonight."

Alice had not a single idea what he was talking about and she told him so.

"Well," said Oliver, "if you don't already know what to fear in Furthermore, I can't imagine you'd want to change that now. Perhaps it's best to be ignorant just a moment longer." And then he held up a finger and peered up at the sky.

A moment, it turned out, was all it took.

The sky exploded with light, shot through with so many stars and moons and glittering planets that it was blinding in a whole new way. It looked as though the night sky had tried to snow but the flakes had fallen upside down and gotten stuck.

It was, in a word, *magical*.

Not just the sky, but the whole village. People appeared out of nowhere, shops and businesses busy in an instant. Food was cooking and chimneys were puffing and children were crying and parents were shouting and the hustle and bustle was all it took to shuffle Alice right along, right into the heart of it, and she felt her spirits soar despite her many worries. Eyes wide-open, Alice took it all in. This was a *real* adventure, wasn't it? This was what she'd always dreamed of. And, oh, to find Father in the process! She nearly ran into the arms of this new world.

But first, she had priorities.

"Alice, no!"

Oliver tackled her.

"But I'm hungry," she said, staring at the flower she'd nearly plucked out of the ground.

"You musn't," he said. "You can't. And you absolutely shouldn't."

"But—"

"No," he said firmly. "Only on special occasions are visitors allowed to eat anything in Furthermore. And this is not one of them."

"Only on special occasions?" she said back to him. "And what are they to do until those occasions arrive?" Her hands were on her hips now. "Are they expected to starve?"

"Yes," he said, and very gently and with a smile she did not anticipate. "Now," he said, clapping his hands together, all business. "Will you be requiring use of the toilets? There's only one set of toilets in all of Slumber and they're right here at the start, so best to use them now if you need to. It'll be a long trip, you know."

"I—well, yes. Okay." Alice dropped her hands and looked away. It was hard on her pride to be treated like an imbecile, and she hated the way Oliver seemed to know so much and she so little. She was fighting no small battle to be cooperative, if only for Father's sake, but her patience had little practice. "But I'm also very hungry," she said, determined to be heard. "I haven't had any noonlunch."

"Good," Oliver said. "That will help us quite a bit."

"And how's that?"

Oliver squinted up at the night sky and, once again, offered no answers. Alice glared at his back. Oliver was secretly relishing his role as leader of the two and, under the pretense of being older and wiser, he hoarded his knowledge, miserly sparing only a sentence or three when he felt he must. But Oliver had underestimated his female companion and her capacity for being condescended to, and he would no doubt pay for his youthful arrogance. With every new slight and casual indifference, Alice was a glass half empty, slowly filling bottom to top with resentment. As for now, all was well enough, as she distracted herself with the splendors of her new environment, but Oliver would later find much to revise in his early moments with Alice Alexis Queensmeadow.

"Now then," Oliver said, glancing at her, "we have only a couple of hours before the sun wakes up again, and a lot to do before that happens. Best to get moving," he said, patting her on the back as a parent might. "And let's get you to the ladies' toilets, shall we?"

Alice grimaced and trudged on, mildly embarrassed and ignoring the urge to pop Oliver in the nose. She sighed loudly whenever they passed a patch of grass and a promising bud, the grumbles in her stomach growing louder by the moment. She knew she would be a terrible companion if she missed too many meals and it worried her; this journey was too important. She needed to be her best self—healthy and full of energy—and Oliver didn't seem to care. He was grinning cheek to cheek, happy in a way she didn't know he could be, and she realized then that Oliver was fond of Furthermore. Happy to be back. Maybe happy to be home.

Strange.

Alice skipped a little as they got closer to the heart of town, abandoning her frustration in exchange for excitement, eager to be seeing and doing new things. This was a thrilling journey for a young girl (and newly twelve years old, lest we forget) who'd never left home in all her life. More exciting still, Slumber wasn't at all like Ferenwood, where everything was an explosion of color; no, Slumber was black and bright, an inky glow, orange-yellow spilling out of corners, puncturing the sky, creeping past their feet. It was cozy and merry and perfectly odd, and if Alice weren't so preoccupied with thoughts of Father, she might've been more inclined to enjoy it.

There was food, everywhere.

Cups full of nuts standing in bowls, jars and jars of honey stacked in storefronts, glasses full of flowers just sitting on tables. Alice wanted very desperately to eat one. Just one, she thought, couldn't have been so bad.

She said as much to Oliver.

"That is not food," he said to her. "Those are decorations. People in Furthermore do not eat flowers. They eat animals."

"Animals!" Alice cried, and shuddered, thinking of all the cows and sheep and birds back home. The people of Ferenwood lived in peace with living things, only occasionally borrowing milk or eggs or honey in exchange for a lifelong friendship with creatures older and wiser than they. Alice was duly horrified and she suddenly remembered Oliver's hair, which had always reminded her of silver herring. She pointed an accusing finger in his direction. "You eat them, too, don't you? *Don't you?* Oh, those poor fish!"

Oliver went pink. "I haven't any idea what you mean," he said, and cleared his throat. "And anyway, no food is to touch your lips, not here and not at all, at least not until I tell you so."

She scowled.

He scowled back.

"Remember what I said earlier?" Oliver scolded her. "About how we aren't to break a single rule if we are to find your father?"

Alice nodded.

"Well, this is the first one," he said. "So don't break it."

"Fine," she said. And she pursed her lips, quietly hating him.

❖

They crept through town quietly, doing little to draw attention to themselves. Strangers offered them a few glances but little else, which Alice thought was kind of them, considering how awful she must've looked with her sea-washed hair and clothes. Her outfit was fairly ruined and her hair was a wispy nest, and though she looked nothing at all like anyone in Slumber, they didn't seem to mind. She realized it was because they couldn't really tell.

In the dark, they were all the same.

"Here we are," Oliver finally said.

He pointed to what appeared to be a ladies' toilet. It was little more than a wooden shack standing in the middle of all the dimness, and when Alice gaped at Oliver, all he did was shrug.

So into the shack she went—*tick tock tick tock*—and out the shack she came.

She shook out her skirts and smoothed out her top before

joining Oliver where he was standing, and did her best to appear proper. She cleared her throat a little.

"I'm ready now," she said.

Oliver glanced at her. "And how are you feeling? Still hungry?"

"Yes," she said. "Quite."

"Good. Very good. Shall we?" He gestured to the main path.

"Where are we going?" she asked as she fell into step with him.

"We have to pick up something important while we're here. I just hope it'll be in the same place I left it."

"Oh?" said Alice. "And what is it?"

"A pocketbook."

Alice laughed. "But you've already got one," she said, nodding at his bag.

Oliver shot her a look. "I most certainly have not."

"Oh Oliver." Alice sighed, rolling her eyes. "We'll get you ten pocketbooks if you love them so."

Oliver was perplexed but let it go. He seemed distracted—nervous, even, as he wove a path through town, but Alice was experiencing no such nervousness. She followed Oliver through the narrow cobblestoned lanes and tried to be present in each moment, appreciating the scents and scenery of this new land. Lanterns were lit along every path and the sky was positively mad with power, but even so, it was hard to see.

Night light made everything invisible around the edges, all slinky silhouettes and occasional spotlights. Alice did her best to keep up with Oliver, but her efforts required more than several apologies to the bodies she collided with. Still, it smelled like cardamom in Slumber, and the pinked cheeks of bundled strangers made her want to stay forever.

Oliver, however, was not having it.

"But that's not fair," she said to him. "What if there are clues here? Clues to where Father has gone? We came all this way—I really think we should investigate the people! If Father has been here, we should shop the shops he shopped and climb the trees he climbed and see how the gentlemen wear their hair and, oh, Oliver, I would dearly love t—"

"Absolutely not," Oliver said, stopping in place. He lowered his voice to a whisper. "Alice, please stop insisting we stay. I already know where your father has gone. I don't need any more clues. And besides it all, you don't understand how important it is that we—"

"But—"

"It's not safe!" he said, finally losing his temper.

"It's not safe? To pop into a shop? Not safe to knock a hello on a neighbor's house?"

"Not safe, no! Not safe at all! We cannot, under any circumstances, go into the *light*," he hissed. "Don't you understand?"

"No, I do not *understand*," Alice snapped. She shook her

head and shook off his hand. "You are being insufferable," she said, "and I'm so tired of it I could fall asleep standing up."

"But—"

"Now I haven't a single idea which feathers you pluck in private—(this was a common Ferenwood expression; I'll try to explain later)—but I can't guess which either. And my right hand to rainlight, Oliver Newbanks, I swear it, if you go on an *inch* more with this nonsense of answering *none* of my questions, I will find a lake and push you in it and then," she said, poking him in the chest, "then you'll discover the only use in having a head so full of hot air."

Oliver had gone reddish.

Humility had gotten lost on its journey to his ego, but the two had finally been reunited, and the meeting appeared to be painful. Oliver swallowed hard and looked away. "Alright," he said. "Alright. I'm sorry. But let us find a quiet place first. A private place. We won't have much time to spare, but I'll do my best to tell you the things you need to know." His eyes darted left and right. "And please," he begged, "for Feren's sake, lower your voice."

Alice sighed.

"Oh, very well," she nearly said. "Fine, fine, let's carry on," she nearly said. She nearly said she was perfectly ready to be amiable.

But nearly said was not quite enough. Alice was distracted,

frustrated, and embarrassingly stubborn, and she had stopped paying attention to anyone but Oliver. So it should come as no surprise to you then, that in that moment, just as she was about to grant Oliver her acquiescence, she was plowed into.

Apologies abounded.

Excuse me and *pardon me* and *oh goodness* collided in the air. Alice was dusting herself off and adjusting her skirts and clambering to her feet (with no help from Oliver, mind you), when she first saw the person with whom her body had collided.

Friends, he was the most handsome boy she'd ever seen.

He was tall but not too tall, perfect but not too perfect, dark hair, dark eyes, dark skin. He looked like molasses had made a man. Her exact opposite in every way. Skin like silk jam, hair as dark as pitch. Eyes with lashes so thick and black and oh, how they fluttered when he blinked. Was he blinking? He was staring. At her.

At her?

Where she looked like nothing, he looked like everything, and she had never been so speechless in all her life.

Be still her heart, he was smiling at her.

Alice was convinced, after a moment or two, that she was most certainly in love with him. It seemed like the only logical explanation for what she was feeling. And it wasn't until Oliver pointed out (rudely) that her mouth was open (only a little, really) that she was startled back into her bones.

She gasped, surprised by how loudly her jaw snapped shut, and wondered how best to ask the beautiful boy to marry her. He was maybe Oliver's age, which meant he was close to Alice's age, which meant none of them had any actual interest in marrying anyone, but that didn't change what Alice said next.

"Will you—" she began to say, and thought better of it.

"Would you—" she said instead, and reached for his hand.

Oliver snatched her arm away and gave her a very mean look. "What are you doing?" he hissed.

"Oh, hush," she whispered, waving him away.

"Good sleep to you," the beautiful boy said to her, smiling wide. "It certainly is a pleasure to be meeting you tonight."

He had a slight accent; his voice was deep and musical, like maybe it wasn't real. Like maybe he was speaking a language she didn't know she could understand.

She didn't much care either way.

"It is a very great pleasure to be meeting you, too," she said quickly, ignoring Oliver, who was already trying to pull her away.

"Yes, yes," Oliver said. "Pleasure. We must be on our way now. Thank you, good-bye!"

"Wait!" said the boy urgently. He scanned Oliver's face for only a moment before turning back to Alice. "You are new here. I have never seen anyone like you before," he said, and as he did, he reached out, tangling a strand of her unfortunate white hair around his fingers.

Alice nearly fainted.

"Would you like to stay awhile?" he asked her. Only her. "I could show you around—"

She was already nodding when Oliver interrupted them, yet again. "Please," he said quietly. His eyes were bright and twitchy and locked on to hers. "A moment of your time in private?"

Alice wanted to ignore him, but the look on Oliver's face worried her. So she excused herself and promised the beautiful boy that she would return shortly.

Oliver, however, was steaming mad.

He had a whole host of unhappy things to say to her about breaking the rules and not listening to him, and though she tried to reassure him that she hadn't meant for any of this to happen, Oliver was adamant that they keep moving.

"And anyway," Oliver said, "I haven't any idea why you're so enchanted by him. Residents of Slumber are very nearly covered in dust." (*Dust*, I should mention, was a kind of slang for *magic*.) Oliver crossed his arms. "He has hoaxed you, be sure of it."

"Oh but Oliver," Alice said, glancing over his shoulder. "Did you not see him? He is so astoundingly beautiful. Just, oh"—she was very nearly melting—"so very, very beautiful. I am sure I have never seen anyone so handsome in all my life." She grabbed Oliver's sleeve. "Do you not think he is the most handsome person you have ever seen in all your life?"

Oliver went purple in the face. He pursed his lips and flailed his arms and almost exploded the words he spoke next. (Honestly, no one could understand a thing he said, so I won't even *try* to recount any of it.) Anyhow, Alice didn't want to upset Oliver—he seemed so very put out by the whole thing—so she prepared to tell the boy that she could not accept his generous offer. But when they returned, he'd already assembled a crowd, and by then—well, by then it was far too late.

And it was all her fault.

Oliver had gone white.

He was milk and paper and ghostly fright. He'd taken her hand and was squeezing so tight Alice had no choice but to shake him off. She yanked her hand back and scowled at no one in particular, realizing all too late that she had caused quite a lot of trouble. She glanced at Oliver. He was frozen in place, eyes wide, horrified by the spectacle they'd become.

The beautiful boy and his crowd of people were close, closer, and a blink later, had circled around them completely. The tallest held a torch and held it high, high above Alice's head, so everyone could get a good look at her face. They were pointing and gesturing, heads cocked and gazes roving over her hair, her skin, her tattered skirts. She felt as though she were locked in a cabinet of curiosities, and she didn't like it one bit.

Alice narrowed her eyes at the beautiful boy, but he didn't seem to notice. He was smiling wide, looking around at his friends like he was proud, like he'd discovered something odd and strange and oh, wouldn't it be tops to poke fun at the nothing-girl tonight. Well, she wasn't having any of that.

Alice was not interested in being stared at, and besides, she and Oliver had a very busy schedule and no time to spare for nonsense.

The beautiful boy stepped forward.

"My name is Seldom," he said. And smiled.

Alice wanted very much to speak, but she was abruptly startled into silence. Seldom had moved into the torchlight and his face—well, it was nothing at all like it was in the moonlight. Here, where the fiery glow illuminated his features, she could see him far more clearly. Tall and broad, he wore a sleeveless shirt with a deep V-cut neckline, very short shorts, and a pair of moccasins. But most interesting was his skin. He was a stroke of midnight—so blue he was almost black—and he was covered, head to toe, in tattoos. Stars, moons—*galaxies*—were drawn upon his body in ink so gold they shimmered in the light. Alice stood there staring at him, just as he stood staring at her.

Mouths agape.

He was beautiful in an extraordinary way. He was beautiful in a way she did not understand.

"What is your name?" Seldom asked.

"Alice, don't tell him!" Oliver said, reaching out as if to stop her.

Alice didn't even have time to roll her eyes at Oliver.

"Your name is Alice?" Seldom asked.

She nodded, pausing just long enough to shoot a dirty look at Oliver, who had now turned a very unflattering shade of puce.

"Yes," she said, and sighed. Oliver had already told him anyway. "My name is Alice. Can I leave now?"

Seldom shook his head. "We would like to keep you."

"Oh," she said, surprised. She looked around at the crowd. They were smiling eagerly, nodding and waving hello. Suddenly they seemed friendly, and she was convinced it was some kind of a trick. "Well, that is very kind," she said, turning back to Seldom. "But I really must be on my way."

She took a step forward.

Seldom stepped in front of her. "Where do you have to go?"

Alice bit her lip and looked him square in the eye, wondering how much to say to him. She wasn't sure how dangerous this situation was—mostly because Oliver was such a mouse he could hardly say a word—but she wasn't going to let anyone keep her here. She knew that if she wanted to find Father, she had to first find her way through this.

(I feel it necessary to mention here that were it not for Father, Alice might not have felt so brave. Love had made her fearless, and wasn't it strange? It was so much easier to fight for another than it was to fight for oneself.)

But how? Alice thought. Escape might require a lie, and she—well she had bound herself to the truth.

And yet, Alice compromised, her truths were meant only for Ferenwood, weren't they? Technically—if we may speak technically—Alice hadn't even known Furthermore was real when she made that pact. And anyway, she quickly convinced herself, these next words wouldn't be a lie. Not exactly. She would tell a story, she'd decided. A fable. A work of fiction.

"I am in charge of the sun," she said loudly. "And I'm on my way to wake him up."

Seldom blinked fast. Shocked.

Oliver inhaled sharply.

The crowd around them went loud then silent in rapid succession.

"Alice," Oliver whispered. He was holding her hand again. He kept doing that. "What are you thinking?"

"I don't know," she whispered back to him. She was still looking at Seldom. "I'm trying to get us out of here."

"But, Alice—"

"You are in charge of the sun?" Seldom asked quietly. His eyebrows had rushed together in confusion.

"Yes," she said. And nodded, too, for added effect.

"Oh." He frowned. "We did not think a person could climb so high."

"I'm very talented," she assured him, this time not lying at all. "There are a great many things I can do."

Seldom grunted.

Alice tried to smile.

"Is that why you're so white?" Seldom asked, with no preamble.

"Excuse me?"

"Because your color's all burnt off," said someone from the crowd. "You're white because you burnt off all your colors, didn't you?"

"Well, I wouldn't say that I—"

"So—you are not a visitor?" Seldom asked. "You're one of us, but your color is gone? Because of the sun?"

"I, um"—Alice cleared her throat and looked around at their anxious faces—"yes," she decided, "yes, that's exactly what happened." And she silently congratulated herself on her storytelling abilities.

"And what about him?" Seldom was pointing at Oliver.

"Oh yes," she said quickly. "Him too. He's seen the sun too many times, too. Not as many times as me, of course, but, you know, eventually, he'll be just as white as I am."

Seldom was crestfallen. He was so disappointed, in fact, that he seemed almost mad at Alice. He and his friends shared some words on the matter, and everyone took turns shooting her unkind looks.

Slowly, they scattered.

When they'd all finally walked away, Alice and Oliver were left to dwell on their feelings—and it turned out they were both very angry with the other.

Oliver was still holding Alice's hand and they were now walking very, very quickly through town, but Oliver was huffing and Alice was puffing and he said, "I can't believe you!" and she said, "You are such a coward!" and he said, "Always causing trouble, never listening," and she said, "Didn't do anything at all to save us, just standing there like a stump," and Oliver stopped so suddenly they nearly fell over.

"Didn't do anything at all to save us?" he said. "*Standing there like a stump?* Alice, have you gone mad?"

"Oh don't be ridiculous, Oliver! I was the one who had to think quickly—I was the one who had to—"

"You did nothing at all!" Oliver nearly shouted. "Do you know how hard I had to work? To get us out of that mess?"

"What?" she said. "What are you talking about?"

"Me, Alice, *me*." He stabbed a finger at his chest. "While you stood there answering questions and making up stories, I had to convince them to believe you, and my head nearly exploded with the effort. I've been working so hard to help you, and all you do is fight me. I take your hand and you shove me away and I'm left grasping, furious—"

"Well maybe I don't want you to hold my hand," Alice

snapped, cheeks pinking. "And anyway, I had been wondering why—"

"I am trying to keep us safe!" Oliver shouted, so angry now he was practically shaking. "I need to be near you in order to quietly convince everyone to leave us be! And what thanks do I get for all this? None. None at all. You're running off, breaking away, charging into strangers! You make everything so much more difficult!"

Oliver threw his hands in the air.

Alice shoved him in the chest. Twice. "Maybe if you'd been *honest* with me about what to *expect*—"

"Maybe if you'd been *patient*, or even bothered to ask *nicely*—"

"I am not incompetent!" Alice cried. "And I don't appreciate your patronizing me! In fact, I've no doubt I could find my own way through Furthermore, without a bit of help from you—"

"Is that right?" Oliver's eyes flashed.

"Right as rainlight!"

"So you really think," Oliver said, stepping closer, "that you'd have gotten five feet farther without my saving you from your own silly stories? You think anyone would've believed you?"

Alice's confidence faltered. Her stomach did a nervous flip.

Oliver looked away, shaking his head. "*In charge of the sun*," he said. "Really. What nonsense was that? Of all the things to say!"

He ran both hands through his hair, losing steam.

"Don't you understand why your father was tasked to me? Why the Elders sent me *here*, to Furthermore, to a land of tricks and puzzles? I have the gift of persuasion, Alice. And, yes, it grants me the ability to know the deepest secret of every person I meet, but the people of Furthermore are nothing like the people of Ferenwood, and their deepest secrets hardly help me at all, making the task infinitely more complicated. And if you think navigating this land is hard for *me*, it would be a sight near impossible for *you*."

"I beg to diff—"

"Forgive me," he said, exhausted. "I didn't intend that as an insult. Truly. It's just that some things in Furthermore are about more than being smart. In fact," he said, "most of it is about lying, tricking, and the luck of just barely surviving." He looked up, looked her in the eye. "Alice, this land is not generous. It does not forgive. And it would kill to devour you.

"There is only one reason I have not yet met your father's fate, and it's that I have the ability to convince others to believe what I want them to believe. So please," he said. "Please trust me enough to do the one thing I'm any good at.

If we don't stick together, we're lost for good."

Alice hung her head.

"But even you couldn't save Father," she said, staring into the darkness. "Even persuasion wasn't enough."

"No." Oliver sighed. "Not the first time, at least. But we'll get it right this time. I swear it."

Alice closed her eyes and hugged herself, more terrified for Father than ever before. Furthermore was brilliant and frightening, and though she'd only seen a small slice of it, she could now understand perfectly well why Father had been so enchanted. But it was becoming clear to her that Furthermore was full of quiet dangers, and it would not be wise to be too easily distracted. It would be simple to get lost here—lost and destroyed—and she had not realized that Oliver had been looking after her all this time, quietly convincing this world to leave her unharmed.

The truth was, she *hadn't* trusted Oliver. Not really. He'd hurt her somewhere deep—wounded her pride and her vanity—and it made her cold and hard and stubborn. But she could see now that she was being difficult, and fighting Oliver would do them no good. Father needed her, and that meant she had to trust Oliver, no matter how *nothing* he thought she looked.

Oliver lifted her chin with one finger, and when their eyes

met, they both apologized. Regrets and reconciliations, all at once.

Oliver almost smiled.

Alice almost did, too.

Then she slipped her hand in his and held on tight.

HERE WE GO

They walked for days. Weeks. Months and years.

"Don't be so dramatic," Oliver said. "It's only been fifteen minutes."

"But I'm cold." Alice sneezed.

Oliver stopped to stare at her. "Yes, I daresay you are." He looked a bit defeated as he looked her over. They were friends again and making their way out of Slumber, feet pounding the cobblestoned path. "Alright," he said, pulling her close. "Don't worry. We're almost there."

But almost there was still too far, and the farther they walked, the farther the town stayed behind, keeping its lights with it. They'd wound their way through the center of Slumber, Alice's eyes eating up what her stomach could not: the fire-like glow; the slinky black backdrop; the hustle and bustle and the sounds that came with it. It was chilly but it was alive, chimney-puffing and storytelling and snips of conversations the strangest strangers left on sidewalks.

They were leaving it all behind.

"So where do we go?" she asked Oliver. "To get the pocketbook?"

"Up," he said cheerfully.

"My goodness, Oliver, have we learned nothing in the last half hour? *Up* is not an answer."

"Right," he said, startled. "Right, forgive me. I meant *up*, you know, in the sky. I hid it in the clouds, you see."

Alice was beginning to realize that the explanations she'd so desperately sought were now only adding to her confusion. She was no longer certain she wanted to understand Furthermore.

In any case, she felt another sneeze coming, so she let go of Oliver's hand and grabbed on to his tunic, bracing herself for the impact. But the sneeze was a false alarm, and when it passed it left her sniffling; she could feel her nose slowly growing numb. The last dregs of the sun's heat had left them, and warmth was in short supply. "So, Oliver," she said, still sniffling. "Tell me. Why did you fail?"

"What?" he said, his body tensing.

"To free Father," Alice said. "Why did you fail to bring him home the first time? What happened?"

"I . . ." Oliver trailed off. "Well . . . I . . ."

He seemed to be making a decision right then; a decision that would say quite a lot about the direction of their friendship. Would he trust Alice with his insecurities? Could he dare to be vulnerable in her presence? Which would it be, hmm? Truth or omission, truth or omission, truth or—

"I just wasn't good enough," he finally said.

(Ah, a bit of truth, then. Refreshing.)

"I hit a dead end. The final steps stumped me, and I knew I needed help."

"And you needed *my* help?" Alice asked, flattered and suspicious all at the same time.

Oliver stopped walking and locked eyes with her. "Yes," he said softly. "But you know why, don't you? You can imagine why?"

"Because he's my father?" Alice guessed, searching Oliver's face for answers. "Because you need to know something about him only I can tell you?"

Oliver's gaze faltered. He offered her a smile and said, "Well, we'll talk more about it later, won't we? For now," he said, perking up as they walked on, "we should pay close attention to where we are. Furthermore is always awaiting our distraction. There's always a trick, always a catch, always a danger smarter or sillier than you think. It's a strange and terrible land to get lost in," he said. And then, more sadly, "It's probably why your father couldn't get out."

"Right," Alice said, startled. "Of course."

It was another tiny pinch of a reminder, but it was enough. Alice had worried and wondered about Father for three years, and now here they were, so close, so close.

And still, so very very far.

Alice had dreamed of a reunion with Father the way some people dreamt of fame and glory; she'd acted out the motions hundreds of times; she'd imagined every smile, every tear, every clinging hug. And yet, somehow, it was much easier to dream of Father from afar, because being this close to him now only filled her with fear. What if their journey went terribly wrong? What if she ruined everything with a simple mistake and Father stayed gone for good? It would be infinitely more difficult to live with loss if Alice had herself to blame for the lack.

She wore her worries like a cloak clasped tight around her throat but, come fear or failure, Alice would tread cautiously into the night. There would be no turning back.

⁂

Alice didn't know where they were going now, but the farther they went, the darker it grew; and the darker it grew, the colder it became; and the colder it became, the quieter it was; and the quieter it was, the more there was to hear.

"My goodness," Oliver said. "Your stomach has quite a roar."

Alice felt a blush creep up her neck. "It's no fault of mine," she said. "I'm not to blame for needing food."

"And how are you feeling?" he asked. He'd come to a complete stop, so she did, too. There was nothing but darkness all around them; not a single thing in sight.

"I'm feeling alright, I think." Her stomach sang another song, and she sighed. "I'm feeling a bit faint, really."

"Are you quite empty, do you think?"

Alice raised an eyebrow at Oliver.

"Empty," he said again. "How empty are you feeling?"

"Very."

"Well I'm thrilled. This is excellent timing."

"Why Oliver Newbanks, what a rude thing to say. My hunger is not a thing to be happy about."

"Hunger is not one but two," he said. "Emptiness is not three but four." He was whispering to the moons, his eyes on the stars, his hands reaching up into the dark, searching for something.

"What?" she asked, eyes wide. "What are you doing?"

But then there it was.

Oliver was tugging on a chain in the sky. He pulled once, very firmly, and it made a scissor-like sound.

A lightbulb illuminated.

It was hanging free and clear, right there, right in front of her, suspended not ten feet off the ground—she wouldn't have been able to reach for it, not even with a stool—right in the middle of nothing.

She was still gaping at the lightbulb, even when Oliver looked back at her. "Are you ready?" he asked.

"Always," she said. "But whatever for?"

And then he took her by the waist and tossed her in the sky.

Alice thought maybe she should scream—it seemed like the right thing to do—but it didn't feel honest. The truth was, she wasn't scared at all, and besides, it was much warmer up here. She'd flown straight up, light as a bulb, and it was only once she'd stopped and stood around that she understood why lighting that first light was so important. It was awfully dark in the clouds.

She looked around for Oliver and it was only a moment before he was standing beside her, both their feet planted firmly in the air.

"It's quite nice, isn't it?" he said.

Nice wasn't the word Alice was searching for. It was not uncomfortable, no, but it was strange, certainly. The cloud they stood on was fairly insubstantial—and she feared she'd slip through at any moment—but when she mentioned this to Oliver, he only shrugged and said, "As long as you're hungry, I wouldn't worry. It's always best to float on an empty stomach."

Oliver was positively beaming.

He kept reaching out around them, touching the dewy cotton of the clouds, running his fingers through their tangled strands. Occasionally he was too rough, and he'd rake his hand right through a stubborn knot of cloud, and the whole thing would burst into rainwater. This seemed to delight Oliver in a most particular way, as the water would then pool in the palm of his hand, and he'd proceed to drink up its contents.

"Hey," Alice said, and tugged at his shirt. "I thought you said we weren't allowed to eat anything in Furthermore!"

"This is not eating," Oliver said, licking his fingers. "This is enjoying."

Alice was beginning to realize that the longer they stayed in Furthermore, the more relaxed Oliver became. (It was also true that he was still very nervous and overly cautious, but somehow, despite his many fears, he seemed happier.) He was nothing at all like the grumpy boy she'd met so few days ago, and Alice was surprised to find that she was actually learning to like Oliver. Just now, she couldn't help but grin at his giddiness.

Though she was a bright, interesting young girl, the difficulties of the last three years had isolated Alice from persons her own age. Now was her chance to start new and shake off the disappointments of her middlecare years, and she couldn't contain her quiet excitement. After all, Alice was now twelve years old, which meant she was nearly grown up. And if growing up meant she'd be making new friends? Well, Alice decided she wouldn't mind getting old.

The clouds were pressed up around them now, soft and warm and doughy. The air smelled like apples and baked bread, and Alice had never known she could feel so safe in the sky.

She peered down to see how high they'd floated, but could see nothing of the ground. Around them was cloud after cloud, and, oh, she could just lie here, she thought, and it would be so cozy and she'd have the best sleep of her life, definitely, definitely. Had she mentioned how soft and warm it was in the clouds? She couldn't remember. Anyway she was so tired. So comfortable. So sleepy. So—

"Alice!" Oliver said suddenly. "Alice, no!" He shook her, hard, the panic in his voice sending a chill through her body.

"What is it?" she gasped, looking around. "What happened?"

"You cannot sleep without a dream," he said urgently. "Never, ever, sleep without a dream." He looked so rattled; she didn't know what to say. "They will always try to keep you here, but *you cannot stay*. Do you understand?"

"No," said Alice, who was still visibly frightened. "I don't understand at all. Who will try to keep me? Why?"

"You really don't know, do you? You truly know nothing of Furthermore?"

"Of course I don't," said Alice, defensive. "I've heard only rumors of Furthermore, and most of them nonsense. Aside from that?" She looked around. "Well, we are standing on a cloud, Oliver. I can't possibly make any sense of this."

Oliver almost smiled. "People are so preoccupied with making sense despite it being the most uninteresting thing to manufacture." He shook his head. "Making magic," he said, "is far more interesting than making sense."

"But we do make magic," Alice pointed out. "It's all we make, isn't it? We spend our lives harvesting magic."

"Yes," said Oliver. "We make magic. And what do we do with it? We turn it into currency. We make laws. We build homes, we bake bread, we mend bones. We use magic so carefully you'd think we had none at all."

"And you think we should do things differently in Ferenwood?"

"No," Oliver said quickly. "Not exactly. But I do think there's much to be appreciated in the oddness of Furthermore. There's something curious about a land that uses magic in a reckless way." He smiled to himself. "I confess I sometimes enjoy the chaos; it provides a great diversion from the safe, sleepy lives we live in Ferenwood."

Alice touched a hand to her face, cold against cold, both warming each other from nothing, and kept quiet for a minute. Oliver's opinions had left her troubled and concerned; and she wondered, for the very first time, whether she hadn't made a very big mistake in coming here.

Alice didn't agree with Oliver, you see.

Alice loved her safe, steady village, and for a girl who'd always longed for adventure, she didn't much care for chaos. In fact, Alice had never even thought of using magic haphazardly, without regard for consequences or the well-being of others. That just wasn't the way of Ferenwood folk; they were kind and caring people who lived mostly happy, straightforward lives. A lawless sort of magic-making seemed dangerous to Alice. Lawless magic, she realized, would make it easy to hurt someone else. And despite it taking her far too long to discern this, Alice was finally grasping something rather important.

"Oliver," she said slowly.

"Yes?"

"Are there people in Furthermore who want to kill us?"

"Yes," he said. "Of course."

Alice felt a pain snatch the air from her lungs.

"Why, Alice," Oliver said, surprised, "there's a reason why the Elders keep Furthermore a secret from Ferenwood. This land is like sinking sand. Once you step inside, you're never really meant to leave."

"Ever?" she cried.

"Never."

"But why?"

"I really *would* like to tell you, but it would take far too long to explai—"

Oliver was silenced by a single, threatening look from Alice.

"Oh, alright," he said with an air of defeat. "We can spare a few—and only a few!—moments to talk this through. And I suppose it's best to start from the beginning if you haven't even a hint of the middle." He looked around for something to lean on and found nothing but sky, so he began pacing the short length of the cloud. "You know the old song, don't you?" he said. "About Furthermore and Ferenwood?"

This much, Alice knew. So she nodded and promptly recited:

Farther is more than Ferenwood!
Go as far as the land may reach
A quick dip in the sea
and you're up to your knees
then cross the sleeping beach.
Time is a hard and heavy rule
You'll find it behind the door
Adventure is there
(he's lost all of his hair)
Beyond is Furthermore!

It was a nursery rhyme Alice had known forever. A tale of nonsense, she was told. Just funny words strung together to trick children into sleep. It was only now, as Alice repeated the words aloud, that she saw the secrets between the silliness.

She grew quiet as she finished the poem, and Oliver nodded, recognizing her silent realization. "Long ago," he said, "in the very, very beginning, Furthermore and Ferenwood were united, despite being split vertically by sea. It was a land called *Anymore.* Things were different back then," Oliver said thoughtfully. "Anymore had opened its borders to the non-magical world."

Alice's eyes went wide. This, she'd never known.

"Magical folk married non-magical folk and things were alright for a while, but—you know how it is. We can't survive without magic, and non-magical folk didn't understand. Mixed magic made it so some children were born with talent while others were not, and they couldn't always tell right away. Non-magical parents would want to take their children out of Anymore, to go back home, and things seldom ended well. To make matters worse, giving birth to magical babies was very hard on non-magical mothers. Many of them died in childbirth. It was a very dark, very unhappy time."

"Oh, Oliver," Alice said, her hand on her heart. "This is a terrible story."

Oliver nodded. "And I hate telling it, so I'll skip ahead. Do you know the origin of Feren and Further?"

Alice shook her head.

Oliver was solemn as he said, "They were twin sisters. Their birth had killed the mother, and they were raised by a grieving magical father. But the two girls processed their father's grief in different ways. Feren, who'd inherited her father's magic, wanted to prevent this sort of thing from ever happening again by cutting ties with non-magical folk. Further, who'd not inherited any magical ability, wanted to honor her non-magical mother by maintaining those ties. It was the beginning of a revolution for the land. The two became figureheads for a controversy that'd been brewing for decades. Wars were waged. Sides were taken. Anymore split in two to become Ferenwood and Furthermore as we know it now."

Alice was so stunned she could no longer stand, so she sat down, legs crossed beneath her, and leaned back on a bit of cloud.

"And then what happened?"

"They never spoke, not ever again," said Oliver. "Both sides lost so much life and magic during the war that they eventually agreed to agree to only one everlasting law: That they would never meddle in each other's magic matters, for as long as their lands still stood."

"Wow," said Alice.

"Furthermore has been true to its founder's wishes and deals with all kinds of visitors, magical and non-magical alike. But the twisty business of Furthermore attracts the wrong sorts of visitors. Few come to Furthermore in pursuit of decent pastures." Oliver frowned. "And it doesn't help that this land has been reckless with their magic. It's a deeply unsteady, turbulent place, and its people have fractured into hundreds of smaller villages, each with its own rules and officials, and each with contradictory laws and confusing legislature. It's a land rife with inconsistencies because the confusion suits their underhanded ways. But they burn through magic faster than the land can produce it and, in their desperation for more, they're willing to do awful things."

"What kinds of awful things?" Alice asked.

Oliver paused, then said. "Well—we live off the land in Ferenwood, don't we? We are made more magical because of the fruits and plants and nuts we eat, are we not?"

Alice nodded.

"Right. So." He cleared his throat. "In Furthermore, they eat more than just fruits and plants and nuts."

Alice nearly jumped to her feet. "I knew it!" she said. "That's why they eat animals, isn't it? Isn't it? Oh, how awful!"

"I'm afraid it's much worse than that," said Oliver quietly.

"What?" Alice stalled. "What do you mean?"

"Furthermore is very hungry for magic, Alice. And *we*—that is to say, you and I—are meant to be"—he hesitated—"well, we're meant to be consumed."

Alice blinked and stared, confused.

"Oh, for goodness' sake," Oliver said. "*Consumed*, Alice. They want to *eat* us. They will eat people for their magic.

Though they do prefer to eat visitors," he added. "Something about it being more compassionate that way. They'll only eat their own in the most desperate situations. And in order to avoid these desperate situations, they've taken proactive measures."

Alice made a squeaking gasp of a sound.

Oliver bit his thumb, deep in thought. "I suppose Furthermore is a lot like a series of increasingly complicated spiderwebs. Each village has a distinct way of catching its prey, which, well—*you know.*" He raised an eyebrow. "It makes it so it's very difficult to stay alive here."

"How awful!" Alice cried. "Oh, I can't imagine, I can't even *imagine*—goodness," she said, holding a hand to her chest, "I can't breathe, can I? I'm sure I can't breathe."

She was wrong, of course; she was entirely able to breathe, but Alice was scared, and so she was, for the moment at least, very short of breath. And it was then, as she struggled to right her breathing and keep from upsetting her stomach, that she decided she hated Furthermore more than she'd ever hated any place in her entire life. She was now fully terrified for Father, and she couldn't imagine what horrors he'd already experienced.

Oliver held out a hand to her. "Right," he said. "Ready to finish up here?"

Alice accepted his outstretched hand and, once on her feet,

shook out her skirts and looked around at the slumbering darkness. She couldn't trust anything anymore. She was sure this velvety night cloaked infinite secrets.

"Oliver," she said quietly.

"Mm?" He was searching his pockets for something.

"How do you know all this? All this history of Furthermore and Ferenwood? I don't remember learning about any of it."

That held his attention.

"No," he said, looking up. "I didn't learn any of it in Ferenwood. My friends in Furthermore taught me."

"You have friends in Furthermore?" Alice said, startled. "But I thought—"

"There are good and bad in every bunch, aren't there?" Oliver shrugged and resumed digging through his pockets. "I've seen many hearts here heavy with the loveliest secrets. Not everyone in Furthermore enjoys eating people, you know."

"But—"

"I'm so sorry, Alice, but now we really must be going. We've already used up a great deal of time and any more than this would be a waste. I promise I'll answer more of your questions when there's time to spare."

"Alright," she whispered, staring at their clasped hands. But then—"Can I ask just one more question?"

Oliver sighed and smiled. "Yes?"

"Is Father in very great danger?"

Oliver's smile wavered, and he would not answer immediately. He looked away before he spoke, and when he did, he only said, "It's so good that you've come, Alice. We've needed you."

"We?"

"Yes," said Oliver. "Your father and I."

Shock shook her.

"You've seen him?" Alice asked, grabbing Oliver's shirt. "You've seen him?" She nearly burst into tears. "Oh, you've seen him, please tell me you've seen him—"

"I—" Oliver said, swallowing hard. "That is—I mean, yes, I have."

"How was he? Did he look healthy? Did he say anything to you?"

"Yes," Oliver said. The stars were so bright behind him. The sky, so dark. "He spoke to me, but—only once."

"And?" Alice was impatient now. Terrified. Horrified. So happy. "What did he say?"

Oliver looked down. "He told me to find you."

Alice stared at Oliver in stunned silence, just until the clouds shook and the moons flickered and the stars swayed in the sky. The air was changing, and Oliver noticed.

He was in a hurry to get moving, but she was still numb, somehow. Still trying to process everything she couldn't understand.

Father had asked for her.

Oh, it made her very knees tremble. It made her miss him more than ever. More in every moment.

But then Oliver pulled a vial out of his pocket, and curiosity pushed her back into the present.

"What's that for?" she asked.

"The sky has something we need," he said, "so we must give it something it wants."

"What could a sky possibly want?" Alice wrapped her arms about herself and fought back a shiver as she spoke. She was suddenly cold. "That seems silly."

"Don't be absurd," he said, surprised. "Everything wants something."

And with that, he uncorked the vial and poured its contents upside down. It was too dark for her to see.

"It's dirt," Oliver said, answering her silent question. "This stretch of sky," he said, gesturing to the air around them, "will never touch the ground. It's a prisoner, all alone, stuck here forever, always gazing down upon the land, always estranged from all the excitement."

Alice had never considered a lonely sky. It was a new thought for her, and she wanted to explore it, but then the wind snapped like a crack of lightning, and Alice and Oliver looked toward the sound. A book hung in the air, big and brown and leather-bound, and Oliver snatched it out of the sky, grabbing Alice's hand in the process. Without a wink or a warning (or a sentence to spare on the matter), she and Oliver were sent crashing down. The weight of the book made them heavy; and though they fell far and hit the ground hard, they were only slightly bruised and out of breath upon landing. Alice opened her eyes to find their limbs tangled together, and she hurried to unhook herself from Oliver, drooping sideways as she stood up. It took her a few moments to find her head. Strangest of all: She wasn't dead.

"Why didn't that kill us?" asked Alice, peering up at the sky. "We fell such a long way."

Oliver shrugged, dusting the dirt off his pant legs. "Falling down would be a tragically boring way to die in Furthermore. They'd never stand for it."

"Right," said Alice, who wondered whether Oliver hadn't gone a bit mad.

Once they'd both recovered their footing, they turned their eyes to their prize.

A pocketbook, Oliver had said.

But this was not that. And Alice told him so.

"What do you mean?" Oliver asked. "Of course this is a pocketbook. What else could it be?"

"A pocketbook is a ladies' purse," she said, tapping the book. "And this is not a ladies' purse."

"A ladies' what?" Oliver asked, frowning. "See now, I haven't the faintest idea what nonsense they're teaching to young people these days"—Oliver cracked open the cover—"but this," he said, "this is indeed a pocketbook."

And so it was.

It was a book. Where every page had a different pocket.

Alice reached out, amazed, to touch one of the pockets, and Oliver jerked the book away from her.

"What are you doing?" he asked, horrified.

"I just wanted to—"

"One does not simply reach into a pocket!"

"Why not?"

"What do you mean, *why not*?" Oliver looked absolutely ashamed of her. "What kind of manners were you raised with?"

"Hey," she said, stomping one foot. "That's not fair. I have very good manners."

"Oh? And your mother taught you to go digging in other people's pockets, then?"

"No," Alice said, going red in the face. Then, more quietly, "I didn't realize they were other people's pockets."

Oliver's expression softened. "Have you never seen a pocketbook before?"

Alice shook her head.

Oliver's voice was gentle and sad when he said, "I take it your mother's hometeaching lessons were not very thorough?"

"Not thorough at all," she said, staring at her feet.

"My apologies, Alice." And he really did sound sorry.

So she looked up.

"Pocketbooks are full of other peoples' pockets," he said simply. "And one must not touch another person's property without permission."

"That seems fair," she said.

Oliver nodded.

"So how do we get permission?" she asked.

"Well, we have to ask them, of course."

"All of them?"

"Some of them," he said, closing the book carefully.

"Won't you please let me look in the book?" Alice asked. "I promise I won't pick any pockets. I'm only curious."

"I have to return this to a friend of mine," he said, "so let's wait until we're in his presence. Besides, there's very little light here, and it's never safe when the sun comes out."

Alice stared at him. "You never told me that."

"I certainly tried to, didn't I? Anyhow, now that we've got the pocketbook, we can turn our attention to other things. There are still a few items we need for our journey, so we'd better get a move on."

Alice rushed forward so eagerly she nearly tripped over her skirts. She trailed too close to Oliver and kept stepping on his heels. Alice was now rightly afraid of Furthermore and its hidden dangers (and if she had to choose between here or home, she'd choose home every time), but everything was so *interesting* here—so different, so suddenly terrifying—that it was somehow addicting. After all, Alice had known loss and loneliness and bone-deep sadness, but she'd never known anyone who'd wanted to *eat* her, and a small part of her wondered what that was like, too. The thing was—now that she'd had enough time to process the shock of it all—Alice found herself rather . . . flattered by the idea. Our young friend had been paid very few compliments in her life and, strange as it was, she was pleased to know that someone thought she'd make a fine meal. That had to mean she was high-quality magic, didn't it? That had to mean she was made of something strong and sustainable. Didn't it?

Of course it didn't. But then, very few grown-people have ever made sense of a young person's mind, and I've no great ambitions to count myself among the pioneers. In any case, Alice was now more fascinated by Furthermore than ever before and she wanted to know everything about life in this strange land. Oliver, however, was reluctant to share.

"But where did you live?" she asked him, half jogging in an effort to match his pace. "Was it nice? Did your mother come to visit?"

Oliver laughed in this strange, incredulous way that twitched his face and pinched his nose. "My mother?" he said. "Come to visit? Alice, be serious."

"But didn't she miss you?"

Oliver raised an eyebrow at her. "I doubt it. Besides, would *you* want your mother to visit while you were on a task?"

Alice blushed. "Well, seeing as I'll never have a task, my answer couldn't really matter, could it?"

Oliver stopped, bit the inside of his cheek, and was generous enough to look ashamed of himself. "I'm sorry," he said. "I forgot."

"Yes. I nearly had, too."

"Do you still have your card?"

Alice nodded, her fingers reaching for the stiff piece of paper tucked inside her skirt pocket.

"I still think you should unlock it," he said.

"Yes, well, I think we should find Father," Alice said, and looked away.

Oliver opened his mouth to speak, exhaled sharply, and said nothing more on the subject.

It was Alice who finally broke the silence.

"So what else do we need to get?"

Oliver glanced at Alice's bare feet and said, "Shoes."

"Shoes?" Alice hurried forward, startled, to catch up with Oliver, who'd already begun walking again. "But I never wear shoes."

"You'll also need to get clearance before we can leave Slumber," he said. "So we'll need to get you a ruler, of course—as all visitors must carry rulers—and then we'll need to get it filled, which—"

But Alice had frozen still.

Oliver was speaking, but Alice could no longer hear him, and it took him a moment to realize she was no longer following his lead. When he finally looked back, he found Alice planted in place, her eyes wide with wonder.

"What is it?" Oliver whipped around in search of danger. He was trying not to worry, but Alice had a bad habit of worrying him. "What's the matter?"

"Why?" she said.

"Why what?"

"Why do I need a ruler?"

"Because," he said. "Despite the many inconsistencies, following rules is very important in Furthermore."

"But—"

"Now, Alice," Oliver said, frowning, "please don't fight me on this. We might be able to compromise on the shoes, but the ruler is very important. A visitor in Furthermore must have a ruler at all times."

"But why?"

"Well," Oliver said, "because it measures our time spent here." He reached into his bag and procured a simple wooden ruler that looked an awful lot like something Alice had seen before.

She took it from him, inspecting it, and was swiftly reminded of Father's ruler: It was the one thing he'd taken with him when he left home. Alice had not forgotten. How could she? Father always took great care of that ruler. He'd kept it wrapped in a thin rectangle of red velvet, tucked away in the top drawer of his dresser, and checked every night to make sure it was still there. The one time Alice had taken it, hoping to engage it in a bit of play, Father had told her very firmly that it wasn't a toy.

He'd said it was special.

Alice had always wondered how a ruler could be special, but now, holding Oliver's ruler in her hand, she was finally beginning to understand. As she remembered it, Father's ruler was much the same as Oliver's: dark and thin and marked along the edges the way a ruler might be. But the greatest difference between the two was also the strangest: Oliver's ruler was much, much heavier than Father's.

"Mmm," said Oliver, nodding. "Yes, it's quite heavy when it's full."

"Full of what?"

"*Time*, of course. Time is the only thing in this land that's actually regulated," Oliver explained. "Furthermore is very, very persnickety about time. It's mandatory to fill and measure the length of any visit because Furthermore likes to keep a close eye on all who pass through."

"Time," Alice said softly, eyes still locked on the ruler in her hand. "How odd."

"Yes. They don't like to waste time here. For years Furthermore let visitors take as much time as they wanted, but so much of it was spent on *thinking* and *wondering* and *deciding* that it's now very strictly regulated." And then, seeing the look on Alice's face, he added, "Studies have shown that thinking and wondering lead to thoughtful decision-making. It's an epidemic."

Alice's mouth popped open in surprise. "You mean to say

that Furthermore doesn't want visitors to make thoughtful decisions?"

"Of course they don't," Oliver said, tugging the ruler out of her hands. "Stupid people are much easier to eat."

"I beg your pardon?"

"If you force visitors to make hasty, hurried decisions, they're bound to make poor choices more quickly, which will more efficiently lead to their demise. But going slowly won't do, either. They'll make a nice stew out of you for wasting time. It's a simple trap," he said. "You lose either way. So we'll have to settle for being quick *and* clever."

Alice relinquished the ruler, but reluctantly. Distractedly. She was done being shocked by Oliver's explanations, but she was now lost in her own thoughts. "Did you know," said Alice quietly, "that Father left Ferenwood with nothing but a ruler?"

"I did."

"So he knew," Alice said, confirming her own suspicions. "Before he left. Father knew where he was going."

"He must've known," said Oliver. "He'd been here plenty of times before—he knew how it all worked. In fact, it was because of his notes and knowledge of Furthermore that I'd known what to do when I got here. I owe him a great debt."

This was too much for Alice to process.

Why would Father come back to Furthermore after all these years? What did he want here?

Alice had long suspected that Father was different from everyone else in Ferenwood—his thoughts were richer, his mind was fuller, his eyes were brighter—but Alice never thought of Father as a man with secrets, and now she was beginning to wonder if she'd really known Father at all.

She bit her lip and bundled her thoughts, setting aside her feelings of unease. Loving Father meant loving all of him—his open windows as well as his dusty corners—and she refused to love him less for secrets unknown. Alice had secrets, too, didn't she? And she was beginning to realize that part of growing up meant growing tender, and that secrets were sometimes wrapped around tender things to keep them safe.

"So," Oliver said as he straightened the hem of his tunic. "Shall we see about getting you that pair of shoes?"

Alice looked down at her feet.

Horrifying, I know, but Alice had never much cared for shoes. She'd only ever worn shoes in the winter, and when she had, they were linen boots lined with cotton flowers; soft and springy and comfortable. But it wasn't winter, and she couldn't imagine wearing them now. "Do I have to?" she asked Oliver.

"There's a tremendous hike ahead of us," he said, making an

effort to look sympathetic. "I do highly recommend it."

"Well," said Alice, biting her lip. "Alright. If wearing shoes will make it easier to find Father, then I suppose it's—oh!" Alice hesitated, remembering something important.

"What is it?" Oliver said.

"I haven't any finks," she said. Then, more quietly, "Do they even accept finks here? How do we buy things in Furthermore?"

"You know, I don't know," Oliver said, smiling. "I just ask people to give me things when I want them."

"But that's stealing!"

"For me, it's asking."

"Oh, Oliver," she said, her eyes narrowing. "You're awful."

"Anyway," he said, cheering up, "I happen to have some currency on my person. Just a moment." Oliver reached into his bag and dug around a bit. He held up a few red coins (they looked a lot like buttons, but imagine them heavier) for just a moment before snapping them all in half, releasing their magic. One fink contained only an ounce of magic, but three finks would be three times as much, and a lot could be done with three ounces of magic. Working quickly with his hands, Oliver fashioned his finks into a simple pair of shoes, which, needless to say, was a complicated task for a thirteen-year-old. Most people didn't bother making things from scratch anymore; most people traded in their finks (red) and stoppicks (blue) and tintons (green) for ready-made products fashioned together by expert artisans.

Alice was impressed.

More impressive still: the shoes themselves. They were simple ballet slippers made of bright blue satin with ribbon-laces trailing like glossy tendrils. Oliver could've magicked together any style of shoe for Alice, but he chose the slippers on purpose; they were the dancing shoes she never had, and Alice was deeply flattered by the gesture.

In fact, for a girl who didn't care for shoes, Alice was surprised to find that she genuinely liked (almost loved) the slippers; but her pride kept her from telling Oliver the whole truth. So she smiled and thanked him, very politely stating that they were perfectly good (when indeed they were great), and entirely sensible (when in fact they felt luxurious), and Alice had already told so many small lies since arriving in Furthermore that she no longer noticed how easily she slipped into a few more. It had become so easy to fib little fibs and tell little fictions that truth had become gray; and Alice had no way of knowing that her one protection against Oliver (and all other untrustworthy souls) had failed long ago.

So she happily tied her blue shoes to her feet, danced around on tiptoe in anticipation, and followed Oliver into the dark.

Slumber really was quite tediously dark. I say this not only because it's true, but because at this point in the story there is little other scenery to comment on. Alice and Oliver were leaving the city lights of Slumber far behind; from here there was no firelight visible, no floating bulb brightening the sky. It was dark. Cold.

Very quiet.

Alice and Oliver had been walking along in companionable silence, each absorbed in their own thoughts. They were heading toward somewhere or other—to a place where Alice would acquire a ruler and other miscellaneous necessities—but neither of the two children seemed, at least in the present moment, much interested in discussing it. Alice was loping along, poking at the dark with one finger and hoping to make a hole in it. She was searching for light, for answers, for Father. Her desperate need for him had led her here: wading through perfect darkness, navigating blindly a world she did not know.

Father had left on purpose.

Alice knew this now, and somehow that changed everything. Had Father left *her* on purpose? Or had he left *Mother* on purpose? What did all of it mean? Why would he leave their home for a land that might consume him? Why take that risk?

For what?

Alice's head had filled with so many questions she'd run out of the space needed for paying attention. So she didn't notice Oliver or the sudden spring in his step or the crooked smile on his face. Alice couldn't have known what Oliver was thinking—so I really shouldn't tell you, either—but I think we know each other well enough now to take care of each other's secrets. So I'll tell you this: Oliver was feeling relieved. He'd told Alice a bold lie not too long ago, and now he was finally sure he'd gotten away with it. Which was the lie I will not say—but Alice, Oliver had realized, was no longer immune to his charms.

Let's not forget this.

Alice, oblivious, was still deep in thought, distracted only by her first glimpse of light in the distance: a single, pulsing beam that grew larger as they drew closer. Alice tapped Oliver on the arm and they were both soon alert, Oliver reclaiming his wariness as Alice grew once again curious.

She turned to Oliver. "What—"

"It's the border crossing," Oliver said briskly.

"Border crossing? I thought I was getting a ruler."

Oliver nodded, and Alice could just barely make out his silhouette in the growing light. "Yes, you'll be issued a ruler as soon as you receive clearance," he said. "Slumber is the point of entry for all visitors. The real Furthermore is still beyond."

Alice's eyes and mouth went round at the same time. "And what do I have to do to gain clearance?"

Oliver hesitated. "I haven't any absolute idea," he said. "It's different for everyone. But we'll find out soon enough, won't we?" He nodded ahead. The light was growing larger by the moment, and now it was nearly blinding. "Just a bit farther."

Alice pressed forward, shielding her eyes against the glare. It was nearly impossible to see anything anymore; the brightness was almost painful. In fact, Alice was just in the middle of thinking she didn't know how much more of this she could stand when suddenly, the light went dim.

It took Alice several tries to get her eyes to focus. She blinked and blinked until the multiple halos disappeared and she could finally be certain of what she was looking at.

There was a single white door planted upright into the ground. In the center of it was a very large doorbell. Above the doorbell were hammered gold letters that read

PRESS HERE FOR ADVENTURE

Alice looked to Oliver for reassurance, and he nodded. Carefully, very carefully, Alice reached one finger forward and pressed the button. It beeped softly, like it might've been sleeping.

A moment later the door disappeared, instantly replaced by a person and a desk, one behind the other.

The person was wearing several shirts in varying shades of piglet pink and Alice couldn't tell if the person was in fact a person (or perhaps a thing) but she didn't have time to deliberate before it spoke.

"Name?" said all the pink. (It turned out that it was indeed a person, the kind who wore a powder-blue top hat.)

Alice startled and hurried forward. She noticed a nameplate on the desk that read

TED ADVENTURE
BORDER CONTROL
VILLAGE OF SLUMBER

"Name?" Ted demanded again.

"Alice Alexis Queensmeadow," said Alice quickly. She tried to smile.

"Business?"

"Business?" Alice repeated nervously. She glanced at Oliver. "I, um, I'm here to look for my f—"

"Fruit tree," Oliver finished for her, jumping forward and

flashing a smile at Ted. "She lost her fruit tree in the town of Slender and she's desperate to get it back. Raised it from a seedling, you know."

Ted blinked at Oliver several times, wordlessly shuffling paperwork around. "Seedling," he finally mumbled. "Yes, of course, I've got that here."

"I'm sure you'll find all her documents are in order," Oliver added with another smile.

Ted nodded again, his head heavy with Oliver's persuasion.

"So if you would be so kind as to issue her the proper ruler and fill it with—oh, I'd say six months' worth of time—we'll be on our way." Oliver slid his own ruler across the desk. "I'll take a refill on mine, too, thank you. Same as last time will be just fine."

"Same as last time," said Ted. "Mmm-hmm."

Ted got to work, quickly stamping papers and rifling through desk drawers, and Alice was—for the very first time—amazed by Oliver's ability. She thought she knew what he was capable of, but she'd never really seen him in action. Not like this. This was truly extraordinary, she thought. And while a part of her felt guilty for tricking her way through Furthermore, another part of her realized that that was just the way things were. It was, as Oliver had said, a land of tricks and puzzles, and Alice and Oliver had to play along if they were ever going to make it through.

"Your ruler," Ted said suddenly.

Alice felt a flutter in her stomach as she stepped forward. The ruler Ted pushed across his desk was different from Oliver's; hers was a bleached wood, a bit shorter (but sturdier), and looked as though it'd been salvaged from a garbage bin. It was riddled with nicks and scratches—clearly used to death—but Alice didn't mind. Her ruler felt worn and well loved and easy to hold. It was solid. Heavy. Full of time. She flipped it over to find a brief inscription carved into the wood.

ALICE ALEXIS QUEENSMEADOW
SNAP IN THREE IN CASE OF EMERGENCY

"In case of emergency?" she said, looking up at Ted. "What does that mean?"

Ted stared.

"Excuse me," she tried again. "What does—"

"Your time is up when the wood loses its weight," Ted said, not appearing to have heard her. "So be sure to get back here before then."

"Alright," said Alice. "But what happens if I don't get back here before then?"

Ted blinked. "You'll be arrested for stealing."

"What?" Alice gasped.

Ted blinked again. "I will now ask you a series of routine questions."

"But—" Alice swallowed hard. "Okay."

"Are you a visitor traveling with a disability or a medical condition?" Ted was reading from a sheaf of paper, at which he now squinted. He shifted closer to his desk lamp.

"I-I don't—"

"Are you traveling with any special items?" Ted asked. He was making small notes on the page as she answered.

"No," Alice said. "I mean I don't think—"

"Are you a visitor aged seventy-five or older?"

At this, Alice frowned. "Obviously not. I've only just turned twelve."

Ted pushed a button on his desk and a shock of confetti exploded over his head and onto the brim of his top hat. (Alice now understood why he wore it.) "Congratulations," he said. "Are you traveling with any food or gifts?" At this, Ted looked her square in the eye, and Alice could see a flicker of his stubborn mind breaking free of Oliver's hold.

"N-no," she said, shooting a worried glance at Oliver. "No food or gifts."

Oliver squeezed her hand, and a moment later, Ted's eyes had glazed over again. He asked her no more questions.

"Don't forget to take your visitor pamphlets," Ted said, shoving some glossy documents across the desk. "And remember to review the *Permitted and Prohibited Items* list, as we've recently updated the—"

"Alright, sure," Alice said quickly, pocketing the pamphlets without looking at them. "But what about earlier—when you said something about being arrested? What did you mean by that?"

Ted had just opened his mouth to answer when Oliver began tugging her away. "Thanks so much! See you soon!" he called to Ted, and quickly tucked his own ruler back inside his bag.

"Best not to talk too much to Ted right now," Oliver whispered. "The more he tries to think, the more easily he'll be able to push through my persuasion, and we can't risk that."

"Okay," Alice whispered back, absently shoving the ruler in her skirt pocket. "But Oliver, what did he mean I'd get arrested?"

"I'll tell you more about that soon, I promise," he said. "But right now we have to hurry, because the sun is about to wake. We need to head straight to the village of Still, and it's going to be rather tricky."

"Trickier than all this?" she asked.

"Much."

"How much?"

"Very."

She stared at him.

He stared at her.

They stared ahead.

The sky, you see, was ripping itself in half.

"Run!" Oliver shouted, and Alice knew better than to ask why.

The sky was actually ripping apart, right in front of them, and though she hadn't the slightest idea why it was happening, she knew the answer couldn't have been good. But strangest of all wasn't why they were running in the face of danger—it was why they were running directly toward it. There were so many questions Alice wanted to ask, but she was doing her best to keep up with Oliver's long legs, and she was already out of breath.

"Oliver," she said, panting. "Why is the sky ripping apart? What's happening?"

"What do you mean?" Oliver asked. "The day is over. Today is getting dressed for tomorrow."

"That," she said, breathing hard, "is one of the silliest things you've ever said to me."

"Why is that so strange?" he asked. He was breathing hard, too. "Don't you change your clothes every day?"

"Well, yes," she said. "But I'm a person."

"Oh?" Oliver shot her a look. "And people are the only ones allowed to care about their appearance?"

Oliver clenched his teeth as they ran the next hundred feet, breathing harder than before. He was almost entirely out of breath when he said, "Alice, if you plan on surviving in Furthermore, you really must change the way you think." He was gasping now. "Narrow-mindedness will only get you as far as Nowhere, and once you're there, you're lost forever."

"You think I'm narrow-minded?" she asked him, clasping a hand to her chest, her heart hammering with each running step. *"Me?"*

Oliver never answered her, though probably because he could no longer breathe. He was wheezing more and more every second, and so was Alice, but Oliver was carrying the pocketbook, which looked very heavy; she was sure his struggle was greater than hers. But even though they were running as fast as they could, it seemed impossible to reach the horizon. Alice wasn't sure what Oliver was trying to do.

"When I tell you to jump," he said, still gasping for air, "we must jump." He glanced at her. "Okay?"

"Yes," she said, trying to catch her breath. "Yes, okay."

The sky was straight ahead, midnight curtains pulling apart as slivers of gold and silky blue peeked out from underneath. It was an infant sky, innocent as a day unknown.

"JUMP," Oliver shouted. "JUMP, ALICE, JUMP!"

Jump, she did.

The wind caught them in an instant, wrapping around their limbs and hushing their gasping, rasping breaths, and when the moment was right—as it seldom was—they were tossed into the center of a changing sky.

Down they fell, from Slumber to Still.

Two thumps later, in Still they sat. Alice and Oliver were sitting on their bottoms, legs outstretched in front of them. The wind was gone from their lungs and aches stirred awake in their joints and Alice had so much to be concerned about, but no time to be concerned.

Still had stopped the clock.

Winter snow and autumn leaves and spring showers had frozen in place. Raindrops shimmered, suspended, like the air wore earrings, and thousands at a time. Snowflakes stuck to the sky like glitter to glue. Autumn leaves had fallen but never to the ground, and they fluttered in the gentle wind, ornaments hung on a holiday breeze, brown and orange and red and yellow, caught in a moment that could not be forgot.

Alice looked up and around in awe, parted lips and clear eyes, and leaned back on her hands to take it all in. It was quiet as a feather, and so calm it was tender. The sky was a smoky lavender and the sun was a yellow cloud puffing along in the distance, lending an eerie golden glow to everything it touched. Homes were made of colorful squares and triangle roofs; gray sidewalks curved down streets made of the blackest stone. Birds sat on stoops and did not sing, and it was all very sweet and all very small. Alice could see straight for miles from where she sat, and there wasn't a person in sight until she stood up.

She gasped.

Stepped back.

The strangest scene was set before her.

Alice couldn't understand why everything was so different so suddenly, but it had been her movements—however small—that disturbed the land of Still, and now she stood facing all of its occupants: A sea of citizens had appeared in silent protest.

There were ladies, ladies, everywhere.

They wore suits. An orange pantsuit here, green over there, purple in one corner, red in another. They were a rainbow of ladies sitting perfectly still on stools and tables and crates and benches, on sidewalks and steps and bicycle seats. Hundreds of them.

And they were all, every one of them, staring at her.

"Oliver?" Alice could feel him standing beside her, but she was afraid to break eye contact with the ladies. "Oliver," she whispered. "What do we do?"

He said something so quietly she could hardly hear him.

"What?" She glanced in his direction.

The ladies gasped. Round eyes and round mouths gaped at her.

"I'm sorry," she said. "I didn't—"

More gasps. Horrified faces. Stunned silence.

Alice was starting to grow nervous. Apparently speaking was not allowed in Still. No speaking, no moving, no disruptions at all. (This was all an assumption, of course, as Alice didn't know the first thing about Still, or anything at all, in re: what she was or wasn't allowed to do here, as Oliver [as usual] appeared to be no help. He hadn't prepared her a stitch for what to expect in Still, and if they were eaten alive by a group of angry young ladies—*well*, Alice thought—he would have no one to blame but himself.)

Now, before we get to what Alice did next, allow me first the opportunity to defend her actions. In retrospect I realize her decision wasn't very constructive, but she wasn't going to stand still for all of eternity (after all, she had Father to think of) so I will say this: In my opinion, her decision was—at least in the moment—a realistic one:

She took a few steps forward.

Someone screamed. Something shattered. Alice knew immediately that she'd made a mistake, but in her haste to correct the error, she made a few more. She scrambled backward, trying to undo what she'd done, but the more she moved, the more it disturbed the ladies of Still, and soon they were shrieking, all of them, screaming and howling and pulling at their hair, their clothes. They raked their fingers down their faces and drew blood, shed tears, and lost themselves in crazed, choking sobs. (Alice felt like crying, too, but for very different reasons.)

The ladies had begun to stand now, but slowly. Their eyes, openly weeping, never left Alice's face, and the sight of it all was so monstrous that Alice's poor heart nearly quit. The ladies' movements were so careful, so slow and methodical, that it was all somehow worse. It would be a slow death, Alice thought, a careful torture, an agony she could not scream through. Terror had so thoroughly overtaken her she was afraid to breathe.

"Alice, run!"

Oliver grabbed her hand and they charged through Still, destroying every bit of composure the village had carefully preserved. They tore through leaves that then crashed to the ground; they whipped through raindrops that broke on their faces and splashed down their necks; they plowed through snowflakes that caught in their hair and clung to their clothes.

The ladies sprang after them.

"Faster!" yelled Oliver. "We must go faster!" And though Alice wanted to kick him in the feet and tell him she was running as fast as she possibly could, she was also in the unfortunate position of being unable to breathe, and so decided to save her quips for a better time. She pushed herself, one small leg after another, to climb up the very high hill that led to the only street that ran through Still and tried very hard not to focus on the fact that they were probably going to die. Admittedly, she was not very good at this.

The ladies of Still were close behind. They were screeching in pain, no doubt agonized by all this exercise that had been forced upon them, and Alice was crying—albeit only a little—but mostly because she was so desperately tired, and because she thought she should very definitely stop running lest her lungs should shatter. But no matter, the ladies of Still did not give a fig about Alice's lungs, and so her legs and lungs would have to soldier through, whatever the cost.

Oliver's hand was wrapped tightly around hers, and he was nearly dragging her up the main street now. Alice had no idea how he was managing all this *and* still carrying the pocketbook, but she was in no position to ask or even offer any help, as she realized rather quickly that the black stone with which this road was paved was in fact quite slippery, and she was already doing all she could to stay upright. They skidded as they ran, slipping and stumbling and holding on to each other for dear life.

The ladies were now silent as snow, catching up to them even without their realizing it, and Alice turned back just in time to catch a glimpse. They were running on tiptoe, knees up and knocking into their chests, and they looked so ridiculous Alice was almost ready to laugh. In agony. Ridiculous though they may have looked, at least they knew what they were doing; these ladies had mastered the road while Alice and Oliver only struggled to survive it. The two children staggered and slipped, constantly readjusting, never fully regaining their footing.

All seemed lost.

Alice's legs felt as though they were melting beneath her, and if Oliver ever said a word to her, she could not hear him. Her breaths, hard and rasping, were all she knew, and the pounding in her chest had spread up to her head and down her arms and she was so blinded by pain that she could hardly see.

She wanted to give up.

She nearly did.

Instead, Alice shook her head and forced herself to focus. Quitting would be easy. Dying would be simple. But neither would solve her problems, and both would leave Father lost forever. She had to find a way to keep the two of them alive.

Well, and Oliver, too.

Suddenly, she had an idea: All this running they'd done, all this energy they'd exerted—it could be put to good use, couldn't it? There was no time to deliberate. She grabbed Oliver's shirt, kicked him in the backs of his knees, and knocked the both of them onto their backs. Before Oliver had even a chance to shout about it, they were flying. Sliding, gliding, they were practically penguins sloping down the shiny street, moving so quickly you'd think they had wings.

Up and left and down and right, the street curved and swayed and dipped and flipped and with it they went, human roller coasters ready to be sick upon stopping.

Eventually, the road came to an end, and with it, Alice's only hope for escape. She and Oliver had been dumped at the outer edge of Still, beyond which was nothing but grass for miles on end. There was no way out, it seemed, and certainly no time to celebrate Alice's temporary stroke of genius.

In the few moments they wasted catching their breaths, the ladies of Still had spent catching up to their bodies. Hundreds of ladies in colorful suits and angry, bloodied faces were waiting to attack two dizzy, dazed, and broken children.

They had nothing left to spare.

Not an ounce of energy. Not a shred of power.

Not a single—

"Alice," Oliver gasped. "Oh, Alice. Bless you. Bless you," he said, "bless you for getting us to the other side, you wonderful girl," and he tugged a stoppick out of his bag, broke it in half with his teeth, turned back for only a moment, and threw it hard in the direction of their attackers.

Everything slowed.

The broken casings spun with no real speed, but the very

presence of magic sent the ladies into a wild-eyed frenzy. They were salivating, faces distorted by tortured excitement as the magic drew closer, but their eagerness turned to anger as the remains of the stoppick froze and shattered in midair. The ladies shrieked and shrank back, clawing at their eyes, as tens of thousands of colorful threads fell from the sky and wove themselves across the land, creating a beautiful and terrifying barricade.

Alice couldn't believe something so simple had worked. She also wondered where Oliver had gotten so much magic, and how much more he had left.

Oliver collapsed.

"Alice," he said, "oh, Alice, you were excellent. That could've gone so badly," he said. "But you did so well."

"That could've gone *badly*?" Alice was staring at him in shock, even as she crumpled to the ground. "You mean it could've gone worse than them nearly killing us? Oliver, have you gone mental?"

Oliver shook his head. He was on his hands and knees, trying to breathe. "You have no idea how much worse it could've been," he said. "The first time I met the ladies of Still"—he laughed, wheezed—"I tried to be charming."

"Oh, Oliver," Alice said, cringing. "You didn't." She coughed twice and prayed for her legs to stop cramping.

"I did," he said, sitting up. His breathing was a little better now, still broken, but evening out. "And it was a most thorough rejection. I did my best, but it proved impossible to persuade such a large number of ladies to believe anything I said."

"So how did you get through?" she asked, as she, too, pushed herself up into a more comfortable position.

"Well, the first time I only broke free by accident. I was very nearly done for. They'd had me strip down to my underpants and climb into a pot over the fire—"

Alice gasped and covered her mouth with both hands.

"—because it had been a long time since they'd had any dinner, you see."

"They were really going to *eat* you," she cried, dropping her hands. "I still can't believe—"

"Yes," Oliver said, "*but*"—he held up one finger—"while they were busy trying to light the fire, one of the ladies tripped over my clothes and stepped on a few stoppicks that'd tumbled out, accidentally releasing their magic." He waved his hand with a flourish. "They went *mad*. They were *thrilled*. All they want is magic, after all—it's the central reason they want to eat us—but I hardly had time to be relieved before they were demanding more. More magic. Everything I had. They took me for every fink they could find and it still wasn't enough. So they were going to eat me anyway."

Alice was shaking her head in horror.

"Luckily, all their procrastination gave me time to form a

better plan. I had one last stoppick tucked behind my ear, and I decided to put it to good use. I was outnumbered and would've been completely useless in any kind of battle; and as I had only a single stoppick—which isn't enough magic to do much damage—I had to think quickly. A temporary barrier seemed like just the thing to help me get away." Oliver nodded at the woven wall he'd built. "This will fade, eventually, but it'll keep for at least several hours or so." He laughed. "Good grief. Getting in and out of Still has proven a highly expensive endeavor, hasn't it? Though I do hope I can say with some confidence that our lives were worth it," he said, still laughing. Oliver was thrilled, grinning from cheek to cheek, feeling far too triumphant to notice the careful narrowing of Alice's eyes.

Using magic to solve a problem felt like cheating. After all, not everyone had spare stoppicks just lying around, and it made Alice angry—now that she thought about it—to know that she'd need more than just courage to survive in Furthermore.

She pressed her lips together.

Alice had been considering Oliver's finks and stoppicks for some time now, often wondering at his casual use of magic and his practiced skills in conjuring and manipulation. These were skills Alice never had access to, and not for a lack of wanting. She had, of course, taken basic classes on the harnessing and transformation of contained magic, but that was all theory. She'd never interacted with much raw magic, and when she did have a few finks her in pocket, they were very precious to her; she used them carefully and thoughtfully. Alice had never known anyone who could throw money around the way Oliver had in the last few hours, and she couldn't imagine what that kind of luxury was like.

Thinking about money made Alice unspeakably sad. She still had much to learn in life, but she'd seen enough to know that money mattered, and though she didn't understand the whole of it, she did understand that a few extra stoppicks in a pocket often made it easier to live. A thousand times Alice had wondered whether having money would've helped her find Father sooner, and thinking about it now put a pinch in her heart.

Alice bit her lip as she looked Oliver over, taking care to really notice him now. She squinted at the simple clothes he wore—the ones she'd so carelessly dismissed earlier—and this time noted the careful stitching, the heavy fabric, and the expertly tailored fit. She noticed his hands, smooth and unblemished, his nails clean and short and buffed. Her eyes roved over his shiny hair, his glowing brown skin, the healthy brightness in his blue-violet eyes. Alice was beginning to realize something about Oliver that she'd never realized before.

"Oliver," she said quietly. "Are you *very* rich?"

Oliver blinked fast. "What?"

"Do you have a great deal of money?" she asked, valiantly ignoring the heat blooming in her cheeks.

"A great deal?" he said, eyes wide and surprised. "No," he said. "I don't think so. Not any more than most people, I imagine."

Alice bit the inside of her cheek and swallowed back all the things she nearly said. *Much more than me*, she nearly said. *I've never touched a stoppick in all my life*, she nearly said.

"Oh," was what she actually said.

Oliver wore a pained expression, his cheeks warmed by a truth neither one of them wished to acknowledge, and Alice was surprised to find that his discomfort bothered her. Embarrassed her, even. So she changed the subject.

"The town of Still seems so small compared to Slumber," she said, staring at the colorful barricade Oliver had built. "Where are we now? Why isn't anyone trying to eat us anymore?"

"Right! Yes!" Oliver said too loudly, relieved to be discussing something new. "Well! The villages in Furthermore are all built differently." He nodded. "Some are big, some are small, some are very, very tall. But Still isn't a proper village—and it's not meant to be. Still is only home to one person."

"One person?" said Alice. "But what about all the ladies who just tried to eat us?"

"Ah, well—the ladies of Still are just a security measure," Oliver explained. "They're here to protect the land from unwanted visitors. But the person we're here to meet has no interest in eating anyone. In fact, he's one of my few good friends in Furthermore."

"Who is he?" she asked. "Who are we here to meet?"

Oliver met her gaze, the moon glinting behind him.

"Time."

Alice sat there a moment longer, waiting for Oliver to tell her he was joking, when he tugged on her braid and said, "Narrow-mindedness, Alice, will do us no good."

Alice scowled and slapped his hand away from her hair. "I'm not narrow-minded," she said. "It's just difficult for me to believe that we are actually about to meet *Time*." She nearly rolled her eyes.

Oliver gasped—and very loudly.

His eyes were wide and horrified, and he dropped his voice to a whisper. "Listen closely," he said. "Do not let those words leave your lips again. You do not disbelieve in Furthermore. Do it enough times and you'll end up there."

"End up where?"

"In Disbelief," he said, and shuddered. "It's a horrid town."

Alice was afraid to ask him why, so she only nodded and said nothing more, keeping her disbelief to herself.

After their lungs had rested awhile, they walked on tired legs into the Still night, where birds were free to sing and crickets were free to dance and frogs would happily croak. They walked through grass that grew up to their knees and ponds that kicked quietly at their shores. Oliver stomped on and smiled at nothing in particular, while Alice distracted herself by peeking into the dark woods that crept just beyond, wondering all the while where everyone had gone, or if anyone had ever been, and what Time would look like, and would Time be nice, and what would happen if Time grew old? What would they do if Time died? And then she had a thought that wasn't relevant at all, because she was reminded in a quiet moment that she'd been hungry—very hungry—not too long ago. Strange. She didn't feel it at all anymore.

She mentioned this to Oliver.

"That's not strange," he said. "Eventually you'll stop being hungry ever again."

"Really?" she asked him. "But why?"

"Because the longer you stay in Furthermore, the farther you get from Ferenwood."

"I don't understand," she said.

Oliver hesitated. Tilted his head.

"Back home in Ferenwood," he explained, "we have to sleep every night and eat frequently throughout the day, don't we?"

Alice nodded.

"Right. So, life without those two things," he said, "would be impossible."

"But not in Furthermore?"

Oliver shook his head. "In Furthermore you sleep for the dream and eat for the taste."

Alice hesitated, considering his words.

"So when they eat people," she said, "they do it only for the taste?"

Oliver was so caught off guard by her question that he laughed and coughed at the same time. "Well—no," he said. "Not exactly. I *have* heard that humans have a very particular taste, and that the magical ones give the meals an extra kick"—Alice shuddered at the thought—"*but*," Oliver said, holding a finger up in the air, "they eat people because their souls are empty, not their stomachs.

"Here, hunger and exhaustion don't exist the way they do back home. The infrastructure of Furthermore was built with so much magic as to make the very air we breathe work differently—it makes it so food and sleep are no longer a necessity, but a luxury. It was an irreversible decadence that magically bankrupted the land. Now people can indulge in dinners and dreams only in the pursuit of pleasure. Because doing so for any other reason," he said simply, "is considered a waste of—"

"—time," she finished for him.

Oliver stopped walking and looked at her. He nodded slowly. "Yes." He smiled, just a little. "You seem to be catching on."

"You think so?" she said. "I don't think so."

"No?"

"No," Alice said. "I don't think I'm catching on at all. I haven't the faintest idea why we need to meet Time, not a clue what it has to do with the pocketbook, and not the tiniest inkling what any of this has to do with finding Father." She sighed. "Oliver," she said, "I have never been more confused in all my life."

Oliver looked worried for only a moment before his worries danced away. He laughed, which made him look lovely; and then he charged ahead, whistling a tune she could not place.

Finally.

They stood in front of a door attached to no house (this seemed to be commonplace in Furthermore), and Oliver was looking nervous. Alice couldn't understand why—it was just a door, after all, and very similar to the one they had encountered at Border Control—though this one was even bigger, and much taller, and bright red and shiny as an apple, with a fancy handle made of gold. It was a beautiful door, but its secrets must've been contained somewhere she could not see, because on the other side of the door was nothing but trees.

She took a moment to inspect it.

"Where—Alice, where are on earth are you going?" Oliver said.

"I just want to look around," she said. "It's only right that I have a chance to see what we're getting ourselves into, isn't it?"

Oliver threw his hands up in defeat. And then he leaned

against the door frame, crossed his arms, and nodded, as if to say, *Please, by all means, take a good look.*

So she did.

They were right at the edge of the woods now and surrounded on every side by very, very tall trees whose densely packed, triangle-shaped leaves were a shade of green so dark she had to squint to see their silhouettes. But when she tiptoed farther into the forest, Oliver panicked.

"Not in there," he said, pleading. "Not—Alice—"

"Why?" She glanced back. The look on his face, really. "What's the matter?"

"Not in the forest," he said quietly. "Please, Alice."

"Oh very well." Alice relented and tried not to roll her eyes, thinking of how gracious, how patient and tolerant she was of Oliver's whining, and turned to leave. But then—

Well, it was strange.

She couldn't move.

She didn't want to alarm Oliver, so she didn't say a word, and anyway she was sure she'd just gotten her skirts caught on a branch or some such. It certainly felt that way.

Maybe if she tugged a little harder?

Hm.

No, that wasn't working either.

She tried again.

Finally, she cleared her throat. "Oliver?" she said loudly. "I appear to be stuck."

"What do you mean?" Oliver was in front of her in an instant, paler than a wax moon, but careful to maintain his distance.

"Oh, it's nothing to worry about," she assured him. "Really." She tried to smile. "It's just that"—she tried tugging—"I can't seem to"—she tugged again—"get free." She sighed. "Will you see if my skirts are caught on something?"

Oliver went even paler. He was such a little turtle sometimes, his neck disappearing into his chest. "I told you not to go in the forest," was all he managed to whisper.

"Oliver, please," Alice said, irritated now. "Don't be such a—"

There was no time to finish that sentence, I'm afraid. No time at all, no, because Alice was suddenly screaming. It was all fairly embarrassing, actually, because the ordeal was over and done with in only a moment.

Alice fell to the ground at Oliver's feet and righted herself in a hurry, dusting off her skirts and whipping around too quickly, trying to get a look at her assailant.

But Oliver's face froze her still.

He was staring at something with a look of shock she could not have anticipated. She thought nothing in Furthermore could surprise him. She thought he'd seen it all. Apparently not.

This was a fox.

An origami fox. A sheet of rust-and-white paper folded expertly into a real, live, deceptively lovely animal.

It scampered about and made little fox noises and yipped and jumped and chased itself; and when it trotted along toward Alice, she wasn't afraid at all.

Oliver had nearly climbed a tree in fright, but Alice stepped forward, hand outstretched, ready to pet the paper fox. It bounded forward and nuzzled her hand before plowing into her legs, and she laughed and laughed and touched the top of its head, awed by the coarse paper of its fur.

"What's your name?" she whispered, crouching down to greet him. Or her. She didn't know. "Are you a boy or a girl?"

The fox jumped around her and bit her skirts, tugging on her clothes. For a fox with no teeth, it had quite a bite. Still, she felt no danger. Her new fox friend held her in place until finally she pet its head again. "Will you let me go?" she asked.

Slowly, it nodded, stepped back, and fell into a bow.

"You understand me?" she asked, astounded.

Again, the fox nodded.

"Alice," said Oliver, his voice high and shaky. He was rifling through his bag with great urgency. "Could we *please* get going?"

"Do you know anything about paper foxes?" she asked him. "Have you ever seen one before?"

Oliver looked up, startled, his maps clutched in one hand, his notebook in the other, and shook his head. "Furthermore is made up of hundreds of villages," he explained, now flipping through the pages of his notebook, "and I've only been to sixty-eight of them." He paused, scanned a few pages, gave a disappointed sigh, and stuffed the notebook back in his bag.

Alice was surprised to see Oliver so anxious.

"I haven't any idea where this fox came from," Oliver continued, "but he's not from here, and your father—well, your father never mentioned a paper fox in his entries, so this can't possibly be good. No, this can't possibly . . ."

"His entries?" Alice said, surprised. "You mean that notebook belonged to Father?"

But Oliver wasn't listening. He'd unrolled a few map scrolls and was reading them upside down and then right side up, collapsing paper staircases and poking open miniature doors and unlocking tiny windows and finding nothing behind them. He even gave the maps a good shake to see if anything new would fall out, all to no avail. He was looking increasingly worried, which Alice, bless her heart, found highly entertaining.

"It's not right," Oliver was saying, jabbing at different parts of the map with one finger. "It's not as it should be. There's nothing here about a fox." He shook his head, hard, and rolled up the scrolls he'd so hastily unfurled.

"Oliver," Alice tried again. "Is that Father's journal you've got there?"

Oliver's jaw twitched. "What? This? Oh," he said. "Yes, well, it was all part of my task, you know, to help m—"

"May I see it?" Alice asked, stepping forward. "Please? I'd dearly love to see what Father wrote down."

Oliver was clinging to his messenger bag so tightly he was nearly vibrating in place. "I'm afraid that's not possible," he said. "The Elders put very firm magical restrictions on the items I've been loaned for my journey, and if they're handled by anyone but me, they'll know."

"Oh," said Alice, crestfallen. She knew how tasks worked and she could imagine the Elders having done such a thing. But more importantly, Alice was still operating under the assumption that she could trust Oliver; she thought she'd be able to tell when he was spinning a lie.

So she believed him.

Oliver was visibly relieved, but Alice, who was once again distracted by the paper fox, didn't seem to notice.

Oliver cleared his throat. "We, um, we should really get going."

"But he looks so sweet," she said. "Can't we bring him along?" Alice had little to hold on to in this strange land and she was proud to have discovered something Oliver had not.

She wanted to contribute something important to their journey and couldn't bring herself to give up on the fox just yet.

But Oliver was shaking his head. "Don't be fooled by Furthermore," he said as he shoved the maps back into his bag. "Please, Alice. Remember why we're here. If we don't stick to my original plan, we might never reach your father."

Any reminder of Father was enough to set Alice's spine straight. "Of course I remember why we're here," she said quickly, cheeks aflame. "No need to remind me."

Oliver nodded and even looked a little sorry to have said anything.

No distractions, Alice scolded herself. No distractions. Think of Father, she thought. Waiting for help. Hurting somewhere.

That was all it took.

She offered a small smile to the fox (who then scampered back into the forest) and joined Oliver at the red door. They were here to meet Time. They were here to save Father.

She took a deep breath.

"Are you ready?" Oliver asked her.

"Always," she said.

And they knocked.

The two of them together, her knuckles and his. Oliver said these were important manners in Furthermore. When two people came to visit, both people should knock.

"Otherwise," he said, "it would feel like a lie, wouldn't it?" He smiled. "Thinking only one person was coming over for tea, when actually it was two!"

Alice raised an eyebrow. She didn't say it then, but she was thinking it: Oliver was growing odder by the moment.

So they knocked on Time's door until Oliver said they'd knocked enough, and then it was time to wait.

"How long?" Alice asked. "How long do we wait?"

"As long as it takes," he said. "We wait until Time comes."

Ten minutes later, Alice was grumpy.

She thought this was all a bit ridiculous. Waiting for Time. Oh, she was losing her mind, she was sure of it. She tried to remember the last time she'd slept, and couldn't.

What day was it? How long had they been gone? Had Mother and her brothers finally noticed she'd left?

Alice was paid such unaffectionate attention at home that it was hard for her to believe Mother would miss her. But Alice underestimated the space she took up in the hearts and minds of those she met and she had no way of knowing how her absence would affect the ones she loved. Nor did she have time to dwell on it. Her days were dizzier than ever here in Furthermore, and though she missed her home, she didn't miss the long, empty hours or the interminable stretches of loneliness. Here at least she had Oliver—a friend unlike any she'd ever had—and constant adventure to fill her mind.

Speaking of which, the big red door had finally opened.

Behind it was a little boy.

He wore denim overalls over a bright red T-shirt and he peered up at them through a pair of spectacles far too large for his face, taking care to stare at Alice the longest.

She and Oliver said nothing.

"Good," the boy finally said with a sigh. He sounded like he'd lived the life of an old man. "Very good that you've brought her." And then he turned around and left, walking back through a door into a world she couldn't see the end of.

Oliver moved to follow him, and Alice shot him an anxious look. "Don't worry," Oliver said, reaching for her hand. "He's my friend. And I've been here before."

❖

They followed the boy through a house so dark Alice almost thought she'd gone blind. In fact, it was so impossible to see anything but the boy that the darkness actually seemed intentional.

Time was private, apparently.

They three tiptoed through hallways and up stairways and under doorways until finally they reached a room that was brightly lit. Inside was a very old desk and very old chairs (you'll find that young people are very good at spotting old things), and every inch of the room was covered in numbers.

Plastered to the walls and tables, framed and hung as photos, upholstered to the chairs; books and books of numbers were piled on floors and windowsills and coffee tables. It was bizarre.

The little boy asked them to sit down, and then, to Alice's surprise, took his seat behind the large desk, laced his fingers on the table, and said,

"Alice, it's a pleasure to finally meet you."

"Oh," she said, startled. "It's a pleasure to meet you, too, Mr.—um, Mr. Time."

"No need to be so formal," he said, leaning back in his chair. "Call me Tim. And please"—he smiled and gestured to his appearance—"forgive my age," he said. "It changes on the hour."

Alice tried to smile.

"Thank you for meeting me here again," he said to Oliver. "I know how much trouble it is to negotiate with my security team, but I can only ever be of use to you when I can stand to be still." To Alice, he said, "I hope my friends didn't frighten you too much. Some people find those pantsuits extremely intimidating."

"Not at all," she said shakily. "I thought their pantsuits were lovely."

But Alice was distracted. Tim was dark-haired and olive-skinned in a way that reminded her of Father. Father's skin was not such a lovely brown as Mother's, but just a shade or two lighter, and Alice's heart was hit with a sudden swell of emotion as she remembered her parents' faces.

"Now then," Tim said as he turned to Oliver, all business. "You brought the book?"

Oliver nodded and placed the pocketbook on the table.

"Very well, very well," said Tim, looking vaguely disappointed. "Thank you for returning it."

Alice glanced at Oliver, all question marks. He still hadn't told her anything about what they were doing here, and she was beginning to realize he seldom did—not until it was too late.

Tim seemed to understand.

"Oliver paid me a visit," he explained, "the last time he was in Furthermore. I'd respectfully requested that—in the very likely chance he should fail in his mission—he return the pocketbook to me. And now he's here, true to his word." Tim folded his hands on his desk and took a moment to smile at Oliver in a kind, fatherly fashion, which, truth be told, was uncomfortable to witness, as Tim had the face and build of a seven-year-old and appeared to be in no position to have fathered anyone.

"But why was Oliver here before?" Alice asked. "What did he need the pocketbook for?"

"Well," Tim said, surprised. "To find your father's pocket, of course."

"My father's—I'm sorry," she said, stunned, "my father's pocket is in there?"

"Yes," Oliver said quickly. "The pocketbook brought me to Tim the last time I was here. I needed to hand over to him the contents of your father's pocket."

"Oliver!" Alice gasped, horrified. "You just handed over Father's things to someone else? How *could* you?"

Oliver sat up in his seat. "No," he said, "it wasn't—I didn't—"

"Your father got himself into a bit of a bind," Tim said gently. "Oliver was only trying to help mend the matter."

"What?" Alice looked at Oliver, panicked. "Why didn't you tell me this sooner?" she cried. "What did Father do? Was it awful? Did he . . . eat someone?"

(Tim flinched at that last bit, but we won't dwell on it.)

"Of course not," said Oliver. "But he took far too much time to make a decision. Remember, Alice—we talked about this—it's a grave offense."

Alice was stunned. It took her a full minute to find her voice, and when she did, she said, "That is one of the most ridiculous rules I've ever heard in all my life."

Tim cleared his throat, visibly offended, studied a chipped corner of his desk and pinched his bottom lip between two fingers. Finally he dropped his fingers and, affecting a tone of sympathy, said, "See, it's quite simple, really. In Furthermore we do not waste time, share time, or spare time, and I'm afraid your father took more than his measure. Because what he took belonged to me, I was the only one with permission to search his pockets." He paused. "Though I'm afraid there wasn't much to reclaim. I had no choice but to repossess his ruler."

Alice's hands fell into her lap as she sat straight up and stared, unblinking, at Tim's round, ticking face. His mouth twitched; his hands twitched. He looked like an old clock.

Suddenly, Alice understood.

"Is that what Ted meant?" she said slowly. "About being arrested?" She looked from Tim to Oliver. "Was Father arrested for taking too much time?"

Tim's eyebrows hiked up an inch and his oversized glasses slipped down his nose. "Yes, I'd say so," he said, pushing the glasses back into place. "I'd say so, yes."

"Oh my." Alice had taken to flapping her hands around as the seriousness of it all finally set in. "Oh, oh, *oh*—"

"I know this isn't much in the way of comfort," Oliver said gently, "but . . . would you like to see his pocket?"

Alice dropped her flapping hands. And nodded.

Oliver checked to make sure it was alright with Tim, and Tim tilted his head approvingly. Oliver gave Alice a warm smile, cracked open the pocketbook, and Alice was on her feet and looking over Oliver's shoulder in the same second it took Tim to sneeze. The old, musty pages of the pocketbook had unleashed a foot of dust into the air, and while Tim used up the moment to blow his boyish nose, Oliver bent over the book with great care. The spine creaked and wheezed like an ancient staircase mounted by mighty beasts, and though Oliver did his best to be gentle, he couldn't help but disturb the peace of the pocketbook.

Alice was no help either.

She was so amazed—so very enchanted—she reached out and touched it.

Jabbed it, really.

She pressed a firm finger against a page and Oliver jolted in his seat, dropping the book in horror. Tim shook his head, sighed, and sneezed twice more into his handkerchief. But worst of all—*worst of all*—the book actually yelled at her.

Oliver snatched the book off the floor—shooting Alice an admonishing look as he moved it out of her reach—and though he tried to turn the affronted page, the affronted page was refusing to turn.

"Oh, be good," Tim finally said, waving his handkerchief at the pocket. "No need to throw a fit," he said. "She was only curious."

"I didn't realize a pocket could be angry," Alice said.

"These pockets belong to actual people," Oliver explained. "Some of them are attached to the clothes they're still wearing. I believe the woman you just poked was sleeping," Oliver said, fighting back a smile. But his search for Father's pocket was taking a lot longer than Alice had expected, and it was making her anxious.

"Is Father's pocket attached to him, too?" she asked, hoping no one could hear the desperation in her voice.

Oliver shook his head.

Her heart sank.

"Pockets," Tim explained, "are usually catalogued only after they've been lost. Abandoned. Sometimes a person will want to index the contents of an important pocket they're still wearing, but most others prefer privacy. A pocketbook is often the best place to search for things we've misplaced." Tim clapped a hand on Oliver's shoulder and smiled at Alice. "Very clever of your friend to go looking for it, don't you think?"

Alice didn't know what to say.

Oliver, seeing the blank look on her face, did his best to explain. "We have pocketbooks in Ferenwood, too," he said. "And when I arrived in Furthermore my first order of business was to try and find one, because I hoped your father's lost belongings had been catalogued."

Clever indeed, Alice thought. But she daren't say it aloud. She didn't want to admit this, but she was beginning to resent Oliver's depth of knowledge and experience in Furthermore. She, too, wanted to be smart. *She* wanted to save the day. It was *her* father, after all. Where were all her good ideas?

Why wasn't she the hero of this story?

"As all pockets are cross-referenced with the date, time, and location of discovery," Oliver was saying, "I knew that even if I couldn't access the contents of your father's pocket, I would at least know *where* he'd lost it. Where he'd been. A little luck and a lot of persuasion helped a great deal in my quest. Ultimately, my discovery led me to Tim, who became a great friend. He's taught me so much about Furthermore."

Again, Tim looked on like a proud parent.

Alice felt herself go numb, feeling more useless by the moment. "Oh," was all she said.

Oliver turned another page in the book and then, finally, "Ah. Here we are." He tapped (gently, very gently) the open page and the book groaned, but quietly this time. "This is it," Oliver said. "This is the one."

And there it was.

Father's pocket.

Alice recognized it instantly. It was the only pocket on his faded denim jacket; she remembered this because he was wearing it the last time she'd seen him, nearly three years ago.

"Oliver," she whispered, her two eyes on the book, and two hands clasped in her lap. "Please tell me what's going on. What happened to Father after he was arrested? Did he manage to get free? Is he hiding somewhere?"

Tim looked to Oliver.

Oliver looked away.

Alice bit her lip; emotion had drenched her heart and she was running out of ways to wring it dry. "What is it? What's the problem?"

"My dear girl," Tim said gravely. "Your father is in prison."

Alice heard her breath hitch.

"And his sentence is very long," said Oliver.

"Oh yes," said Tim. "It was made up of many words."

Alice turned to Oliver, her eyes filling fast. "So when you said you knew where Father was, this was what you meant? You knew he'd been imprisoned?"

Oliver nodded. "The last time I was here," he said, "I tried to get him out the proper way. I thought if I followed the rules I'd be able to get him released." He shook his head. "But now I know that the only way to get him out is to break him free."

Alice sniffed away her tears and tried to be brave. "So we have to do something illegal?"

Oliver nodded again.

"Well," said Alice, pulling herself together. "Go on then." She looked from Oliver to Tim. "What is it? What do we have to do?"

Neither of them had a quick answer.

Tim finally leaned forward, studied the two children before him, and said, "Oliver, have you never told Alice what you need her for? Does she not know why she's here?"

"Of course I know why I'm here," said Alice, interjecting. "I'm here to help find my father."

Tim raised an eyebrow. "I'm certain you are," he said. "But did you not ask *why* Oliver needed your help? *Your* help, specifically?"

"Well, yes, I did, but—" Alice stopped short to glance at Oliver, whose face had turned a fine shade of tomato. "Well," she said hastily, "Oliver said that it was Father who asked for me. It was Father who told Oliver to find me. I'm not sure why Father asked for me, exactly," she admitted, wringing her hands. "But it doesn't matter, does it? Father wants me here. Father asked for my help."

Tim removed his glasses and sighed. Alice looked from him to Oliver and back again, growing more anxious by the moment.

"Oliver," said Tim, disappointment heavy in his voice. "I didn't expect such scheming from you. You should've been honest with her about your hopes and expectations on this journey."

"What hopes?" said Alice, turning frantically to Oliver. "What expectations? What's going on?"

Oliver had turned maroon. He refused to make eye contact with Alice, no matter how hard she looked at him, and Alice was suddenly accosted by terror; she felt a fist of panic clench around her throat and, despite her efforts to shout angry things at Oliver, she struggled to speak.

"Alice, dear," Tim said to her as he replaced the glasses on his face. "Oliver has never met with your father. He's never spoken a word to him."

Alice nearly fell out of her chair. "But—but he said—"

"I'm afraid he lied to you."

"No," Alice gasped, looking desperately at Oliver. "That's not possible. You see I made an ever-binding p-promise—"

Tim was shaking his head. "Oliver has never seen your father—at least not in Furthermore," he said firmly. "He's never made it that far."

Alice, poor thing, was beginning to hyperventilate.

"Breaking your father out of prison is a fine idea," Tim went on, "but the problem is no one knows exactly where the prisons are located. There are dozens and dozens of them; each an entire village unto itself, and all secured by intensely private entrances. They're meant to be nearly impossible to access. Don't you see? It's not as simple as—Alice? Alice—?"

Alice's mind was spinning.

Oliver had lied to her. Which meant Oliver had been *lying* to her. But for how long? How many lies had he told? And how had he managed to trick her? And how could she ever trust him now? How would she ev—

Tim rapped the desk to get her attention.

"Young lady," Tim said sharply. "Are you listening at all? I said I need to see your visitor pamphlets. I do hope you *have* your visitor pamphlets," he said with a frown. "You should've received them at Border Control. You did go through Border Control, didn't you? It would make matters infinitely worse if you were here without a ruler."

"No," Alice managed to say. "I mean yes. Yes, I have my ruler. And the pamphlets." She dug through her pockets, unearthed a stack of glossy brochures, and pushed them across the desk. She was dizzy with fear and couldn't bring herself to look at Oliver anymore.

Tim adjusted his glasses and picked up the first (and thinnest) of the bunch, which was titled

— WHAT TO KNOW BEFORE YOU GO —
A Quick and Easy Guide to Furthermore

When Tim opened the slim pamphlet, it unfolded itself across the desk and onto the floor until it grew to be no shorter than ten feet in length, every inch of which was covered in cramped, spasmodically capital-lettered print, and was more than occasionally punctuated by overzealous exclamation points. Alice found the entire business overwhelming and was silently grateful she hadn't bothered to peruse the other pamphlets—

— FURTHERMORE PHRASEBOOK —
How to Understand the Languages You Don't Speak

— DESTINATION GUIDE —
The Top 10 Villages You Should Visit This Year

and

— SHOP LIKE A LOCAL —
Insider Secrets to the Best Gifts in Town

—because it all looked like information for tourists, and Alice didn't consider herself a tourist. She considered herself the brave heroine of an unlikely tale.

"Ah," said Tim, tapping a bit of text on the page. "Here—do you see? Under the *Permitted and Prohibited Items* list. It's been recently updated, you know." He glanced at Alice and scooted closer, making room so she could get a better look.

> Time is permitted until it is prohibited, that is, until it has expired, which is to say: until it is no longer valid under the terms and conditions it was originally acquired (said terms and conditions having been agreed to upon the receipt of 1 [ONE] Furthermore Standard Issue Ruler, the procurement of which is required for all visitors as of sixty-and-two years hence [*see* section 172-5.42]), and as such, the illegal acquisition of Time shall be punishable by The Law of All Lands, and the punishment shall be no

> fewer than five years Enslaved Imprisonment in Isolation, (hereafter referred to as EII), a sentence bound by The Laws of Exile, the duration of which may vary. **Amended to add: In an effort to emphasize the severity of Time Thievery, EII shall be henceforth effectuated by The Laws of Complex Color.**

Alice sat back and collapsed in her chair. She was sure her bones had come loose; in fact, for a moment she thought she could hear them—elbows knocking against wrists cracking against knuckles—but it wasn't that at all. It was Tim; Tim who was rapping the desk again, trying to get her attention.

Alice jerked in her seat.

"Alice? Alice," Tim was saying. "Do you understand what you've just read?"

"I do." Alice's voice was steady, but she couldn't make herself look at Tim. "Father has been enslaved for wasting time."

"Yes, my dear, but it's more complicated than that. Furthermore has been reinforcing all prison sentences with The Law of Complex Color."

Alice blinked.

Tim leaned in. "Do you know what that is?"

Alice glanced at Oliver one final, awful time in an effort to make him speak, but Oliver was determined to look at the floor.

The coward, she thought.

It made her hate him, to know that he'd known all this and never told her. She'd thought they'd moved past these obstacles; she'd thought they were equals now, that he would've shared all truths with her. Instead he'd tricked her into trusting him and had lied to her the moment he was able. She felt more foolish than ever. He'd pretended to be her friend, and it was all a lie, wasn't it? (*No, it wasn't, but we'll get to that.*) Alice was angry and hurt and heartbroken and she would stand for this no longer. Her pride wouldn't bear it.

"Alice?" Tim again.

"No," Alice finally said, a little angrier than she meant it. "I don't know what The Law of Complex Color is. Should I? It didn't sound as awful as everything else I just read."

"But it is," said Tim. His glasses had slid down the bridge of his nose again; he pushed them back up. "It's terrifying. Don't you see? They've stripped him of his color."

"What?" Alice startled. She felt Oliver flinch.

"His color, my dear. His color."

"But I don't understand," she said. "How could they—"

"You should understand better than anyone, coming from Ferenwood as you do," Tim said. "The laws work the same in Furthermore: Living off the land gives us our color; it's the magic we consume that makes us bright. Without it—well,"

Tim said, gesturing to her face. "I'm sure you know better than anyone the effects of having little magic."

Alice felt she'd been slapped in the face.

She'd always known what people thought of her; she'd heard the whispers around town. Ferenwood folk had skin and hair and eyes as rich and bright as the land itself; it was the magic in the fruits and plants they ate that gave the people their hue. Being colorful was the mark of being magical, and Alice, having no color, was presumed to have no magic, either. And after her recent display at her Surrender, Alice was sure she'd finally proven true all their false suspicions. She hung her head in shame. She didn't even try to refute Tim's point.

"So Father looks like me, now?" she said quietly. "He has no color at all?"

"It's a bit different than that," said Tim. "Once an inmate is placed in solitary confinement, he is stripped of all rich color and left only as a grayscale version of himself. He carries not a single bit of brightness, not in his eyes, not in his cheeks. But you, Alice, you exist in full-color, not grayscale," Tim explained. "The bit of brown in your eyes—or maybe the soft pink in your cheeks—these are full and real colors, despite their limited presence.

"But prisons in Furthermore are built only in scales of gray. Currently, your father possesses no full-color of any kind, which makes him incompatible with the real world. If he tried to go home as he is now, the physical demands of a full-color existence would crush him. It's a security measure that makes it impossible for him to escape."

A single sob escaped Alice's lips before she clapped a hand over her mouth. There was such a sudden influx of awful news to contend with that Alice didn't even know where to begin.

At least she finally understood why Oliver so desperately needed her. He wanted to solve *his* task by using *her* talent. The talent Alice hadn't shared with anyone. The one she should have surrendered, and had not.

The talent she hated.

Oh, she could kill him for it. For lying to her. For deceiving her. For making her think he actually cared about her or Father or any of the pain she'd suffered in Father's absence. Oliver didn't care about *her*, Alice thought. He cared only about completing his task.

Oh, how could she ever trust him again?

She couldn't. She wouldn't.

"Alice?" It was Tim again. Tim, the only person willing to tell her the whole, ugly truth. "Do you understand? Do you now understand why you're so desperately needed?"

"I do," she said softly. "But there's still one thing I don't understand."

"Yes?"

Alice didn't know how to put this delicately. "Why didn't

they just eat him?" she asked. "Why put him in prison?"

Tim was suddenly and visibly uncomfortable. "*Well*," he said airily. "You mustn't see us all through the same lens, Ms. Queensmeadow. We don't all approve of eating visitors, you know. In fact," he said, holding up a finger, "in fact, just the other day I initiated a petition to spare the young ones, you know, whose magic is most pure, and thus most coveted—"

"All the same," Alice said steadily. "Why is he still alive?"

Tim cleared his throat. "Well, you see, it's the law that requires it. The law says that prisoners must be made as useful as possible before they're . . . sold off to the highest bidder."

"Right." Alice nodded. "So, just to be clear: You enslave us, work us nearly to death, sell us, and only *then* do you eat us."

"Why, Ms. Queensmeadow, when you put it like that it sounds almost inhumane—"

Alice stood up carefully, collected her pamphlets, her dignity, and her broken heart, shoved them in her pockets, and turned to Oliver. "Our deal is done, Oliver Newbanks. You may return home now. I will find Father on my own."

And with that, she turned on her heel, stormed out the door and down the stairs and through the hall and back outside, and left in her wake a stunned Oliver and a disheartened Tim, and did not cry but six tears before she sniffed the rest away.

And then she ran.

She ran as far as she could get from Tim's red door, ran directly into and through the forest Oliver had told her to stay away from (Alice didn't care a whit what Oliver thought anymore) until she reached the edge of the woods and could go no farther. It was there, in the middle of nowhere (not to be confused with Nowhere), that Alice fell to her knees and hugged herself through a crush of heartache.

Father was in Enslaved Imprisonment.

This was a truth Alice's young heart could not handle. Three long years Alice had been lost and tortured, hoping and wishing that Father would come home. She'd always prayed he was okay, that she would one day know what had happened to him, but now that that day had arrived, she was sorry for it. Her heart seized, her lungs squeezed, and Alice fought through the pain for a gasp of air. She felt infinitely powerless in the face of Father's enslavement, but being angry gave her something to do, so she took hold of it with both hands and refused to let it go. Oh, there was so much to be angry about.

Speaking of which: *Oliver was a liar.*

This, another truth that broke Alice's heart. She'd trusted him, befriended him, and Oliver had lied. He'd manipulated her. He'd withheld information from Alice over and over and he'd kept secret the most critical details of her father's imprisonment. He should've told Alice exactly what he needed from her; he should've secured her voluntary participation in all parts of his plan. He'd made a series of increasingly stupid, shortsighted decisions.

He was entirely at fault.

But between you and me, dear reader, I would dare to share my humble opinion that Oliver's stupidity alone was flimsy reasoning for Alice abandoning her otherwise well-traveled, well-informed partner at such a critical juncture in the story. If Alice had any sense of self-preservation she would've waited for a safer moment (or a safer place) to have walked away; but Alice and Oliver had more in common than they realized: The two possessed passionate, rumpled spirits and they were both guilty of crimes committed of childish ignorance.

Alice had neither the maturity nor the self-awareness to wonder at Oliver's ability to be such a consistently talented liar; she did not think his skills could be a symptom of some greater problem. So she couldn't have known then that Oliver's lies were motivated not by cruelty, but by fear. Fear of rejection, of abandonment, of interminable loneliness. There was very little she knew about his interior life, simply because she'd never asked.

Oliver, too, had made no effort to understand Alice. His young life had always been safe and boring and predictably comfortable; he'd never known the weight of grief or poverty.

He did not understand that a broken heart long untended would eventually cease to beat. And Alice, whose heart had been badly broken for some years now, desperately needed a body upon which to unburden her pain. Tonight, she chose Oliver. In this moment, anger was a magic all its own: It gave Alice energy, adrenaline, and a distorted sense of self-righteousness that would, for a short time only, power her through a pair of unwise decisions.

Abandoning Oliver would be the first.

KEEP UP!
THERE'S NO TIME
TO WASTE!

Oliver Newbanks was equal parts terror and anguish. He'd dashed out of Tim's home and was running around in a blind panic, checking under every lake and hill for a glimpse of his friend—but she was not to be found. If only Oliver had known where to go looking for Alice, he would have had no trouble finding her, as she was making no effort to disappear. In fact, she'd made quite a spectacle of herself when she thought no one was looking.

Alice was sitting on her bottom in the middle of the woods—her head dropped into one hand, her skirts bunched up to her knees—and was currently in the process of turning the entire forest an electrifying shade of blue. She'd changed the color of these woods several times now, but couldn't decide which hue would do. And then, as she squinted up at the trees and allowed herself another brief, self-indulgent little cry, she thought, *Oh, those leaves would look better in pink, wouldn't they?* and then turned the trunks pink, too. Playing with magic had always made her feel better.

Clever reader: I'm sure by now you've guessed it, haven't you?

I know I've not kept it much of a secret—and maybe I should've done—but I'm glad you've guessed it, because I'd like to finally be able to say this honest thing: Despite her protests to the contrary, Alice's gift was never to be a dancer. Her true magical ability was to be a living paintbrush.

Alice could change the colors of anything without lifting an eyelid. She could turn a person blue and a thing green and a place yellow and even though she should've been proud of her skill, she resented it. Hated it. Denied it so vehemently that she'd actually convinced herself it wasn't a real talent. Because Alice—*no-color Alice*—could change the color of anything and everything but her own colorless self.

She was sure it was a magic that existed to mock her.

Still, the motions of making color always helped calm her heart, and when she'd finally had her fill, she dusted off her hands and dug through her pockets for the pamphlets she'd neglected to read earlier. She'd had enough of relying on Oliver to make all the decisions and to tell her where to go. She could figure it out on her own, she'd decided, especially now that she knew the basics of Furthermore. And besides, she had information right here, right in her hands; all she had to do was study it.

But Alice couldn't focus.

Her hands were shaking and her thoughts were clouded and the truth was, she was scared. Alice had hoped to be brave—she'd hoped she was stronger than her fears—but Alice was injured on the inside; and though her anger kept her upright, it couldn't keep her steady, and from moment to moment Alice would slip.

She was tired and she was worried and she was consumed by thoughts of Father, of what his life had been like these past years and how she'd ever reach him. He was in danger, she knew that now, but she also knew Furthermore would do its best to keep him from her. This would be no ordinary task, she was realizing, and suddenly the seriousness of it all was weighing down on her. She wasn't sure she was strong enough to save anyone anymore, not even herself.

Alice ran absent hands across her face and rubbed at her eyes. She picked up her pamphlets, put them down, and picked them up again. She wanted to rest, but there was no time for that. She wanted to bathe, but there was no time for that, either. She felt tattered and dirty and she desperately needed a washing but there was Father to think of. Father whom she loved. Father who left when she needed him most. Father who got lost and couldn't find his way back to her. There was never a day she didn't think of him. Never a day she didn't need him.

She missed him with a fierceness that crippled her sometimes. She missed everything about him, about them, about how they used to be. She missed the way they used to fight, she and he, every day.

He would tell her she was beautiful and she'd call him a liar and they would argue until she gave in. He never let her win, never let her convince him she was right. He fought harder for her than she ever fought for herself.

Alice closed her eyes.

"Enough," Father said, shaking his head. He was pacing around the room. He was angry: His cheeks flushed, his eyes pinched, his brows furrowed. "I hate hearing you talk about yourself like this. You're a blank canvas, Alice. No person is better primed for color than you are."

Alice looked up at him, frustrated and exhausted. "Then when?" she asked. "When will I have color of my own? When will I look like you and Mother?"

"Darling Alice," he said, reaching for her. "Why must you look like the rest of us? Why do you have to be the one to change? Change the way we see. Don't change the way you are."

"But how?" she asked, her little fists clenched around his fingers. She tugged him closer. "How can I do that, Father?"

"You're an artist." He smiled. "You can paint the world with the color inside of you."

The memories tugged on her joints; her fists unclenched. Her heart ached.

It was a moment of weakness, and she allowed it. She felt

she'd earned it. She'd decided long ago that life was a long journey. She would be strong and she would be weak, and both would be okay.

So she bit the inside of her cheek, let her chin fall against her chest, raked all ten fingers through her knotted, tangled hair, and she let herself feel weak.

But then—

Well, it was strange, she'd just realized, that she hadn't thought much of her white hair at all lately. Certainly not as much as she used to. Before coming to Furthermore Alice could seldom move from moment to moment without being reminded of her nothing-hair and her nothing-skin. But not here. In fact, it struck her as silly now, to be bothered by her missing colors. What did it matter what she looked like when she had purpose?

She sat up a little straighter.

So what if Oliver was a liar? So what if she'd failed her Surrender? So what if she was lost in a strange land with no idea how to get home? *Father needed her*, and need didn't care what nothing looked like. Alice had a proper mission now, and she would not back down. She would fight harder for Father than he could fight for himself.

Nothing would stand in her way.

Alice had only managed to take one step forward before the fox found her again.

He seemed to have appeared out of nowhere, suddenly sitting in front of her, proper paper tail wagging in the fading light. He looked calm and sweet and bowed his head every time Alice looked at him. She wanted to pick him up and take him home.

Alice could hear the ghost of Oliver's voice in her head advising her to be careful. She could almost picture the fear in his face, the warning in his eyes. But Alice didn't care about Oliver's advice anymore and she was determined to prove she could make wiser decisions without him.

She bent down in front of the paper fox and scratched him (or her?) under the chin; the rough copper-colored paper felt strange and warm against her fingers. He seemed to like that, so she pet him between the ears and he nuzzled right into her hand.

"Hello, Fox," she said.

Fox jumped back, bit her skirts, and crinkled his paper nose at her feet.

Alice laughed and felt the cracks in her heart mend, bit by bit.

She took it as a sign. Maybe the fox was the thing Oliver had missed. Maybe the fox was sent especially for *her.*

What if the fox was trying to lead her to Father?

Alice already knew what Oliver would say about her theory, and even his imaginary condescension made her angry. So she made a sudden decision.

"Fox," she said. The fox yipped and its paper tongue lolled. "Fox, will you take me to my father?"

The fox nodded eagerly.

Alice clapped her hands together in joy. "Oh, you *do* know what I'm saying, don't you?" she asked.

Again, the fox nodded.

"So you'll help me?" she said. "Will you help me save Father?"

Once more, the fox nodded.

Alice cried out and wrapped her arms around the fox. "Thank you!" she said. "Oh, thank you!"

The fox jumped around and yipped again and was already bounding ahead of her through the forest, turning back every few feet to make sure she was following. Alice didn't know what was waiting for her but she was excited to be taking charge and making decisions for once. She felt certain that this was right, that she would make her way through Furthermore in a way Oliver couldn't. Oliver had never even made it to Father, so what did he know about saving him? She was sure that this fox was the key.

This optimism carried her through the next half hour.

Wherever the fox lived, it was far from where he found her, and the farther they went, the stranger the landscape became. Alice assumed they were still in Still, but she couldn't be sure. For just a fleeting moment Alice caught herself wishing Oliver was around to tell her where they were headed, but she quickly checked the impulse and focused instead on her certainty that the fox would help her find Father.

But the truth was, she was beginning to worry.

The ground beneath her was losing its grass, becoming sparer and drier as they went. Night had tilted into day, and the sun swung back into the sky. Heat filled the gaps in everything, and though Alice felt her instincts prick, denial kept her from registering the warning.

Alice was in a daze by minute thirty-four, one foot following the other and neither knowing their way. She blinked once, twice, so many times before the horizon stood upright and everything slipped sideways. It was strange, she thought, so very, very strange, how her feet kept moving even when she didn't want them to. Not only did she not want them to keep moving, she wanted them to do the very opposite of keep-moving, but there was no one to tell her feet anything at all, as her mind was always missing when she needed it most.

Her throat was awfully dry.

She licked her lips and the sky flew in and filled her up, so hot it stuck to her teeth. The earth beneath her was crisping at the edges, every inch fried sunny-side up.

Oh, it was hot.

Horribly, suffocatingly hot.

Alice ached for miles from heel to toe, wincing in the blinding light of what seemed an endless summer, and wondered, in a moment of clarity, if Oliver was worried about her.

She had no idea where she was.

She tried to look around but the moment she turned her head she was flat on the ground. She was pancake thin, plastered to the earth; she was physically impossible. She was suffocated by her eyes, her lips, the length of her face, the impossible weight of her bones and the skin that zipped her in too tightly. She was too human, too many dimensions for this world, and she only realized her eyes were closed when she decided it would be wise to wrench them open.

Sheer force of will pried her eyelids apart. She gasped and wheezed, her eyesight flattening at the edges, and when she blinked again, once more, and three and four times after that, she found herself staring upside down at a bright paper sun stapled to a spinning, glittery thread. She couldn't have known it at the time, but Alice had just come upon the village of Print, a two-dimensional town that could not sustain her.

Alice sat up slowly, reaching one arm forward to steady herself, and heard the crunch and rustle of something very wrong; her eyes shuttered, broke open, and focused on a world made entirely of paper everything. Paper clouds chugged alongside a paper sun, their bottoms taped to the tops of red-and-white-striped straws. A crumpled, folded-and-refolded half-moon was pinned to the blue construction-paper backdrop. Paper trees stood tall and not, and fat and not, and animals hop-walked around parallelograms of pasture. Homes were rectangles and triangles stapled together, chimneys puffing swirls of smoky tissue straight into the sky. Hills were pasted, one on top of the other, in different shades of green, and stick-figured people stomped around flat and sideways, an entire dimension of being snipped right off.

It was confounding. Astounding. She was out of breath with excitement. Amazement. Alice had no idea she was in danger—how could she? Eagerly, she leaned into her arm to push herself up and onto her feet, but fell forward, her arm now limp where a limb should be. And when she looked down at herself, she felt the strangest sensation.

She heard the strangest sound.

Alice was very likely screaming, though if you ask her about this today, she denies it, and I don't know why. Pride, I suppose. I'd not guilt her for screaming had she done so; her histrionics would have been for good reason. The fox, you will remember, was still with her, except that he now had Alice's arm in his mouth, and was very desperately trying to tug her sideways into his paper world. Alice was on the cusp of entering the village of Print, and she was still suffering the effects of being just close enough to a village that could collapse her. She was now moments from being dragged inside and made two-dimensional forever, and she was fighting for her life.

It was Fox against Alice.

Alice tugged and tugged, but it was difficult to know how hard to fight, because in so many ways she felt nothing. Part of her felt half real. Paper-thin. She could only sort of feel the pain of being pulled in different directions, because some part of her had suddenly become something else, and she didn't know what that was. She hadn't realized that the fox had managed to pull one of her arms all the way through to the two-dimensional town, and it wasn't until she heard a great roaring *rip* that she understood how tremendously wrong all this had become.

Technically, she won the fight.

The fox was scampering away, so Alice must've won the fight. Why, then, was Alice screaming so much louder now? (Again, she denies this.) What was there to shout about? And while we're asking questions, I'd like to wonder, why, in that very same moment, was Alice feeling so much regret?

Well, I will tell you what I think.

I think Alice was wishing she'd never run away from Tim and Oliver. I think she was wishing she'd never left Ferenwood at all. I think she was wishing Furthermore had never existed and that she'd never had a twelfth birthday and that she'd never Surrendered the wrong talent.

Oh, I think Alice was filled with all kinds of regret.

She ran blindly, wildly, charging back down an impossible path of impossible gravity, one foot pounding harder than the other in the blazing heat of an impossible sun.

Alice was sorry.

She was sorry for everything. She was sorry Mother didn't love her and sorry Father had left her and sorry for ever thinking she could save him. Alice ran until she tripped, until she fell to her knees and her face hit the ground, until she felt tears falling fast down her face. Only then did Alice understand true loss.

Only then did she discover she was missing an entire arm.

She wasn't bleeding, and this was the first thing Alice noticed. The second thing she noticed was that her right arm had been ripped off at the shoulder, and as she was only now beginning to regain the full use of her mind, the third thing she noticed was that she had been partly turned to paper.

Where blood should have been there were instead wisps of tissue, and where bone should have been there was instead a strange breeze. And though she felt the inclination to bend her arm, to make a fist, to shake herself out of hysteria and tell herself to stop crying—(*It's alright, I'm alive, I'll survive*, she would say)—she could do nothing but stare at the space where something important once was. And then, dear friends, the fourth thing she noticed:

Her bangles were gone.

The loss of an arm and an entire arm's worth of bangles (the latter, of course, being the greater loss) was too much to digest, especially like this. Like this: her head aching from the hit, her legs cramping from the run; still climbing to her feet and stumbling to stay upright, still moving, now panting, two short legs trying not to trip; her two feet pounding the earth, hard hits like heartbeats against the cracked dirt beneath them. She was off balance, unsteady with only one arm but she wouldn't stop, she wouldn't think, she refused to acknowledge any of this, not even for a moment, not until the dirt turned back into grass and the sun fell over sideways and night climbed over day and she was back where she started, forever moving forward just to move backward in time.

Finally, Alice fell to the ground.

She rolled over in the grass, adrenaline keeping her from collapsing into panic, and took a moment to marvel at the twilight she'd returned to. Just above her head was Tim's big red door, and just in front of her was wide-open nowhere with a pond nearby. The crickets sang to scratch an itch and the frogs croaked along because it was a catchy tune; the tall grass danced with a sultry breeze and the moon sat atop an unwashed cloud, shining over everything. Somehow, even in this moment of perfect terribleness, the Still night was still lovely, fragrant, and awfully enchanting, and Oliver Newbanks stood before her, looking like he'd been spun from glass.

Oliver Newbanks, who appeared to be catching his breath. Oliver Newbanks, who was looking at Alice, eyes wide, chest heaving, sweat beading at his brow, and he said once, softly, "Alice?"

So she whispered once, softly, "Oliver?"

"Alice," he said, urgently now, eyes tight and shining, "are you alright?" His voice was pitched low, like he was afraid it might crack.

And Alice shook her head. *No.* No, she wasn't okay.

The moon was quickly rising, and with it, a veil of darkness that partially obscured Alice from view. So Oliver drew closer, and only then did he see what had happened to her. He jerked back, clapped a hand to his mouth, and cried, "Oh *goodness*, Alice!"

She didn't know what to say.

Oliver reached out to touch the place where her arm might've been, and she saw his hand shake.

"Are you in pain?" he whispered, his voice trembling.

Alice shook her head again. *No.* In fact, she felt nothing at all. She hadn't yet processed the shock of losing her arm, so she wasn't sure how to react. Should she be scared? Should she be strong?

"Will it grow back?" she asked.

Oliver's eyes went so wide Alice could see the white rims around his irises. "No," he said softly. "The effects of Furthermore, when they can't be fixed, are always final."

That's when Alice began to feel.

His words stabbed at a corner of her brain; it was a twisty, piercing pain that exploded behind her eyes and took her breath away. For no reason at all she was suddenly desperate and aching, *aching*, where her arm used to be, and suddenly there was nothing in the world she wanted more than to have two arms. Suddenly all she could think about was having two arms. Suddenly there were a million hundred trillion thousand things she wanted to do with her arms and suddenly she couldn't, *suddenly she couldn't*, and it was all too much. The stabbing pain caught fire and dropped a flame down her throat and this shocked her heart into a terrible, tripping beat, and in less than a moment she was so thoroughly and absolutely shattered she couldn't calm down long enough to make herself scream.

She looked at Oliver.

". . . have to find a painter," he was saying.

"What?" The word was more of a rasp than a word. Alice had already lost a father, the length of her right arm, and an entire set of bangles, so it made sense that her voice would follow suit.

"Yes," Oliver was saying. "It's the only way." He was on his feet now, arms crossed, pacing the length of the same five-foot stretch. "The problem is, I don't quite know how to find one. I'd only ever heard rumors, you know?" He looked up at her. "And the trip will take us off course, of course, and cost us a great deal of time." He looked away again, mumbling. "Though obviously the expense would be worth it." He seemed to be speaking entirely to himself.

"Wait," she rasped again. "What do you mean?"

Oliver stopped pacing, looked up in surprise. "We have to get your arm fixed," he said.

"But I thought you said—"

He shook his head, hard. "No, no, it won't grow back. But we could get someone to paint you a new one."

Alice was about to ask more questions, but a sudden hope had taken up too much room inside of her and she couldn't think around it. She made the strangest noises. Startled, squeaky sounds that made it too obvious she was trying not to cry.

"Alice," Oliver said quietly. "Will you tell me what happened?" He offered her a handkerchief and she took it. "Where did you go? Who did this to you? How did you get back?"

So Alice told him the story. She told him about trusting the fox she shouldn't have trusted, about the paper world she saw, about the fox ripping off her arm as she tried to escape.

Oliver was devastated.

Alice was ashamed.

They were each convinced of their guilt, and they were right to be; they two had torn holes in each other, and the wounds, unhealed, had only led to more pain. The simple truth was that they were both to blame for what had happened. Oliver for his reluctance to trust Alice and for his failure to make her feel like a true partner; and Alice for making decisions motivated by anger and hurt and recklessness.

But young hearts are more resilient than most. They would both recover.

"Shall we?" said Oliver tentatively. "Time is such a tricky thing. We can never take too much." His eyes were nervous, asking all the questions he couldn't bring himself to say aloud. He was worried, Alice knew, that she would abandon him again.

So when Alice nodded, Oliver smiled, relief sagging his shoulders.

"Where will we go?" Alice asked. "To fix my arm? How will we get there?"

Oliver looked stricken as he stared at her, and Alice thought it was because he felt sorry for her; but that wasn't it at all. Oliver felt much more than sorry for Alice. His heart had grown ten sizes since he'd met her, and the hours he'd lost her had nearly broken him. She was injured and he knew it to be his fault—to be a result of his selfishness and stupidity—and he wasn't sure he could forgive himself.

"I don't honestly know," Oliver said softly. He looked out into the distance. "But not-knowing is only temporary when we've got the minds to figure it out. We'll find a way."

Alice nodded.

She had no fewer than a thousand questions and concerns, but she managed to swallow them down. Right now, she would make do with this reconciliation, and the rest, she hoped, would come.

Oliver knelt in front of her and smiled. A single tear had escaped down the side of his face, and the breeze touched his tunic, folding it gently between its fingers. Oliver closed his eyes.

"I'm so sorry, Alice," he whispered. "Please forgive me."

And because she was a girl made of more heart than hurt, she forgave him on the condition that he, too, forgive her.

Easily done.

Oliver took her only hand and held it right up against his chest, and then they sank, he and she, together, the two of them, right into the ground.

When Alice opened her eyes again, she felt the blazing heat of a familiar sun beating down her back. Alice's whole body stiffened, and Oliver, who was now paying close attention, misunderstood her fear.

"Sorry about that," he said. "These emergency exits can be a bit uncomfortable."

"Emergency exits?" said Alice, distracted.

Oliver nodded. "If you want to get to the next closest village as quickly as possible, you always exit downward. But the transitions can be a bit rough." He laughed. "One time I down-exited directly into a mass of dead sheep and I couldn't get the wool out of my mouth for days after. I was coughing up hairballs for hours—"

"Oliver, we should leave. Now." The ground beneath them was blisteringly hot, and Alice was beginning to see spots. "This is where the fox took me. This is near the entrance of that paper village. I'm sure of it."

Oliver froze, words still caught in his mouth; luckily, his shock lasted only a moment. He took Alice's hand and began to run, but just as they picked up speed Oliver was knocked sideways, hitting the ground hard as he fell. Alice cried out, panicked, and tried to help him up, but she was abruptly yanked backward, tossed face-first into the dirt, and dragged off by the hem of her skirts. She kicked and screamed and managed to break free twice before being pinned down again, but fear had finally paralyzed her.

The paper fox had returned, and this time, he'd brought his friends.

⁂

Four paper foxes had cornered them. Three of the four were built of a rather normal (read: dull) shade of brown paper, and these three had Oliver cowed on the ground. The only fox built of a vibrant copper color was the one standing directly over Alice's body. This was her fox. The very same one from before.

"Alice!" Oliver shouted. She could hear him struggling. "Alice, are you—" But his voice was quickly muffled. Alice chanced a glance his way only to find that one of the foxes had wrapped its tail around Oliver's mouth.

Alice felt her pulse racing. The heat was sweltering; sweat was beading at her brow. The fox had locked eyes with her and she was doing all she could to stay calm. Alice knew she should say something, but she wasn't sure where or how to begin. This was a paper fox, after all, and as far as Alice was concerned, there was no such thing as magic that could make animals talk.

Still, she had to try.

"What do you want from me?" she said.

The fox stared at her for just a beat longer before pawing aggressively at her skirt pockets.

"What is it?" Alice pulled herself up to a seated position, and the fox retreated a few steps. She patted her pockets with her single hand and unearthed their contents: four visitor pamphlets, her black card, and her blond ruler. Alice held them out to the fox. "What do you want?" she asked. "Which one?"

The fox nodded through her wares, took one of the pamphlets into his mouth, and made a strange whine, indicating with his head that she should retrieve the pamphlet from him. Alice wasn't sure what was happening, exactly, but she was relieved to know that at least her life was no longer in immediate danger. She tugged the pamphlet out from between the fox's paper jaws and glanced at the title.

— FURTHERMORE PHRASEBOOK —
How to Understand the Languages You Don't Speak

Alice inhaled sharply. She looked from the fox to the pamphlet and felt her heart pound quickly in her chest—but this time, Alice wasn't afraid. She was excited. She flipped open the pamphlet with an eagerness that dispelled any lingering fears she might've had, but Alice's eagerness quickly turned to dismay.

Every inch of the inside pages was blank.

Heartbroken, she hung her head. Perhaps the fox (or maybe Ted?) had made a mistake. (Or, you know, there'd been a printing error.) Whatever the reason for her misfortune, Alice was disappointed. She'd already begun refolding the pamphlet when a gentle, handsome voice said,

"Leave it open."

Alice froze.

"Ms. Queensmeadow, please. Look at me."

In that moment Alice was certain she'd misplaced the whole of her mind; but let me reassure you, dear reader, that she was in full possession of her faculties. The fox was most definitely speaking to her, and—

Can I just say? I don't know that I understand the extent of her shock. The fox, like most animals (paper or no), is fully capable of speech. That we make few concerted efforts to understand the fox language is a fault entirely our own.

Now, where were we?

"Ms. Queensmeadow, please," said the fox. "Look at me."

Alice looked up, astounded.

"You are in danger, Ms. Queensmeadow. You must leave here at once."

"Of course I'm in danger," said Alice. "You've tried to kill me twice already!"

The fox shook his head. "I was not trying to kill you. I was trying to *hide* you. I do sincerely apologize for what happened to your arm—"

Alice harrumphed.

"—but I thought you'd be safer in my world. You should go, Ms. Queensmeadow. Go back to where you came from."

"And why should I? Why do you care what happens to me?"

"I know why you're here. We all do. And we know you've lost no fruit tree in the town of Slender."

Alice gasped.

"Your journey to find your father is a noble one," said the fox. "But he had no right to meddle in our affairs, and neither do you."

"What do you mean?" said Alice. "What did Father do to meddle in your affairs?"

The fox tilted his head at her. "Our lands agreed long ago not to go poking in each other's magical matters. And your father—who is publicly known for consorting closely with Ferenwood Town Elders—was found here in Furthermore asking too many questions about our magic and how we use it."

"But he was arrested for wasting *time*—"

"Yes," said the fox. "He was indeed arrested for time thievery. But he was also charged with suspected espionage."

"What?" Alice felt the blood drain from her face.

"Tread carefully," said the fox. "Furthermore knows you're here to find him, and this land will not give up a spy so easily."

"But he's not—he can't be—"

"Go home, Ms. Queensmeadow. Unless you, too, would like to be held accountable for his actions."

"But—if you think my father's a spy—" Alice faltered. "Why are you trying to help me?"

"You are an innocent." The fox tossed back his head. "And I don't agree that you should be harmed for seeking out a lost loved one. Besides," he added, "I don't approve of eating children. It's uncivilized."

Alice didn't know what to say.

"You don't have much time, Ms. Queensmeadow." The fox was growing anxious; he'd begun circling around her. "Everyone here is waiting for you. Go home. Now. Before you're found."

"Who?" said Alice. "Who's waiting for me—?"

There was a sudden rustle in the distance and the fox's eyes darted around. He looked back at Alice with a wild nervousness. "Snap in three in case of emergency."

"What . . . ?"

"Trust a friend who looks like one."

"What are you—"

"We know," said the fox. "We all know."

Alice felt a prick of terror pinch the back of her neck. She couldn't explain how, exactly, but she felt certain that something was about to go terribly wrong.

"Please," she whispered. "I just want to find my father. Can't you help me?"

"I'm afraid I can't. You would do better to return home." He turned to leave.

"Wait!" Alice grabbed the fox's leg.

He stopped and stared at Alice's hand.

"Will you let my friend go?" she asked.

The fox narrowed his eyes. "You may go freely on your way, Ms. Queensmeadow, but I'm afraid the boy will have to come with us."

"What?" said Alice, stunned. "But I thought you didn't approve of eating children—"

"I don't approve of eating *good* children. But your friend is an untrustworthy, duplicitous lout, whose long list of infractions could fill the many trunks of our trees." The fox held his head high. "Little liars will not be rewarded in Furthermore."

"But—he didn't mean any harm—"

"Liars have the longest tongues, Ms. Queensmeadow. A delicacy we all enjoy. And we've all been hungry for so long, you see, that it's hard to deny ourselves a fresh meal when it's so well deserved. I'm sure you understand."

With that, the fox took a deep bow, broke free of Alice's hand, and scampered off in Oliver's direction.

❖

Alice sprang to her feet, shoving her belongings in her pockets as best she could with one hand. The four foxes were already busy carting Oliver off into the distance, and now that his mouth was unmuffled, Alice could hear him screaming into the sunlight.

She ran forward, horrified but determined, and snatched the ruler from her pocket, charging at the paper creatures as though it were a dagger. She swung and swatted at the foxes, kicking and yelling as they yelped and fell away. Alice hadn't managed to do much real damage to the animals (who, for paper creatures, made formidable opponents), but her own friendly fox looked so heartbroken by her betrayal that Alice was tempted to feel sorry for him. Fortunately, her guilt was quickly wicked away. She didn't care that her life had been spared—no fox would eat her friend, no matter the lies he'd told.

But the foxes would not be beat.

They threw themselves forward more quickly than Alice could shove them back. She managed to land a few hard *thwacks* with her ruler, but her single arm was quickly tiring, and though Alice was now huddled protectively over Oliver's body, the foxes were showing no signs of letting up. Alice had underestimated the power of animal hunger; these creatures had been promised a meal and they would not leave without it. Oliver tried several times to aid in his own defense, but the foxes were thrashing about so forcefully—growling and snapping—that Alice was worried they'd bite his head clean off.

"Down-exit!" she cried, crouched low over Oliver's back. "Down-exit, please!"

But nothing was working. (Oliver, to his credit, had tried desperately to persuade the foxes to let him go, but his talent had been withered by fear; his occasional flickers of success weren't strong enough to fight all four foxes.) Alice, meanwhile, was becoming increasingly panicked. She was fumbling, losing her grip on the ruler as her arm weakened under strain, and all it took was a moment's hesitation—

Alice was flung backward.

She landed heavily on her only arm, her head slamming hard against the ground. It took her a few seconds to blink away the dizziness, but she clenched her jaw against the dull, throbbing pain and drew herself up, determined not to sway. Alice could still hear Oliver shouting and fighting, landing kicks and punches wherever he could, and she was just about to charge forward again, ruler clenched tightly in her hand, when she felt the ground shift beneath her. One of the foxes had slammed its head into Oliver's jaw with a resounding *crack*—and Oliver had gone still.

The foxes snapped around his limp figure, fighting to see who'd get to take the first bite, and Alice felt her brain disconnect from her body.

"NO!" she cried.

She stumbled as she threw herself forward, falling hard onto her knees, her agonized screams ringing out across the barren landscape. She bent into the raging heat and blinding light of this strange town and felt the fresh pain of fear and loss pry open an iron door in her chest and all at once—everything changed.

The land, the sky, the foxes, and even Oliver: disappeared.

Alice had reduced the color of all things around her—the large, the infinitesimal, and everything in between—to a single shade of black, and she was so wholly unaware of the magnitude of what she'd done that it wasn't until she heard the confused, frenzied foxes knocking into one another that she realized she'd snuffed out the sun. Alice alone stood in stark contrast to the painted night. She examined her single arm—the white of her skin glowing neon in the dark—and for the very first time in her life, Alice Alexis Queensmeadow felt powerful.

Alice heard the foxes scamper off into the distance, the four of them no longer brave enough to fight blindly. When she was finally sure they were gone for good, Alice closed her eyes, drew in a deep breath, and—with the simple twitch of her mind—reset the colors she'd so fully distorted.

She spotted Oliver instantly.

He was on his back, his arms and legs splayed, his lip bloody—but, thank heavens, he was still breathing. Alice ran to her friend, tossed her ruler to the ground, and pulled him up against her.

⁂

She shook him, but he wouldn't wake. She slapped him, but he wouldn't speak. "Oliver, please!" she cried. But he wouldn't stir.

Tears were streaking fast down her face and though she fought valiantly to hold on to hope, she wasn't sure how to fight *this*.

Panic had overtaken her.

Alice was just in the middle of giving Oliver another good shake when her eyes hit upon the ruler she'd dropped so carelessly onto the ground. The inscription in the blond wood was staring up at her.

SNAP IN THREE IN CASE OF EMERGENCY

If this wasn't an emergency, Alice was a dill pickle.

She didn't hesitate—desperation had left her no options. She grabbed the ruler, held it in place with her foot, snapped it twice—leaving her with three broken pieces—and cried, "Help! Help! This is an emergency!"

And everything slowed.

The scene before her went soft and blurry, and a moment later, all things froze. The bees went still in midair; sitting birds went silent mid-chirp. Only Alice was free to move, and when she did, she stood up.

❖

A crack, a zip, and an exclamation point later, three extremely thin, ludicrously tall, bright orange doors were set before her. Hung on each door was a different sign:

STEP THROUGH TO FIX YOUR ARM

ENTER HERE TO SAVE YOUR FRIEND

OPEN ME TO FIND YOUR FATHER

And then, in small print under each sign,

CHOOSE ONLY ONE DOOR OR DIE A PAINFUL DEATH

It's a great testament to the tender heart of our dear Alice that she did not agonize over this decision. Alice Alexis Queensmeadow knew right away what she would do.

(She'd decided to save Oliver, of course.)

Alice would no longer be bullied by the tricks and games of Furthermore. She didn't care what the doors said. She would have her friend *and* her father. (And maybe her arm, too.)

She would find a way.

So she marched right up to the door she'd chosen, turned the knob with great conviction, and tripped—in the most unflattering way—straight over the threshold. With a sudden twist in her stomach and the uncomfortable displacement of her heart to her throat, Alice fell forward, screaming, into a strange sky. She flipped upside down only to tumble right side up only to plummet horribly to her death, and it was only the sound of someone else's blistering screams that so swiftly silenced her own.

Oliver came barreling through the sky like a bullet, slamming into Alice so hard she nearly knocked her head against his nose. She righted him as best she could and then took hold of his hand, squeezing it tightly, relief and joy flooding through her. She had no idea how much she'd come to care for Oliver until she'd nearly lost him.

"Don't worry," was the first thing she said to him. "Everything will be alright."

And Oliver beamed at her.

After ascertaining that he was indeed in one piece and not two, Alice quickly explained everything that'd happened with the fox and her ruler and the emergency doors, careful to leave out the part about things changing colors. (Alice wasn't ready to talk about that yet.) Oliver's head was spinning with the weight of all this frightening new information, but somehow, despite the horrors they'd seen, a huge smile had hinged itself to his cheeks. (Alice had chosen *him*, you see. Alice had chosen to save *him*, and Oliver was euphoric. It was all rather sweet.)

But Alice was thinking of other things now.

The thing was they'd been falling through the sky for quite a long while now, and they still hadn't reached the bottom of anything—and it was beginning to make Alice anxious. To make matters worse, it was taking a great deal of effort to keep her skirts out of her face (and with only one arm, my goodness), and she was growing tired.

"Oliver," she said.

"Yes?" he said.

"When do you think we'll reach the bottom?"

"Of what?"

"Of . . ." Alice looked around at the emptiness surrounding them. The bluest skies, a couple of clouds, and no sun she could see from where she sank. "Of this," she said, nodding at nothing in particular. "When do we get to the bottom of this?"

"I haven't any idea," he said simply. And right then they hit the ground.

Alice and Oliver landed with two great *thumps*, one after the other, the impact rattling their teeth and bruising their knees.

"Right," said Alice, as she picked herself up off the ground, dizzy and light-headed. She squinted at the scene set before them. "I take it you've never been here before, have you?"

Oliver shook his head.

They were standing in a narrow lane walled in by hedges three times taller than Oliver and packed so densely with roses and lilies and peonies and lilacs (and gardenias and freesia and hyacinth) that the two of them could hardly breathe. The flowers were stunning, but the sweet scent was so intoxicating as to be sickening, and the farther they walked, the more difficult it was to tolerate.

"Well," said Alice. "I suppose we're about to die, aren't we?"

"You jest," said Oliver, raising an eyebrow. "But it's entirely possible."

Alice shot him a halfhearted grin. "Well then, should we down-exit?"

Oliver laughed. "You can't just down-exit your way through Furthermore, Alice. You're only allowed to do it once every five villages."

"See—how do you even know that?" Alice said, throwing her only hand up in defeat. "I haven't any idea how to go about unearthing information like that." She sighed, then mumbled, "And anyway I was wondering why it hadn't worked for me earlier."

Oliver offered her a sympathetic look. "To be fair," he said, "I've had your father's journals to guide me. I'd have been lost without them."

Alice sighed, kicked at a patch of dirt, and trudged on. Quietly, she said, "I suppose I've now thrown us entirely off course, haven't I?" She looked up. "I've made a great mess of things."

"Not at all," Oliver said brightly. "I know it might not seem like it, but you're doing exceptionally well in Furthermore. Most people don't make it this far."

"Oliver," she said, visibly embarrassed, "I tried to make it on my own for five minutes and I had my arm ripped off! The result of which forced us to take an unknown path that ended with our being attacked by a skulk of foxes who nearly bit off your head and forced me to snap my ruler in three." She put her hand on her hip. "I don't think that makes me any good at this."

"Well"—he hesitated—"no, maybe you're not an expert, but—"

"Oh, don't bother, Oliver. I'm terrible on my own and we both know it."

Oliver bit his lip. His mouth twitched.

And Alice couldn't help it: She started laughing.

So Oliver did, too.

The two of them laughed and laughed until tears streamed down their faces, and for just a moment, neither child was bothered by the strange floral lane they walked through or the dangers they'd survived or the ones they'd soon encounter. This was a time of ease and release, and while it was possible they'd sniffed one too many sweet blooms and were unnaturally moved to silliness, it was far more likely that they'd just discovered one of life's greatest tricks: Laughter was a silk that would soften even the roughest moments.

"You're right," Oliver was saying. "We should probably stick together from now on."

"Yes, please," said Alice, still giggling. "I've no interest at all in doing this on my own anymore. And I hope you will at least *try* to stop me if I attempt to abandon you again."

"I'm glad to hear it," said Oliver, eyes shining. "I'm so glad."

Alice smiled.

Oliver smiled back.

Alice was missing an arm, and somehow it didn't matter;

she was much happier now than when she had a spare.

"Alice," said Oliver, once the laughter had subsided. He was looking at her only hand.

"Yes?" she said.

"Did you really snap your ruler in three parts?"

Alice nodded and, after tugging them out of her pocket, held up the broken pieces for him to see.

Oliver looked suddenly anxious. "You know," he said, "snapping your ruler like that—that is, I'm terribly grateful—but—"

"What is it?" Alice narrowed her eyes. "What's wrong?"

"It's just—your ruler is a container. If you snap it open, its contents scatter—and you lose all the time you've been allotted. And . . . if you lose all the time you've been allotted, you'll have to live on borrowed time; and if you're caught borrowing time, you'll be arrested for stealing."

Alice's mouth had fallen open. "Then why does it say to snap my ruler in case of *emergency*?"

"For its own selfish reasons, I suppose. You'd get your emergency sorted out just in time to be carted off for Time Thievery."

"So I'm going to be arrested?"

Oliver said nothing.

"Oliver!"

"Probably?" He looked anguished. "Maybe? I don't know, Alice, I have no real experience in this matter. Only theories."

Alice groaned.

"I'm truly sorry. And I could be wrong, you know."

Alice sighed, defeated, and looked off into the distance. Time had turned against her, and she didn't know how much she had left. "Maybe," she said, trying not to sound too hopeful, "maybe if I get arrested, you could use your emergency option to help me?"

Oliver shook his head. "I wish I could. But all *Tibbins* are different. Mine isn't the same as yours."

"Tibbin?" Alice said. "Is that what it's called?"

"Yes. Furthermore likes to pretend its rulings are fair and forgiving, so every visitor is offered one bit of help on their journey through the land. But the help is different for everyone, and it's always decided at Border Control. Once it's been issued, it's inscribed on the back of your ruler. It's called a Tibbin."

Alice frowned. "How could they know what bit of help I'd need on my journey before I'd even begun?"

Oliver raised an eyebrow. "How do you think?"

"But, Oliver," she said, confounded, "using magic to tell the future—they couldn't possibly—"

"Couldn't they? Furthermore does what it wishes."

"But *happenstance* is the most unstable, imprecise kind of magic—surely even Furthermore would know better than to rely on magic that grants only flickers of the future."

"You think too highly of this land if you think it wouldn't resort to lowly tactics," said Oliver. "Remember: Furthermore has no interest in playing fair. They could snatch us up at any moment, Alice. They could kill us right now if they wanted to. Don't you see? We're alive only because they want us to be."

"That makes no sense."

"It makes perfect sense. Furthermore doesn't want to kill and conquer its meals with no fuss or fanfare. It's far too easy that way—too boring." Oliver shook his head. "No, this is a land that likes to play with its food."

"But Oliver," said Alice slowly, carefully. "Do you think it's possible they're torturing us a bit more than they do most people?"

Oliver's eyebrows shot up his forehead in surprise. "What makes you say that?"

"Something the fox said to me." Alice looked away. "He said that Father was charged with suspected espionage. They think he's a Ferenwood spy come to meddle in their magic."

"*Wow.*" Oliver let out a low whistle. "This is entirely new information to me. But goodness, it would explain a lot."

Alice looked up. "You think so?"

Oliver nodded. "Your father's early journals never expressed such fear as I've felt on my journeys. It would make sense that your father had done something to anger them; that we were on some kind of hateful watch list as a result—and that our path would be more intentionally treacherous." He hesitated. "Which is why I'm now even more concerned that you've used your Tibbin."

Alice bit her lip. "Is it really that awful to spend it? Have you never used one before?"

"Not ever. I had one the last time I was here, too, but I never trusted it. I don't like accepting offers of help from Furthermore."

Alice bit her knuckles. She was growing more anxious by the moment. "Well, I had no choice, did I? Anyway what does your Tibbin say this time?"

Oliver didn't even have to look. He'd already memorized it. "*Trust a friend who looks like one.* And I haven't any idea what it means. Gibberish, most likely."

But Alice had just remembered something.

"Oliver," she said, "the fox—"

"Yes?"

"The fox said that *very* thing to me. Just before he walked away. First he said *Snap in three in case of emergency*, and then he said *Trust a friend who looks like one.*" Alice frowned. "At first I thought it was nonsense, but now I think he was—"

"Telling you our Tibbins?" Oliver's mouth had popped open. "They're supposed to be private information!"

Alice shook her head. "All the fox said was *We know. We all know.* He also said he knew I was here to find Father."

Now Oliver looked convinced. "They're definitely watching us. They know our Tibbins *and* they know I lied to them at Border Control. Goodness . . . he was a very helpful fox, wasn't he? I might've even liked him if he hadn't tried to eat me."

"Me too," said Alice softly. "He was very kind otherwise. It was all very strange. He was a strange fox." And then, more thoughtfully, "I do wonder . . . what *do* you think Father was doing here?"

It was a very good question, though perhaps one Alice should've asked sooner. The thing was, Alice hadn't really wanted to think about why Father was here, because she hadn't wanted to believe that Father had left home on purpose. (Alice, you will note, had a bad habit of ignoring matters of unpleasantness in her life [*see also* Alice's fervent denial of her true magical ability], no matter the consequences.) Alice still hoped Father had been trapped or tricked or had been forced to come to Furthermore; she couldn't understand why he would leave her voluntarily nor what he'd hoped to do here, in a land so far from Ferenwood.

"Well," said Oliver, clasping and unclasping his hands. "It—it could've been for any number reasons, couldn't it?"

"But why was he meddling in Furthermore magic? You don't think he was really a spy, do you?"

"No," Oliver said firmly. "I definitely don't think he was a spy. I will say, however, that I think Furthermore is more than a little paranoid."

"But then why would he come here? Why do visitors *ever* come to Futhermore?" Alice prodded. "What's the draw?"

"Vacation?" Oliver said too loudly. "Perhaps a bit of travel—"

"Oliver, please," said Alice. "You mustn't hide things from me anymore. I can handle the truth, whatever it is." She stared at him. "Really, I can."

"Honestly, Alice." He sighed. "Your father's motives, I don't truly know. I have only my assumptions."

"And they are?"

Oliver shrugged. "Visitors only ever travel to Furthermore when they want something they can't otherwise procure. It's a land that deals in the dangerous and the unlawful; if what you want exists nowhere else, it's likely to exist here. But *getting* here is incredibly complicated. It's a perilous journey, and the stakes are too high for nonessential wants and needs. No," Oliver said, shaking his head. "People only ever come to Furthermore when they are in desperate need of something important. Something worth all the risks." He looked up, locked eyes with Alice. "So, you tell me," he said. "Is there something your father wants more than anything else in the world?"

Alice hesitated, thinking carefully before answering. "I

don't think so," she finally said. "I confess I wouldn't really know."

Oliver shook his head again. "It's inconceivable that he'd come here for no reason. Think, Alice. You're overlooking something wildly obvious."

"What's that?" she asked.

"*You.*"

"Me?"

"Yes," said Oliver. "You're underestimating how much your father loves you."

"What?" Alice's heart was kicking around in her chest. "You think Father came here for *me*?"

"What I think," said Oliver, "is that what your father wants, more than anything else in the world, is for you to be happy."

Alice blinked, her eyes stinging with emotion, and looked away.

"And what does your father think will make you happy?" Oliver asked. "What is the secret desire of your heart?"

Oliver knew.

Of course he knew.

He'd known the secret desire of her heart since the first time he met her; this was a part of his talent. And Alice's deepest secret was more than just the truth of her real ability; it was also her deepest wish. Her forever fantasy.

"Color," she said, her voice catching. "I want color."

"And don't you think," Oliver said quietly, "that your father, knowing your pain, would come here for you? In search of a solution? Furthermore uses magic in ways Ferenwood never has; it's a place of endless experimentation and infinite possibility. It makes sense that he would search here, especially if he's been here before."

Alice's heart was thrown into chaos.

She could hardly speak and, even if she could, she didn't know what to say. To think that Father had put himself in such danger—that he'd risked so much—for *her*? It was impossible to describe her heart's simultaneous pain and joy; so she was silently grateful she didn't have to. Because just as she parted her lips to respond, Oliver did her a great kindness and changed the subject.

"So anyway," he said, staring off into the distance. "I do hope we'll still be able to find him."

"What do you mean?" Alice said sharply, the gentle moment forgotten. "Why wouldn't we be able to find Father?"

Oliver clapped a hand behind his head and looked off into the distance. "It took me sixty-eight villages just to unearth the basic facts of your father's imprisonment. And when I failed to reach him, I thought we needed to start over in the same pattern—only I figured we'd need to do it better this time. It'd taken so much work just to be able to get a glimpse of where your father had gone that I was too afraid to do anything differently; I didn't want to lose track of him. But ever since we left Tim, we've been taking paths I've never traveled, and I don't know what that means for us."

"Well, I don't want to lose Father," Alice said nervously. "Maybe we should go back to the original plan, Oliver, I think that might be—"

"No," he said. "Absolutely not. We will find your father, yes, but we will fix you first." He looked at where her right arm used to be. "This is an emergency," he said softly. "It's not a waste of time. In cases of physical wound or peril, Furthermore has been known to overlook the expense; your father won't suffer for our delay. I can promise you that."

"You're sure?" said Alice anxiously. "Because I've already got one arm, and I'm sure I don't need two. I'd really rather find Father."

"Alice," Oliver said with a laugh, "you are so very, very strange." He was staring at her, a gentle smile strung from ear to ear, and it was then that Alice realized how different he'd become in this short time. Alice couldn't explain why, exactly, but she knew now that things had changed between them. Oliver had become her friend in an absolute, uncomplicated way. She was done fighting him, and he was done lying to her.

Their friendship had changed seasons.

And now, after all they'd fought through, she couldn't imagine returning to Ferenwood life without him. She couldn't think of sleeping with the pigs and fighting with Mother and sharing a room with her tiny brothers and finding ways to pass the time on her own. How could she forget the excitement of an adventure with Oliver? What would her life be like when they finally returned home?

Strange, she hadn't thought of it until just then.

It scared her a little.

"A new adventure awaits!" Oliver cried, charging forward.

"I'm very glad you're excited"—Alice laughed as she ran to catch up to him—"but we still haven't a single idea how to get to a painter to fix my arm. What do we do now?"

"We figure it out." Oliver grinned. "Furthermore is a land of tricks and puzzles, so we must use the only tools we've got."

"And what tools are those?"

Oliver beamed. "Our brains, of course."

Alice and Oliver had been wandering a long while before the floral hedges finally opened up to an expansive clearing. Endless green hills rolled off into the distance, their gentle slopes dotted with wildflowers. Soft, golden light filtered through spider-webbing tree branches, creating an impression of sweetness that the land of Furthermore did not deserve. Most curious, however, was the great, glimmering lake set just beyond the hills. A long wooden pier had been built out to the middle of the water, where the path was then split in two: Separate footbridges led to either ends of the lake—one going left, and the other, right—but where those paths went, Alice could not see.

"Oh, this is splendid," said Oliver, awed as he looked around. "And much more interesting. I thought for sure that we were in another village."

"And we're not?"

Oliver nodded at the lake. "Your emergency door dropped us

inside of an intersection." He looked at Alice. "This is a Traveler's Turning Point."

"So we have to choose which way to go?"

"Yes."

"And . . . I'm guessing it won't be easy," said Alice.

Oliver laughed.

They didn't speak as they climbed the gentle hills, but Alice was studying the idyllic scene like it was something to be feared. Birds were pirouetting through the air and lambs were bleating their woes and flowers dipped and swayed in the wind like this was just another perfect day. But Alice wouldn't believe it.

And when they finally, reluctantly, stood at the end of the pier in the very middle of the lake, she and Oliver didn't know which way to turn.

"So," said Alice. "Left or right?"

"Wrong," said Oliver.

Alice raised an eyebrow.

"We have four choices, not two," he said. "Up, down, left, or right."

"Down?" said Alice, taken aback. "You mean—down into the lake?"

"And up into the sky. Yes."

"Oh, for Feren's sake," Alice said, and sat down.

Alice hadn't the faintest idea which way to go, but she didn't say as much because her vanity wouldn't allow it. Oliver was now relying on them to use their brains to navigate Furthermore, and as she was currently the smartest person she knew (outside of Father, of course), Alice didn't want to lose that title to Oliver. She wanted to prove herself. She wanted to be useful.

(She wanted to be smarter than Oliver.)

And then she had a sudden stroke of inspiration.

"Perhaps the answer is in the pamphlets!" Alice cried, and not a moment later she was digging papers out of her pocket and soon she was unfolding "What to Know Before You Go," all ten feet of it rattling and unfurling across the pier.

Oliver flit about anxiously as Alice perused the papers, shooting her skeptical looks and claiming *he'd* never had to rely on pamphlets to get him through Furthermore and "it's all nonsense anyway, not meant for anything but confusing" but Alice paid him no mind. She carried on perusing, and soon his anxiety gave way to acquiescence, and moments later he was sitting by her side. The two of them pored over the pages in hopes of finding a single useful word, and though it took them nearly ten minutes to come upon it, they eventually found their answer in large, shouting capital letters:

<u>CONSTRUCTION NOTICES: ALL INTERSECTIONS</u>

UP AND DOWN EXITS PERMANENTLY CLOSED FOR REPAIR!!! DO NOT ATTEMPT DOWN-EXIT WITHOUT PERMIT. DO NOT ATTEMPT UP-EXIT ON MONDAY THROUGH FRIDAY OR SATURDAY AND DEFINITELY NOT SUNDAY!!!! IF EXIT IS NECESSARY, RIGHT AND LEFT ARE UNDER CONSTRUCTION BUT CURRENTLY OPERATIONAL. PROCEED WITH CAUTION!!!! NOTE: DOWN-EXIT DISALLOWED ON MONDAYS FROM 2:00 to 6:00 p.m.

“Well, that wasn’t helpful at all, was it?” Alice said with a sigh.

“What do you mean?” Oliver was beaming. “It says here that up- and down-exits are closed! Narrows things down, doesn’t it? Now we only have to choose between left and right.”

“Well, yes,” Alice said, “but do we go left or do we go right?”

“Oh,” Oliver said, the smile gone from his face. “I don’t know.”

“Let’s go left,” Alice said, deciding. She got to her feet. “Everyone is always going right, and if so many people are going right, it’s bound to be wrong, I think.”

“Okay then,” Oliver said, looking at her like he was proud.

And surprised. But mostly proud. “Left it is. Left we go.”

“Left we go!” Alice cheered.

So that was that. They took the Left footbridge and ran as left as it would go—

until they ran into a wall.

They were knocked backward with two short screams, one after another, and landed painfully on their backsides. Oliver moaned. Alice groaned.

"My head," he said.

"My eyes," she cried. "I can't see a thing."

"Alice?"

"Oliver?"

"Yes?"

"Are you alright?"

"Just fine," said Oliver.

"Oh, good. Me too."

They were both silent a moment.

"Well," Oliver finally said. "I can't see a stitch."

"No," said Alice. "Neither can I. And it smells like dirt."

"And wood," Oliver said. "It smells like dirt and wood."

"It does, doesn't it?" A pause. "Where are you?"

Alice hadn't any idea where they'd landed. She stumbled to her feet and tread carefully, single arm out, feeling for familiarity. Alice and Oliver both breathed sighs of relief when they collided, and he quickly took hold of her only hand, holding tight as they forged forward, sniffing and sensing and listening for a hint of what would come next.

They hit wall after wall of old, musty wood—strange, the wood felt damp—until they finally stumbled upon a door. Alice's heart did a happy flip in relief, and Oliver laughed a nervous sort of laugh, and then . . . they hesitated.

Alice wanted to turn the knob, but Oliver said they had to knock. "It's the Furthermore way," he reminded her. "It's improper to walk, uninvited, through a door that isn't your own. You always have to knock."

"But what if no one answers?" she asked. "What if we knock forever and no one comes?"

"Nonsense," Oliver said with a wave of his hand. "There's no door in Furthermore that isn't aching to be opened."

Alice took a deep breath. "Very well," she said. "If you're certain."

"Quite certain."

They were both quiet a moment.

"Are you ready?" said Alice.

"Always," said Oliver.

And together, his knuckles and hers, they knocked on the door made of damp, musty wood, and tried not to think too hard about what might be waiting for them on the other side.

✦

After only a moment, the door creaked open. Wood straining against wood, the door no longer seemed to fit in its frame. It was so old and warped it was almost as though it'd never been opened until that very moment.

Alice was goose bumps everywhere.

Inch by inch, light poured into the dim room they stood in, until soon the lengths of it were flooded with light, and Alice and Oliver had to squint to see who stood on the other side.

Alice blinked and blinked until a figure finally came into focus, but even then she was confused. It was either an owl or a very old man, she couldn't be sure. All she did know for certain was that he was very happy to see them. She knew this because the first thing he did was burst into tears.

"Honorable guests of Left," he said, sobbing, "you are most welcome to our land. Oh honorable guests," he wept, "bless you for bestowing your good graces on our home. Bless you," he said, "for choosing Left when you could've gone Right. Bless you," he said, his voice cracking, "for we've wanted for visitors for so long. We hoped and danced for the chance to speak to another. Waited and waited for a moment with a new friend.

Oh honorable guests!" He was half bent, hands clutching his knees and weeping (Alice could see now that he was indeed an old man, and not an owl), and she was so startled, so moved, so touched, and so tentative, she wasn't quite sure what to do.

She looked at Oliver.

He shrugged.

"Please," the old man said (after he'd pulled himself together), "please," he said, gesturing toward the light. He moved just outside the door to allow them room to pass. "Step into the land of Left. The land of my home. A land," he said with sudden pride, puffing his birdlike chest into the air, "no longer ignored. No longer neglected. Oh joy, oh joy," he said. "What a day, what a day!"

Oliver stepped forward cautiously and peeked his head out. She heard him gasp, and then he looked back, eyes wild, and made an effort to smile. "It's okay," he whispered.

Alice took Oliver's outstretched hand and followed him out the door. She didn't know what she felt more: nervousness or excitement, or a nervous sort of excitement, but, oh, where they were she didn't know and didn't mind, because it was beautiful and strange. The little old man was beside himself with joy, and she didn't think anyone had ever been happier to see her than he was just then.

Friends, they had just stepped out of a tree trunk.

These were trees as tall as giants who were tall for their

size. Trees as grand as mountains, tree trunks as wide as tree-tops, trees chock-full of leaves so green she could barely stand to look at them. They were high, high above the ground, but in the land of Left there was a clear bottom: Many thousands of feet below them was an expanse of green that seemed to go on forever; she could see little yellow flowers dotting the tall, wild grass. But most interesting wasn't the web of interconnected trees. It wasn't the many busy people tending to their lives in a brilliantly lit forest. Well, I mean, it was—it was all of that—but it was more: Here, their homes were made from empty egg-shells; mostly whole or one-quarter missing, each one painted a different geometric design. They were bright and steady and somehow unbroken, hung from branches with thick, glittering white rope. Inside each one was a little world, a home that held hearts and minds; and it was immediately obvious to Alice—and Oliver—that the people of Left were a happy sort.

But experience had taught her to be suspicious.

The little old man was waiting for them under a canopy of branches. There was just enough shade to protect them from the sun, but occasionally the light would slip through a crack and remind them all how dim they were without it.

Alice and Oliver carefully balanced their way down a branch and followed their new guide. Suddenly he came to an abrupt stop, jumped straight up in surprise, and turned back to face them.

"My goodness," he said. "I have taken leave of my manners." He shook his head and bowed slightly. "Please forgive the oversight," he said. "It's only that I am so very pleased to see you that I forgot everything but my own excitement." He lifted his head and looked them in the eye. "I am Paramint," he said. "And it is my great honor and privilege to meet you both."

Alice and Oliver introduced themselves, and as they did, Alice noticed that Paramint was wearing an outfit she'd never seen any person wear before: a mustard-colored buttoned-down shirt with a bright-blue vest and a red-on-rust pinstriped jacket paired with olive-green velvet trousers. He wore chocolate-brown boots so shiny Alice swore she heard them glitter, and he carried in his hand a very tall candy cane, presumably for walking.

So many clothes for a man. Alice was impressed.

Alice had only ever seen father wear loose tunics and linen slacks. (And occasionally his denim jacket, when it was cold.) But not only was Paramint wearing a shirt, a vest, trousers, *and* a jacket, he was also wearing some kind of knitted cloth—a scarf, perhaps?—knotted around his neck, and he'd stuffed a handkerchief in his jacket pocket. It made her wonder if he sneezed a lot.

But never mind all that, because Paramint was the nicest, cleanest old man she'd ever met. He explained that it was his job to guard the Visiting Door, and to always be ready for guests; he said it was all he did, all day long. He made sure he was prepared (and looked presentable) for the day the land of Left would finally receive a visitor.

He said he'd been waiting fifty-six years.

Paramint ushered them down one branch and up another, all the while announcing very loudly to anyone who would listen that Alice and Oliver were the honorable guests who'd finally arrived. There were many gasps, a few short screams, and occasionally, someone would faint. (Oliver had a bad habit of laughing very nervously when this happened.)

The whole of Left was dressed in complicated clothes. A few of the ladies wore suits much like Paramint's, and though they were well tailored and colorfully done, the truth was Alice hated suits just as much as she hated pants, so really, it was only the gowns she loved. There were a few ladies (and even a gentleman or three) who wore the most beautiful gowns—flowing skirts and intricate tops—and did very interesting things with their hair. Alice looked down at her own tattered clothes and touched her matted, knotted hair and, for just a moment, was silly enough to be sad she wasn't a bit more presentable. She imagined that she and Oliver must've looked very strange indeed. What a pair of dirty visitors they were. Were it not for the blue shoes Oliver had made for her, Alice would've had nothing to be proud of, because those blue shoes were now the most beautiful things she owned. And no matter her running, jumping, and nearly dying, the slippers still looked brand-new. Oliver had done some very skillful magic.

Speaking of Oliver, he was currently engaged in the practice of awe. He was looking around, bright-eyed and blooming, truly wowed by the land of Left. Alice thought Oliver had seen all there was to see in Furthermore—she thought he could never be wooed again, not the way Alice was when she first arrived—but clearly she was wrong. Oliver had grown accustomed to the things he'd already seen, but beyond that, he was just as vulnerable as she was. She knew then that they'd have to be even more vigilant now; without Oliver's constant caution, they'd have to work even harder to keep from falling prey to the fancy twists and feasts of Furthermore. Alice took a nervous breath and squeezed Oliver's hand. He squeezed back.

Neither one of them was an expert here, and here, in the land of Left, they'd be faced with an entirely new challenge.

OLIVER SAYS I'M TERRIBLE AT CHAPTER HEADINGS

Paramint never wanted them to leave.

He'd been waiting fifty-six years for visitors, which meant he'd had fifty-six years to plan all the things they would do when visitors finally arrived.

Alice only realized this when they'd reached Paramint's home. The hanging homes were quite spacious and sturdy, despite their eggshell exteriors, which made Alice wonder where these eggs had come from. What kind of creature could lay an egg so large? She decided she didn't want to think about it. But then, she also didn't want to think about the very large scroll Paramint was pulling out of a trunk in the round of his home, but there wasn't much she could do to stop it happening.

"We'll start with a celebration, of course," Paramint said as the scroll unfurled at his feet. "And it will be a very grand day indeed. A feast for all, even the little ones! We'll have dozens of cakes and every fresh berry and pitchers of fairysnip and candied-corn husks. We'll have a musical jamboree! We'll sing every dawn and dance every night!"

(Alice and Oliver were sitting on Paramint's very small pumpkin-orange couch, not saying a word.)

"Of course, we must first alert the queens," Paramint was saying, "who'll then alert the princesses, who will then alert the twincesses, who will then—"

"Paramint," Alice said, clearing her throat quietly.

"Yes, your honorableness," he said, dropping the scroll in an instant. "What good thing may I do for you?"

Alice smiled an uncertain smile, unaccustomed to such attentions, and said, "We are so, so grateful for all your kindness, and so excited to be in the land of Left—"

"It really is the most lovely place," Oliver said, smiling as he looked around.

"Oh, thank you, sir," said Paramint, blushing. "Thank you so much."

"But I'm afraid we can't stay for very long," Alice said carefully. "Is there any chance we could cut short the festivities?"

Paramint was deathly still for only a few moments before he began nodding, very quickly. "Of course," he said. "Of course. Forgive me, your honorableness, I should not have assumed you would want to celebrate so much."

Alice smiled, relieved.

"I will make the proper changes to our schedule," Paramint said, still nodding. "I'm certain that with the right planning, we may yet have a wonderful time—and celebrate just as thoroughly!—over a ten-year period." Paramint was smiling a pained sort of smile. "Will that be alright, do you think? It will be difficult, yes, and it will mean a lot of very busy days, but I'm sure, together, we can make it work."

Alice looked from Paramint to Oliver, and from Oliver to the eggshell house, and from the eggshell house to the world that lay beyond it, and she began to panic all over.

Every inch, panicking.

And she didn't know what to do.

Oliver didn't appear to either.

They said nothing, the two of them. Alice sat there like a stone, turned solid from the inside out, and Paramint didn't even seem to notice. She was all dread and worry and fear and she didn't know how they'd get themselves out of this one, she really didn't. She rolled Paramint's words over and over in her mind.

How many queens were there? How many princesses? How many twincesses? More importantly, how angry would the twincesses be if Alice and Oliver tried to escape? And where, *where*, did those eggshells come from?

Alice wasn't sure she wanted to know the answers to her own questions. But she knew they needed a plan.

Paramint had left them alone for a stretch (he was seeing about their baths, he'd said) and she and Oliver were still sitting on that little couch in the eggshell house, staring at each other like they thought they could summon solutions out of each other's brains. Speaking of brains, using theirs had turned out to be a very bad idea, and Alice said as much to Oliver.

He didn't seem bothered at all.

"Oh, don't worry about Paramint," Oliver said, waving a hand as he got to his feet. "That's what I'm here for, remember? I can always persuade him to let us go. I'm not worried about that."

Relief flooded through Alice so quickly she would've needed to sit down if she weren't already sitting. "Well, why didn't you say something *sooner*?" She collapsed backward on the couch, every tense muscle in her body coming undone. "And why didn't you try to convince Paramint while he was still here?"

"Because I haven't the faintest idea where we'll go if we leave right now," Oliver said. "We need a safe place to stay until we figure out how to find a painter. Perhaps Paramint will be able to help us."

Alice made a small sound of agreement before letting herself melt more completely into the couch. Alice was so tired and so full of fears and worries that she could almost understand what it was like to be a real grown-up. In any case, she desperately needed a break and she was grateful for the chance to let her guard down for just a moment longer.

But Oliver wouldn't allow it.

"Up, up, *up*," he said abruptly. "Now's not the time to be lazy, Alice. We must remember to pay extra attention while we're here, especially now that we know we're being watched more closely than most."

Alice threw Oliver a grumpy look and stumbled up to her feet.

"Now, I don't think Paramint is the one to worry about," said Oliver, "but all the same, we must keep our eyes and ears open for anything that seems interesting or suspicious. Perhaps if we listen closely we'll be able to unearth something new. In the meantime, I'll see what I can do about finding a painter."

It wasn't much to go on, but it would have to do.

Alice sighed. It was a struggle to remain optimistic. Everything had already gone terribly, horribly wrong, and for every minute they spent searching for anyone but Father, Alice grew more anxious. She was being crushed by the guilt of her own perceived selfishness—and if they didn't find a painter soon, she would insist they abandon the plan to fix her arm. Her priority was Father above all else, and she couldn't risk losing him again.

Alice and Oliver desperately needed a bath.

Paramint led them down a mossy branch that led to a ladder nailed into the trunk of a nearby tree. They climbed until they reached the very top of the trunk, which had long since been hacked off and flattened out. The top of the tree was now a large, flat, oblong expanse of polished wood, and atop it were dozens of gleaming porcelain tubs.

Ladies and gentlemen dressed much like Paramint were awaiting Alice's and Oliver's arrival with towels, robes, bouquets of flowers, and pots and pots of something warm.

Alice was so excited to be clean again that she was already untying the ties of her skirts. Oliver, ever the gentleman, saw Alice half undressing and began to fidget, clearing his throat and stuffing his hands in his pockets and studying a tree branch very carefully. Unfortunately for Oliver, his discomfort was no discomfort of hers, as Alice was unaware of his blushing and fidgeting. She hated clothes and was happy to be rid of them.

Alice gladly followed a smiling lady to an empty tub and let herself relax; she was about to have a bath and, just this once, she would allow herself to enjoy something in Furthermore. She would bathe, and it would be beautiful. She couldn't wait.

The lady helping Alice introduced herself as Ancilly, and Alice decided she liked Ancilly's smiling, honey-hued face and frizzy shock of red hair. Ancilly helped Alice step out of the rest of her clothes and into the tub, and there Alice sat, using her one arm to pull her knees to her chest. She shivered as a cool breeze blew past.

And then: pure, undiluted delight.

Friends, this was not a bath of hot water, but of warm milk: rich and silky in a way that made Alice's very bones unclench. Ancilly poured pot after pot of warm milk into the tub until it was sloshing against Alice's shoulders. She sank down and let her limbs melt into the milk, and just as she thought the beauty of this moment had reached its maximum, Ancilly brought out the bouquets she'd been carrying. She broke off the blooms one handful at a time and carefully tossed them into the tub. The flowers bobbed at the surface, rainbow icing on the cake of a delicious experience, and Alice closed her eyes, enjoying every minute. Their fragrance soothed her, and the warm milk soothed her, and the colors soothed her, and soon Alice was cocooned in pleasure, and she was reminded, all at once, why Furthermore was so dangerous. Alice knew she could lie there, in that tub, forever, and she knew then that she had to be even more cautious as the moments passed.

Soon, she thought. Very soon she would be cautious.

But right now—*for right now*—she would relax.

❖

Too soon, Ancilly had returned with a warm towel, and too soon, Alice was dry and clean and smelling of sunshine. Alice was swiftly wrapped in a toasty robe, and Ancilly set to work running a comb through her wet hair.

Ancilly hummed as she worked out the knots and, once that was done, she sang a sweet, sad song as she braided it all together. Her voice was low and soothing—almost a murmur—and Alice, who was nearly drunk on relaxation, could only just make out the last few words.

In the sky
In the sky
I fell one day
Into the sky
In the sky
In the sky
I fell one day
I learned to fly

Alice had very nearly fallen asleep. She startled her eyes open just in time, ever fearful of Oliver's warning to never sleep without a dream. But Ancilly's song was so rich and somber that Alice's heart had turned to jelly. Our young friend was warm and loopy, and Ancilly's gentle hands were busy weaving flowers into her hair. Alice stifled a small yawn. The unexpected pop of color from the flowers against the bright white of her hair and skin made Alice very, very happy.

Alice thanked Ancilly profusely and the lady blushed, waving off Alice's gratitude. "Please, your honorableness," she said. "It's a treasure to have you here. If you would please wait a moment, I will return with a gift."

So Alice waited. She sat on a little chair and thought about how pleasant it was to be clean, and how strange it was to have only one arm, and how frustrating it was to want to use the lost limb only to have to keep reminding herself that it was gone. These thoughts occupied her until Ancilly returned, and her patience was soon rewarded with something extraordinary. In Ancilly's hands was the most beautiful gown Alice had ever seen.

This dress was a true explosion of light. It was clear that it had been designed by a proper artist and made from only the richest materials; and it was certainly more beautiful than anything Alice could have sewn herself. The many skirts and bodice were a cascade of color: ruby melting into dusk, golds becoming greens, blue and plum and raspberry drenching the hem. Each layer was pieced together delicately and deliberately, a thousand sheets of onion thin silk scalloped and shimmering like the broken wings of a butterfly. The skirts were full and robust but still weightless, ethereal. Alice was sure she could float away in this dress. She could fly in this dress.

"Ancilly," she cried, clutching the gown to her chest. "Did you make this yourself?"

"Oh no, your honorableness," she said, and bowed her head. "This dress was made by the greatest seamstress of the land of Left. It is Left tradition to present our visitors with only our finest gifts." Her voice caught. "We never thought we'd have another visitor," Ancilly said, looking like she might cry. "We are so proud, your honorableness. We are so grateful to you for bestowing your graces on our humble home. Left is so often overlooked."

"Oh, Ancilly," Alice said. "The pleasure is all my own." And even though Alice meant what she said, she couldn't help but feel guilty, too. She knew she had to leave—and soon—and in order to do so she'd have to disappoint an entire village. It broke her heart, but she knew there was no other way.

Ancilly helped Alice into the new dress (Alice noticed it had no sleeves, which suited her one arm very nicely), and she took a moment to admire its details as she tucked her pamphlets, black card, and the broken pieces of her ruler into the deep pockets of the skirt. A spray of feathers was built into the collar, up and outward, creating the illusion that Alice wore wings; every stitch was a work of art, and Alice couldn't help but admire the finery. She'd never worn anything so elegant in all her life. She spun and swam with each step, the silk ebbing and flowing against her legs. It made her miss the quiet moments she'd once resented, dancing alone in the forest, her heartbeats synchronized to the sounds of the world.

Alice was in tears.

It was all so very, very lovely. Alice was genuinely touched and couldn't believe for a second that Ancilly would ever want to eat her. After all, Oliver had said there were good and bad in every bunch, and *these*, Alice thought, these must be the good ones.

Which made her wonder.

"Ancilly," said Alice, still admiring her gown. "If you have a seamstress here in Left—do you have a painter, too?"

Ancilly looked surprised. "I'm afraid we don't, your honorableness. Why do you ask?"

Alice nodded to where her arm used to be. "I was hoping to repair the damage," she said. "And I've been told to find a painter." She sighed. "You wouldn't happen to know where I could find one, would you?"

Ancilly shook her head.

Alice was disappointed. She knew it was Oliver's job to persuade information out of others, but Ancilly seemed like someone Alice could confide in. Besides, she and Oliver had very few options. They were already out of time; they had to get to a painter *soon*.

So Alice tried again.

"Is there *anyone* here who might know where I could find a painter? Maybe the seamstress?"

Ancilly stiffened.

"Perhaps," said Alice quickly, "perhaps the artists of Furthermore know each other—"

But Alice had said the wrong thing.

Ancilly's warmth went instantly cold, and she turned away so Alice couldn't read her face. When Ancilly next spoke, her words were clipped. "The seamstress might've known where to find a painter, but she was pushed off the branch long ago."

Alice startled. "Pushed off the branch? Do you mean—"

"She is gone."

"But I thought you said she made this dress?" said Alice. "How could she be gone?"

"She worked for many years, making clothes in all shapes and sizes in preparation for the day our visitors would arrive. We had to be ready," Ancilly said quietly, "even if we couldn't be sure anyone would come."

Alice touched her arm. "Oh, Ancilly," she said, "I'm so sor—"

"Please excuse me, your honorableness." Ancilly stood in

one swift motion and immediately began tidying the bath things. She said not another word to Alice.

Alice was dismayed—certain she'd done something to offend—and attempted to apologize. "I'm truly sorry," she tried to say, "I didn't—"

But Ancilly had begun humming very loudly and pretended not to hear her. Alice looked away, dejected.

And then she heard Ancilly sing.

It was the same song as before—she recognized the tune—but this time, Alice paid closer attention.

I fell into the sky one day
And it didn't hurt at all
I fell into the sky one day
But I didn't fall at all
I saw a lady reach for me
She told me not to fear
I saw a lady speak to me
She told me help was here
Oh, I didn't know
A truth from lie
She looked so strange to me
But when she pointed
At the sky
I knew where I should be

In the sky

In the sky

I fell one day

Into the sky

In the sky

In the sky

I fell one day

I learned to fly

Oliver was waiting for her back at the eggshell house.

Paramint had given up his home for them that evening—and for the duration of their stay—and Alice was immensely grateful for his sacrifice. In fact, she'd lost track of all the kind things Paramint had done for them since they'd arrived.

It felt indulgent to take so much time for themselves here in the land of Left, but when Alice was being honest with herself, she was able to admit that a bit of rest was necessary. Jumping from village to village was beginning to wear on her, and she wanted to be at her best when they finally found their way to Father.

She'd plopped down on the couch next to Oliver and had already begun telling him all about Ancilly and the peculiar case of the seamstress when she noticed he was looking at her in a very odd way.

"What is it?" she asked him. "What's happened?"

"Nothing," Oliver said. "It's just that you look . . . different."

"Do I?" She looked down at herself. "I think it's because I'm clean. And because of this staggeringly beautiful gown, *obviously*." She laughed and looked admiringly at her skirts. She and Oliver had already marveled together at the gifts they'd received. Oliver had been given ropes and ropes of their finest pearls, which he currently wore draped around his neck and chest, creating the illusion of a collared bib.

Oliver tilted his head. "Perhaps."

"Well, you look the same," she said to him, looking him over. "How do you always manage to stay so clean?"

He smiled and ignored her question. "Alright then," he said. "Tell me more about the seamstress."

Oliver was wide-eyed by the end of her story. He was so full of thoughts and questions he could hardly sit still. In fact, he was already up and pacing the length of the room. "This is very, very interesting news," he said. "Very interesting."

"And the song," Alice said. "So strange, isn't it?"

Oliver met her eyes from across the room. "Very strange. It sounds like Ancilly was trying to tell you something without *actually* telling you anything."

"Yes, I quite agree," Alice said. "I wonder what it all means."

"Me too," said Oliver, hesitating. "But I have to say, I can't see how the secrets of the seamstress would lead us to a painter."

"Well," Alice said, grasping for a connection. "They're both artists. Maybe they *did* know each other?"

Oliver frowned. "Possible. Unlikely, but possible."

Alice sighed.

“But that song,” said Oliver. “So strange.”

“And so *sad*,” said Alice. “To think that the seamstress was pushed off the branch! Oh, how I wonder what happened.”

Oliver raised an eyebrow. “Do you think the song is true, then? You think the seamstress has flown away?”

“If by *flown away* you mean *fell to her death*, then yes,” said Alice, “I think it’s true.”

“A dead end, then? Pardon the pun,” he said, fighting back a smile, “but I’m assuming a dead seamstress wouldn’t have much to say.”

“Well, it’s all we’ve got for now,” said Alice, defeated. She slumped lower on the couch and kicked up her feet. And then, very, very quietly—so quietly she almost hoped Oliver wouldn’t hear her—she said, “I hope we haven’t made a serious mistake choosing to fix my arm over finding Father.”

Oliver joined her on the couch.

“Alice,” he said gently.

Alice mumbled something.

“Alice,” he said again. “Please look at me.”

She did so, but reluctantly. Oliver’s eyes were such a striking shade of violet. So bright against his skin.

“Finding a way to fix your arm,” he said, “will never be a mistake. Please understand that.”

Alice looked away. "But what if we never find Father because of me?"

"That won't happen."

"But—"

"It just won't," Oliver said.

"Oh, alright," Alice said, and sighed. "But I do hope we figure out the next step soon. We can't afford to stay here much longer."

"I know," said Oliver, and he laughed a little. "And it's too bad, really. Under any other circumstances I think we'd actually have a nice time in the land of Left. I mean—I know better than to believe anything good can come of Furthermore, I really do, but they're just so terribly nice to us here. I'll feel bad leaving them, especially as they've waited fifty-six years for a visitor." He shook his head. "I can already picture Paramint's grief-stricken face."

"Me too," Alice said quietly. "I was thinking the same thing earlier. And I don't think they could ever want to eat us, do you? Don't you think they're the good ones?"

Oliver nodded. "I read Paramint's heart when we first arrived here, and do you know what his greatest secret was? His greatest wish?"

Alice thought she could guess, but she let Oliver tell her anyway.

"He wanted to be able to open that door," said Oliver. "His greatest, most secret, most ardent wish was to have a visitor come to the village of Left."

"Oh, now I feel awful," said Alice. "But what choice do we have?"

"I know. We must forge ahead. After all," Oliver said, "we belong in Ferenwood, not Furthermore," and this made Alice smile.

"And while I do love a good adventure," Oliver went on, "I'm very much looking forward to going home. I think I've had enough of Furthermore to last me a good long while."

"Me too," Alice said. "Me too." She dropped her eyes and touched the only bangles she had left. "But I want Father to come home, too. I don't want to go back without him."

Oliver nodded, just once, and said, "I know."

"What about you?" Alice asked him, perking up. "What do you miss the most about home?"

"Me?" Oliver said, surprised. He tilted his head like he'd never considered it before. "Oh, I don't know. Perhaps the comforts of not nearly dying every day."

Alice laughed and said, "Really, though—are you close to your parents? Don't they miss you while you're gone?"

"I don't think so." Oliver shrugged. "I'm not sure. I don't really know my parents, and I'm not sure they really know me."

"What do you mean?"

"My talent"—Oliver sighed—"is both a blessing and a burden. I learned from a very young age how to manipulate my parents into doing exactly what I wanted—into being the kind of parents I wanted them to be.

"I only discovered many years later that a five-year-old's idea of the perfect parent is far from ideal. But by then it was too late. When I stopped interfering and let them take over, they couldn't remember how. They barely even knew me—I'd taken away the most critical years of our life together. They could hardly remember how I'd grown up. And the problem wasn't with just my parents. I'd done it with everyone.

"I never really meant to," Oliver said quietly. "I was just so little—I couldn't understand the consequences of my actions. It was when my father got sick with the fluke that I realized how frail he was—and that one day I would lose him. I was sorry I'd never given him a chance to teach me what he knew. To be my father the way *he'd* wanted to be." Oliver laughed a sad, humorless laugh. "I'd single-handedly destroyed every important relationship in my life by the time I was ten years old." He hesitated, then said, "I have no idea what kind of parents I would've had if I hadn't changed them so early on."

Alice drew in a deep, shaky breath.

"Oh, Oliver," she said, and took his hand. "That's just the saddest story I've ever heard."

"Sometimes," Oliver said, "I feel like my entire life is just a story I tell myself. A lie atop a lie; nipping and tucking at people until they're exactly what I want." He sighed. "I hate it."

"Well," said Alice. "Why don't you stop?"

"Stop what?" said Oliver.

"Stop changing everyone," she said. "Stop manipulating people. I know it won't change the past, but it'll certainly change the future. It's not too late to get to know your parents."

"I suppose it's not," said Oliver, but he was very quiet now.

"But you don't want to?"

Oliver shook his head. "It's not that I don't want to. It's just—I don't know," he said quietly. "I'm afraid."

"Of what?" said Alice.

"Don't you see?" Oliver closed his eyes. "No one would like me if I didn't trick them into it." And then he looked at her, really looked at her. "That's why I was so terrible to you in middlecare," he said. "It wasn't because I thought you were ugly. I didn't think that at all. It was because I knew you didn't like me, and I couldn't convince you not to. I didn't understand then why my persuasion wouldn't work on you—I didn't know about your ever-binding promise—and it scared me. Here was the one person in all of Ferenwood who wasn't swayed by my lies, and she didn't like me. It confirmed all my fears: If I let people be themselves, they'd all abandon me. My parents wouldn't love me."

"But, Oliver," she said, squeezing his hand, "I didn't like you because you were one of the most sincerely rude people I'd ever met. You were arrogant and unkind and a horrible, raging skyhole."

Oliver groaned and got up to leave.

"Wait!" she said quickly, grabbing his tunic. "There's more, I promise."

Oliver shot her a hard look.

"There's more and it's *nice*," Alice amended.

Oliver relented, sinking back into the couch. "Alright then," he said. "Go on."

"Well—look at you now! You're the nicest person, and so friendly and loyal! Who wouldn't like you now? Your parents would adore you. And anyway, *I* think you're wonderful, and you can trust *that* to be true. No tricking required."

Oliver had turned a blotchy sort of red. "You really think I'm wonderful?"

Alice beamed at him, and nodded.

Oliver looked away and mumbled something she couldn't decipher, but he was smiling now, the silliest look on his face, and Alice was smiling, too, looking even sillier than he did, and they just sat there a moment, neither one of them being skyholes, and Alice realized right then that Oliver was her first best friend.

It was a moment she would never forget.

Finally, Oliver cleared his throat.

"Now I've told you all my secrets," he said. "Will you tell me yours?"

Alice bit her lip and looked into her lap. Her heart had begun to skip in nervous beats. "You already know my secrets, Oliver. I wish I didn't have to repeat them."

"Alice," he said gently, "I don't understand. Why won't you accept that you have an incredible talent? Why does it bother you so?"

Here it was.

Her greatest heartbreak of all.

The talent she didn't want, the one she wished she never had, the one she convinced herself wasn't really hers, and all because it didn't work where it mattered most. Alice wanted to tell Oliver the truth, but she was afraid it would make her cry, and she desperately didn't want to cry. Still, it was high time to talk about it, and Oliver had earned the right to know.

"So," she said, nodding. "I can change the colors of things."

A chill coursed through her; her stomach was already doing flips. She hadn't talked about this since long before Father left.

Oliver took her hand and squeezed.

"I can change the color of anything. The sky," she said. "The sun. The grass and trees and bugs and leaves. Anything I want," she said softly. "I could make day into night and night into day. I could change the color of the air we breathe, of the water we drink."

"But you don't," said Oliver. "You don't. And I don't know why. So much talent," he said. "So much talent and—"

Alice shook her head, hard, cutting him off. "So much talent," she said, "and I can't even change the color of *me*." She looked up, looked at him, her eyes wild and desperate. "I could change you," she said, and touched a finger to his cheek, his face flipping colors from brown to red to green. "I could turn you ten shades of blue in the time it takes to blink," she said softly, and dropped her hand. "I can change the colors of everyone else, but I can't change *this* skin," she said, raking her fingers down her face. "Can't change my eyes. Can't even make myself look more like my own *family*," she said, her voice breaking. "Do you know how hard it is," she said, "to have the power to change everything but myself?"

"Alice—"

"I have no color, Oliver." Her voice was a whisper now. "No

pigment. I don't look anything like the people I love."

"But, Alice," Oliver said softly. "The people who love you wouldn't care if you had giraffe skin."

Alice focused on the rug under her foot, and nearly smiled. "Father probably wouldn't mind," she said. "Father would probably love me no matter anything."

"And your mother," Oliver said, "she loves you, too," but Alice shook her head.

"I don't know," she said, and bit her lip. "Mother was so excited when she first learned of my ability—Father was the one who told her, even though I asked him not to." She hesitated. "But after Father left, something happened to Mother. Something changed in her, made her mean." She paused, remembering. "Mother made me practice—every day in the mirror—she made me practice turning myself a different color. But it never worked, and Mother soon tired of me. But then she remembered how much she liked ferenberries—"

Oliver gasped.

"—and made me go hunting for them." Alice looked away. "Gathering ferenberries is the only thing I'm any good for."

"But I thought ferenberries were invisible!" Oliver said, eyes wide. And then he whispered, "And I thought they weren't allowed under the Ferenwood Code of Permissible Food Things."

"They're not really invisible," Alice said, scrunching up her face. "They're just very good chameleons. They blend almost perfectly into any background, so they're hard to find." She shrugged. "But all I had to do was find a single one, and I could change all of them to a color I could see. So I'd pick dozens at a time."

Oliver was visibly impressed.

"And I didn't know they weren't allowed under the Ferenwood Code of Permissible Food Things," Alice added nervously.

Oliver was so stunned he had to stand. "Well," he finally said. "Your mother sounds absolutely hideous." And then, "Forgive me," he said, clapping a hand over his mouth. "I spoke out of turn. It's not my place to—"

"That's alright," Alice said with a shaky smile. "Mother will be better when Father comes home. He always made her nicer. But I think I've disappointed Mother since even before Father left. Perhaps in every way.

"And now," she said quietly, "the only person who ever really loved me is trapped, hurting somewhere, lost in a world that wants to keep him forever, and I'd do anything to get him back. Anything at all." Alice touched the silk of her skirts. "You know," she said quietly, "Father used to tell me I was beautiful."

Alice's eyes had filled with tears, so she knew it was time to stop. She stood as elegantly as she could, excused herself, and told Oliver she needed some air.

He let her pass without a word.

When Alice stepped outside, her hardships were easily forgotten. Here, in the land of Left, was more to enchant the eye than possibly anywhere else. The sun had begun its descent, and the sky had turned a dusty, smoky blue; ambers and golds and violets melted along the horizon and kaleidoscoped through the branches, snowflaking spectacular shapes of light across the land. Everything was vivid green and richest brown and the air was so full of freshness; one deep inhale and her tears were zipped away, carefully stored for another day.

Alice closed her eyes and let the breeze wash over her.

She was stronger than Mother.

And if she wasn't, she would be. She would be strong enough to fight for Father and not fall apart without him. He needed her to be smart, to stay alive, to keep fighting. Her love for Father made her brave. It made her better.

It made her ready.

MORE CHAPTERS
STRAIGHT AHEAD

"Is there anything you'd like to taste?" Paramint asked them.

He'd popped his head into the egghouse to see how they were doing. She and Oliver had been sitting together on the floor, making a list of all the things they'd do with Father when they finally brought him home. It was Oliver's idea, to make the list. It was the first thing he'd said to her when she came back inside. He said that Father would want to know what had happened while he was gone, and since an awful lot had happened while he was gone, they should probably make a list.

"He'll want to see the new ponds and the fishing trees and, oh—we'll have to show him the boats that fell in Penelope's garden, we can't forget that." Oliver was already reaching for a sheaf of paper. "Or how about the penny bushes near the brook? They're so big now! Don't you think he'd like to see that? Alice?"

Alice was so touched she could hardly speak.

So there they sat, he and she, making plans for the day Father would come home, when suddenly Paramint was asking them whether there was anything they wanted to taste.

"Taste?" Alice said, sitting up straighter. "What do you mean?"

"Well," Paramint said, still standing at the door. "We have a very generous tasting menu at our disposal. Perhaps not as grand as you're accustomed," he said, blushing, "but we do have a divine center-cut filet mignon that I'd humbly recommend for your tasting pleasure." He bowed just a bit. "It was specially prepared for you by our resident chef, seasoned to perfection with rock salt and tea leaves, set on a bed of spiced couscous and served with a side of truffled risotto. Though of course if that is not to your liking we do have any number of sandwiches and roasts and hams to choose from—"

"Oh my," she said, glancing at Oliver, "I'm afraid I don't know what any of that is."

Paramint had frozen solid with full words still stuck in his mouth. To his great credit, he thawed rather quickly, and said, "Is there something else I might offer you, your honorableness?"

Alice thought for a moment and said, "Do you have any tulips?"

"We . . ." Paramint looked a little confused, but mostly he looked terrified of disappointing her, which made Alice feel awful. "Well, your honorableness, we have, um, we do have a great many flowers, but none in bloom at this hour, I'm afraid."

"Dear Paramint," said Oliver, "please don't concern yourself with the flowers. Alice is only teasing you," he said, shooting her a swift look that said, *Let me handle this.* "Perhaps we'll skip the main tasting this evening, and go straight for the desserts," Oliver said. "It's been a long journey, and something sweet sounds nice."

"Oh, a *fine* idea, your honorableness!" Paramint was so excited he actually jumped in place. "A *fine* idea! I'll bring out a great selection of cakes and pies and muffins for you to feast on!" He was smiling with every bit of his face, so eager to do anything to make them happy. "Is there any other good thing I might do for you, your honorablenesses? Perhaps after you're done tasting, you'd like some time to dream?"

This last bit caught Alice's attention, and she was nodding before she'd even asked for details. "That sounds wonderful," she said. "I would dearly love to dream."

"Very good, your honorableness," said Paramint, beaming. "So very, very good. I shall return swiftly." And with a bow and another smile, Paramint was gone.

Alice immediately turned to Oliver, overcome with excitement. "I've missed dreaming so much! I dearly love dreaming, you know. It's my favorite part of sleeping."

Oliver laughed. "I can't believe you're more excited about sleeping than you are about dessert."

"Oh," said Alice, distracted. "That reminds me. What is a *filet mignon*, exactly?"

Oliver froze, his mouth caught open in a neat little O. "Nothing you need to worry about," he said hastily. "Nothing at all."

Alice had never realized what a pleasure it could be to simply wake up in the morning. She and Oliver hadn't stayed in any town long enough to enjoy the luxury of sleeping (or dreaming), and now, for the first time in what felt like a very, very long time, she blinked open bleary eyes and yawned her way into dawn, stretching one arm and two legs as far as they'd go.

She was muddled and foggy and still a little dozy, but she was happier than she'd ever been in Furthermore, and feeling ready to face the beginning of another endless day.

Alice sprang to her feet and headed to Paramint's private toilets (which he'd said they might use) and splashed fresh water on her face, stopping to taste the few drops that fell on her lips.

Minty, she thought.

She'd dreamt all night long: topsy-turvy dreams no doubt inspired by her days in Furthermore. She'd been running upside down, her feet stomping along the ceilings of homes she didn't recognize, chasing a man she thought to be Father. The problem was, every time she got close enough, Oliver would pop out of a window and rip her arm off, and she'd lose track of Father all over again. She'd had to remind herself three times already not to be angry with Oliver for being such a nuisance in her dreams, and just as she was reminding herself for the fourth time, she stepped out of the toilets to find him waiting for her.

"Good morning," she said with a smile.

"Good morning," said Oliver, but he looked awful. Half asleep and a little sickly. "Excuse me, Alice," he said, and nodded toward the toilets. "May I? I'm afraid I'm not feeling very well."

"Oh, Oliver," she said. "Is there anything I can do?"

He made a weak effort to shake his head. "I think I'll just rest here a while, and hope the feeling passes." He rubbed at his face. "I vow I shall never eat a pie again," he said, and tried to laugh.

Alice gave him a sympathetic look and nodded. While she'd taken only a few tastes, Oliver had tasted nearly half of everything Paramint brought them last night. She'd asked Oliver several times to take care—which is likely the only reason he hadn't devoured all ten cakes, seven pies, fifteen muffins, and four puddings—and now she was glad to have guilted him so.

She hadn't known Oliver had such a fondness for these decadent things, though he certainly seemed sorry for it this morning. She patted him on the shoulder and let him pass.

While Oliver locked himself in the toilets, Alice tidied up the rest of the house. She hoped it would be their last day here, so she wanted to do good by Paramint and make sure they left his home just as nice as it was when they arrived. She rolled up the dreaming-bags Paramint brought them (they were little sacks with pillows sewn all along the insides, very soft and cozy), and rearranged all his papers, careful to fold away the list they'd made for Father. She tucked the list into the pocket of her new silk gown (which, for a gown, had proven very comfortable) and then sat down on the pumpkin-orange couch, and waited for Paramint and Oliver.

Except she soon tired of waiting and decided to step outside.

It was a beautiful day, just as she'd expected. The sun had only barely begun to rise, and the land of Left was already in bloom. Its occupants scurried about, hanging freshly laundered clothes and buying freshly baked bread and stopping to chat with neighbors about one fascinating topic or another. The sight of it all made her miss home more than ever.

"Good day to you, your honorableness!" It was an eager and smiling Paramint, who seemed surprised to find her up so early.

"Good day to you, too, Paramint," she said, smiling just as wide.

"Did you dream well?" he asked. "Did you enjoy the tasting?"

"Yes to both," she said happily. Then, more quietly, "Though I'm afraid Oliver may have tasted a bit too much."

Paramint's eyes went wide for just a moment before he laughed a hearty laugh. "This is excellent news, your honorableness! I'm thrilled to hear he enjoyed himself."

Alice didn't have the heart to tell him that Oliver's enjoyment was short-lived. "He certainly did," she said. "Thank you again."

"You're quite welcome!" Paramint was bouncing up and down on his toes, bursting with excitement. "Well, I can't keep it in any longer, your honorableness!"

"Keep wh—"

"We have GREAT news, your honorableness. GREAT NEWS!"

"Oh?"

"Yes, indeed, today will be the MOST excellent day, your honorableness. Last night we had the MOST exciting evening, and today we've had the MOST exciting morning. Such INCREDIBLE news!"

"How . . . lovely," Alice said politely. She couldn't articulate why, exactly, but Paramint's eagerness was making her uncomfortable. "I do hope good things are in store for the land of Left."

"They are! The best things! The very BEST things!"

"Well, that's very nice. I better get back t—"

"You," Paramint said, wagging a finger at her. "You have done a very bad thing, your honorableness. A very, very bad thing! But your bad thing has been the best news for the land of Left! The best news!"

Alice swallowed hard, forcing herself to speak even with the surge of panic seizing her body. "I'm not sure I know what you're talking about," she managed to say.

Paramint laughed and laughed. "You've broken the law! You've stolen time! Hours and hours you've stolen! We were notified just last night that we had a criminal in our midst." He beamed. "*The land of Left!* Can you believe it? *Our* visitor—a criminal! Oh, you've made us famous, your honorableness. We've not been contacted by the Elders for fifty-six years," he said, "and now, here we are, with a visitor who brings attention to our land! What a day, what a day!"

"Is *that* what you're happy about?" Alice nearly collapsed with relief. "Well," she said meekly, "I'm certainly glad to be of service."

Paramint lowered his voice and leaned in. "Now, we're going to do our best to keep the Elders from arresting you, but we can't hold them off for long. We'll have to be quick about things! So come with me, come with me—lots to do!"

Alice refused to move. "What do you mean? Where are we going?"

"To prepare the feast, of course!" cried Paramint. "We wouldn't normally plan the feast until the end of your stay," he said in a low voice, "but now that we know you've broken the law, there's no reason to wait. Besides, your getting arrested will only complicate matters," he said, waving a hand. "But if we take care of things before the authorities arrive, everyone will be so pleased! The queens haven't had a full meal in far too long, and you and your friend are sure to satisfy a large appetite. The twincesses will be thrilled!"

Alice stood frozen, sick with fright, and nodded as best she could before Paramint—kindly old Paramint—darted away, expecting her to follow. Alice's skin was clammy with cold sweat and sudden, horrible, slithering fear, and she could feel her throat beginning to close. Why she had ever allowed herself to feel safe in Furthermore she did not know, but now she knew there was only one thing left to do.

Run.

Alice flew back into the room as fast as she could, heart beating hard, hoping she could get to Oliver and out the door before Paramint ever came back. She pounded on the toilet door, shouting Oliver's name several times, but there was no answer. She had no choice but to break a very important rule in Furthermore and open the door without permission.

Thank heavens she did.

Oliver was lying on the floor, half conscious, mostly limp, and extremely heavy. He looked half dead already. Suddenly her talk with Paramint put everything in perspective: This was no matter of overindulgence. Paramint had tried to *poison* them in preparation for the impending feast. He wanted them weak and pliant; he wanted them drugged. And it took every bit of strength she had to keep from panicking.

Instead, she slapped Oliver in the face.

He blinked his eyes open.

"Oliver," she said (still trying—and failing—not to panic),

"Oliver, please—please wake up, please wake up—"

"I'm sorry, Alice," he said, breathing hard, "I'm afraid I'm not"—he swallowed—"not feeling very well."

"Yes, yes, I know, dear friend, but you must get to your feet," she said. "Please, please try to get to your feet, because we need to go. We must leave right this instant."

"What?" Oliver blinked at her again. "Why, Alice? What's the matter?"

Alice hesitated, terrified, then said, "They want to eat us."

Oliver's eyes flew open. He knew better than to waste time asking why. Maybe at another time, in a different state of mind, Oliver might've been able to persuade them out of this, but he was painfully sick and not himself, and she knew she couldn't ask him to save their lives.

For the second time, she had to save *him*.

And somehow, even now, during one of the most terrifying moments of her life, she felt a rush of true affection for Oliver, because she knew he'd decided right then to put his life in her hand(s), and to follow her lead.

"Let's go," he said. And in an act of great determination, he pulled himself to his feet.

Alice slung his bag over *his* shoulder, his heavy arm over *her* shoulder, and allowed Oliver to lean against her much-smaller frame. And though at any other time this might have seemed impossible, their weights didn't matter now; they were both adrenaline from head to foot, and moving on instinct.

Still, Alice felt like it took forever to reach the front door. In her mind their every slow movement brought Paramint closer, and every sudden sound meant Paramint was around the corner, waiting to pounce. In fact, Alice was so focused on outrunning Paramint that it hadn't even occurred to her *where* they'd go to outrun him; not until they reached the door, and Oliver said,

"Where now, Alice?"

But she didn't know.

She was in a real panic. She looked left, looked right: They were surrounded on all sides by the busy bodies making up the land of Left, and there was no other place to go, no other person to trust. Eggshell homes had been strung from nearly every branch as far as she could see, and there was no doubt in her mind that if they tried to hide here, they would too easily be found. For a moment Alice even considered turning everything black again—after all, it had worked on the foxes—but they were not on flat land, which made everything more dangerous. Alice and Oliver would be running across a series of treetops—it would be too dangerous to run blindly; one misstep and they'd plummet to their deaths.

But maybe—

Maybe they stayed put. Maybe they stayed here and bided their time, played nice with Paramint until they formed a real plan—until Oliver was feeling better and could persuade them to have someone else for dinner. Maybe they'd be able to think more clearly in a couple of hours. After all, Paramint wanted to plan a *feast*. They wouldn't be eaten in the next five minutes.

Maybe Alice had gotten ahead of herself; she was too anxious and panicked; she was sure that was it. In fact, now she was sure they would do better to stay. Racing around with no rational plan couldn't help them at all, she thought. So she exhaled a deep breath and glanced back at the eggshell home, ready to tell Oliver her new idea.

Except that when she glanced back, there stood Paramint, hovering just to the side of his own front door, smiling at her in a way that she no longer trusted. He carried in one hand a very large linen sack. And, in the other, a very large butcher knife.

Something inside of Alice screamed, but she didn't say a word.

Paramint's eyes were locked on to hers, and when he next spoke, his voice was suddenly too high, too happy, all wrong. "Where are you going, your honorableness?"

At any other time, they might've been able to dash past Paramint and head back from whence they came, but Oliver could barely stand, much less sprint. Alice scanned the forest floor for options and found little solace in the thousand-foot fall below them. Oliver had said that falling in Furthermore was too anticlimactic to be deadly, but Alice felt certain that this drop would be an exception. After all, if it were safe to fall so far, why was the seamstress pushed off the branch?

All these thoughts rushed through Alice's mind in only a snip of a second, but this last question reminded Alice of something she'd nearly forgotten. It was something Ancilly had said—something she sang.

I fell into the sky one day
And it didn't hurt at all
I fell into the sky one day
But I didn't fall at all

Was it possible? Was Ancilly trying to tell her how to escape?

Well, Alice had no idea, but trusting Ancilly was her only option at the moment, as Paramint was still holding a butcher knife within slicing distance. Alice was out of options and fully tapped of time but she'd not yet lost her hope. So she took a deep breath and whispered,

"Fall, Oliver, fall."

And they did.

She and Oliver clung to each other as they fell, and in her mind Alice was already apologizing to him for being the reason he died. Alice was half hope, half horror, split vertically down the middle about her chances at survival. She wanted to believe there was merit to Ancilly's song, but how could she? She was currently plummeting to her death. Worse still, this didn't feel anything like flying. This felt like dying. Though at least this death, Alice thought, would be a less brutal one. Alice had no interest in being eaten.

So there they were: falling to their deaths.

Neither one of them screamed (as it seemed to serve no purpose), and all Alice saw were Oliver's eyes, wide and scared and sad, so she closed her own, wrapped her single arm more tightly around his, and prayed for a quick, relatively painless exit from these worlds. But no matter how dramatic they tried to make the moment—muscles tensed, whispering quiet goodbyes to the ones they loved—their imminent demise was running a bit late.

Eventually Alice opened her eyes and found that Oliver had, too. They were indeed still falling, and there was indeed a ground coming up beneath them, but something strange was happening, too: The farther they fell, the slower the fall, and soon they weren't rushing to the ground at all, but floating; floating, gently and steadily, all the way down.

They landed on the forest floor with their feet flat on the ground. She and Oliver were so surprised to still be alive that they spent the first few moments just staring at each other.

"Are you alright?" Alice finally said. Oliver was standing on his own now, and he looked wide awake. "Are you feeling okay?"

Oliver nodded. "I think that just scared the sick out of me."

"Well, thank heavens for small presents," Alice said, now feeling weak in the knees. She sank to the ground.

"You don't think they'll jump after us, do you?" said Oliver.

Alice looked up, startled. "I don't—"

"They might," said a voice she didn't recognize.

Alice jumped straight up and back and hit her head against Oliver's chest. His heart was beating as hard as hers; he steadied her shoulder against him, and they both looked toward the stranger.

The voice had come from a woman, the likes of which Alice had never seen before—except perhaps in a mirror. She was pale as moonlight and exceptionally tall, and she wore a cloak made entirely of golden leaves: vibrant yellow, dingy mustard, lemon and honey and saffron and sunlight. The leaves layered together looked like a collection of slivered wings, creating the illusion of something both monstrous and beautiful, all at once.

The lengths of the stranger's robes dragged beneath her, swallowing up her arms and legs; only her hands—paler even than Alice's—could still be seen. The hood of her cloak, also created from leaves, did not mask her face; she wore her hood only halfway, and the long, impossibly yellow locks of her hair—nearly indistinguishable from her hood—fell to her shoulders, and her face, ghostly white, was lit only by a pair of matching golden eyes.

"They might," she said again. "So you'd do best to come with me."

There was something terrifying about her—glowing and beautiful and looming over them—but there was something else about her, too; something in her eyes. This woman had felt true pain before, and somehow Alice knew this was true.

Again, Alice thought of Ancilly.

Ancilly, whose song had saved their life.

I saw a lady reach for me
She told me not to fear
I saw a lady speak to me
She told me help was here

"Who are you?" Alice finally managed to ask.

"I am Isal," she said. She did not blink. "Would you like to die?"

"No," Oliver said quickly; Alice could hear his heart quicken. "Of course we wouldn't."

"Then come with me," she said, and turned away.

As she walked, she left a trail of golden leaves behind, like a snail that could not help but make a map of its travels. But Isal was no snail; that much was obvious, and Alice envied her steady, quiet strength. She *wanted* to follow her.

And anyway, they had no other choices.

She and Oliver marched along behind her, sending each other sideways glances that did little more than remind them that they were not alone. They followed Isal deep, deep into the maze of the woods, but walking wasn't without its challenges: The forest floor was zigzagged by giant trunks of gigantic trees, the tops of which made up the land of Left. The roots that covered the forest floor were monstrously large; they were among the widest and tallest Alice would ever see; these trunks were thicker than most homes. As she and Oliver did their best to scramble over the mountain-sized roots, Alice was suddenly grateful for Isal's colorful cloak—without it, they'd have lost her long ago.

Finally, they reached a small clearing where a dilapidated cottage had been shoved unceremoniously against a tree trunk wider than the cottage itself. The home was simply made; the exterior whitewashed a dull shade. There were two windows cut into a wall not obscured by the tree, but the glass looked dingy and yellow, like the ancient windows had never seen a breeze.

Tall, wild grass grew up the sides of the house, and the roof looked like it'd collapsed a bit, right in the middle, and Alice could see why: Five forevergreen trees had planted themselves on top of the cottage, nearly suffocating the slanted brick chimney, while haphazardly grown tufts of grass and roots gripped the roof in a proprietary fist. This home seemed to have been planted here. It was as if it had grown in and within the forest itself.

Isal opened the front door and turned to face them. "You may come inside."

But Alice and Oliver hesitated.

"Who are you?" Oliver said.

Isal stepped forward. "I am Isal," she said.

"Yes, but that doesn't help us at all, does it?" said Oliver.

Isal looked confused. "Your companion is wearing my designs," she said to him. "And yet you do not know who I am?"

"The seamstress," Alice whispered.

Isal nodded at Alice. "Yes," she said, before looking away. There was a stroke of sadness in her eyes. "I was the seamstress. I am not anymore."

Alice was too struck to speak. There was so much to be afraid of—so much to be concerned about in that moment—but Alice couldn't help but be awed by the woman standing before her. Isal, even in her loneliness—even in her sadness—was entirely too elegant to be real. She was everything Alice had ever hoped to be: strong, brave, dignified. And yet, Isal was *here*. A gem, buried in the forest.

An outcast.

Alice felt a kind of kinship with this stranger and she couldn't find the words to explain why.

Isal stepped forward and touched the feathers on Alice's dress. "I remember this gown," she said softly. "It took me two years to collect enough featherlilies to finish the collar." She dropped her hand. "Ancilly sent word that you were coming."

"She sent word?" Alice said. "But—"

"She was my apprentice many years ago," Isal said. "Long before I was pushed off the branch."

"So they really pushed you off the branch?" Oliver said, aghast. "Why?"

Isal finally blinked.

"Fifty-six years ago," she said, "when we'd had our last visitor—a young girl, not much older than you," she said to Alice, "I tried to warn her away. I knew that ultimately, she would be sacrificed for the queens." Isal looked away. "I did not agree with the queens' methods, and my actions were not appreciated. I was considered a traitor, and pushed off the branch."

Alice's eyes went impossibly wide.

"So they thought you would die," Oliver said.

Isal nodded. "But there is great magic at the bottom of the trees, and it does not wish to do harm. I have been safe here."

"Do they know?" Oliver asked, gesturing to the sky, to the land of Left. "Do they know it's safe down here?"

"They suspect it might be," she said. "But they do not know for certain. So we must hurry. We do not know if they will come looking for you. Please," she said. "Come inside. I can help you."

"But you say you've been here all this time," Alice said nervously. "And yet you've never been discovered. How can we trust that your story is true? What if you're working with everyone else? What if we step inside your house only to be stuffed in an oven?"

Isal smiled a strange, sad smile and pulled back her hood. Her golden hair, no longer framed by the yellow of her cloak, was dimmer now. Desaturated. She looked almost as white as Alice did, pale on pale; all color sapped from her skin. And when she spoke, she spoke only to Oliver. "Perhaps you should trust a friend who looks like one."

Oliver couldn't shake off his shock. "How did you know?" he said. "How did you know my Tibbin?"

Isal considered him carefully. "Furthermore is only occasionally as helpful as it pretends to be," she said. "All Tibbins are created purposely—in conjunction with Furthermore citizens—and in accordance with the happenstance of your path through this land. The moment you arrived, your future was measured, hypotheses were made, and I was sent notification of my role in your journey. Now that you're here, I'm tasked with providing you one piece of advice that will aid you in the rest of your excursion. Once the help is received, my bit is done."

Alice and Oliver were stunned.

"We are never allowed to speak of our roles in all this," Isal said, "but as I gave up on my loyalty to Furthermore long ago, I don't see the harm in telling you. But to deny a Tibbin is a moral offense, not a legal one, and so I am honor bound to assist you." She bowed her head forward an inch, and let her eyes rest on Alice's and Oliver's slack-jawed expressions. "No one has ever found me, you know."

"Yes," Oliver said, and looked around. "I can imagine."

"No," said Isal. "You don't understand. A Tibbin pinned to me is most ungenerous. Left is a land long forgotten, and I, Isal, am the most unremembered of them all." She paused, studying the two of them carefully. "Assigning a Tibbin to me means the Elders were never trying to help you. In fact, it's likely they expected you to fail many moves ago. That you were clever enough to find me means that you are close to achieving what you desire. But tread carefully; the Elders cannot be happy about this."

Alice and Oliver swallowed their fear and said nothing.

"Now," said Isal, and clasped her hands. "I have more than answered all your questions. So I must insist, for the final time, that you come inside. If you stand here a moment longer I will not be responsible for your deaths."

Alice and Oliver stumbled after Isal into her humble home, hearts racing in unison. Furthermore was meaner and twistier than even Oliver had imagined. They knew for certain now that their every move had been mapped and choreographed; the odds had been deliberately stacked against them. Their combined talents had kept them alive just long enough to move from one village to another, but the longer they stayed in Furthermore, the faster their luck would run out, and they would have to be sharper than ever if they were to have any hope of surviving the rest of their journey. They were now fugitives, on the run.

And both Tibbins had been spent.

Alice was shaken back to the present as she walked into the organized chaos of Isal's home. Her cottage was little more than a glorified storage box. Every inch of wall space was covered in ornately framed oil paintings—"All my things were saved and pushed off the branch by dear Ancilly," she'd said—while the interior square footage was set aside for her sewing supplies. Pins and needles and spools of thread and endless bolts of luscious fabrics were stacked up to the ceiling. Dress forms, boxes of jewels and baskets of feathers were arranged in tidy rows. Her home was small, but it was colorful and clean, and once they'd stepped fully inside, Isal removed her cape.

Isal managed to be beautiful in entirely her own way. She wore soft blue silks that draped around and across her body, and they made her look like a barely remembered dream: blurred at the edges and impossible to grasp. It was the first time Alice had ever thought a pale person could be beautiful, and it gave her great hope. Isal was not like Alice, not entirely, for she had depths of gold, even in her paleness, but even so, she looked very different from everyone back home in Ferenwood.

"So," Isal said abruptly, "you are looking for a painter."

"Yes," Oliver said, startled. "How did you know?"

Isal narrowed her eyes at Oliver like he might be a bit bent in the head. "Your friend is missing an arm."

"Right," he said quickly. "Right, of course."

"And you are certain," Isal said, "that this is the one piece of information you seek? There is no greater question you'd care to ask?"

Alice's heart kicked into gear. She looked frantically at Oliver. Would this be their only chance to ask for help? Shouldn't they use it to ask about Father?

"Oliver," she said, "don't you think—"

"This is not your decision," Isal said swiftly. She gave Alice a look that was not exactly unkind, but a bit cold. "It's not your Tibbin to interfere."

"But—"

"I'm certain," Oliver said firmly. "We need to get her arm fixed."

"Oliver, please—"

"We can still do both," he said to her, taking her only hand. "I promise, Alice. We'll find a way. Even if we have to start all over again. But before we do anything else, you're getting your arm back."

Alice swallowed hard. She was nearly in tears.

"Very good," Isal said. "Your solution is simple. Pick any

painting"—she gestured to her walls—"and step inside."

Oliver's eyebrows shot up. "That's all?"

Isal nodded.

Alice and Oliver looked at each other, faces breaking into smiles, relief flooding through their veins.

"Alright," Oliver said, grinning up to his ears. He looked over the paintings. "How about—oh, I don't know—how's this one?" he said to Alice.

Isal stepped in front of him. "Choose wisely," she said. "If the painter refuses to let you enter his home, you will remain here," she said, touching the canvas, "in the painting of your choosing."

"What?" said Oliver.

"For how long?" said Alice.

"Forever," Isal said.

Sudden horror buckled Alice's knees.

"What do you mean?" Oliver demanded. "What nonsense is this? Why didn't you tell us there was a catch before you gave us our answer? You said the solution was *simple*," he said, his neck going red with anger.

"It is not my job to protect you from the consequences of your own questions," Isal said unkindly. "You wanted to know how to find a painter. I told you how to find one. My duty is done."

"But—"

Suddenly the ground groaned and the walls shook; just outside the window a storm of yellow leaves had thrown itself against the glass. Alice knew instantly that it was a sign. Those were the leaves Isal had left behind, and now they'd come to find her.

"They're here," Isal said softly, staring at nothing as she spoke. And in the time it took Alice and Oliver to catch their breath, there were four knocks at the door: one for every set of knuckles, which meant four people were waiting outside.

Alice knew they wouldn't be polite for very long.

Isal grabbed her cloak. "Choose wisely," she whispered. "Choose wisely, and good luck."

Oliver met Alice's eyes in a sudden panic, and she knew there was no time to deliberate. She took Oliver's hand, scanned the frames for a scene that reminded her most of home and love and Father, and pushed their clasped hands through the painting.

It really was that simple.

Their bodies were sucked through by a force Alice could not name, and soon they were pulled and pushed through a tightness that squeezed their chests until she was sure they would burst, and when Alice next opened her eyes, she and Oliver were standing in what looked like an ancient prison cell; it smelled like mold and rust, the ceiling so low Oliver was forced to stoop.

The two of them didn't even have a chance to panic before a slim panel in the wall was forced open, letting a slice of light slip through. Alice squinted against the brightness.

"What's your business?" a voice barked at them. It sounded

distinctly male, but there was no way to be certain.

"I-I've come to fix my arm," said Alice nervously. "I heard you were a p—"

"Which arm is it?" the stranger snapped.

"My right."

The man grunted, but said no more.

"Please," she said. "Please help us—"

The panel slammed shut.

Alice was nearly in tears with worry.

This was their last chance, and she didn't know what they'd do if the painter didn't allow them clearance to pass. And no sooner had she begun to wonder whether the painter wouldn't simply leave them in that cell to die, when one of the cell walls swung open, and she and Oliver were ejected unceremoniously into a foot of fresh snow.

Once she shook the snow out of her eyes, Alice tried to take in their surroundings; but no matter how many times she blinked, she couldn't get the colors to come into focus. The trouble was, there were no colors here at all.

It was like a scene clipped from a newspaper and made whole unto itself. They were in the middle of an eerily flat, snowy landscape, not a single tree in sight, and every shade and shadow was a variation on white and black. Compared to this world, Alice was practically neon, and her whiteness seemed suddenly nuanced, layered: its own kind of color.

Where she and Oliver felt real and full of life, everything in this world looked drab and dim and, frankly, a little dead. It was as though all color had been snuffed out, sapped of life, and in its place were gray skies, gray wind, gray cold. Before them and beyond them was absolutely nothing, save one single, solitary structure:

A giant half globe, made entirely of gray glass.

Its contents were spare, but visually arresting: the pops of black that made up the furniture contrasted starkly against the very white snow, making for a stunning, simple presentation of beauty in contrasts.

More romantic still: It was snowing.

Confetti flakes fell from the sky, piling up all around them and frosting the top of the gray-glass globe. It looked like a lost ornament, fallen and frozen in the snow of a holiday season. The more Alice looked at this black-and-white scene, the more she began to appreciate the subtleties of light and shadow, and though Alice eventually found it quite lovely, it was also entirely foreign to her. They were not in the painting she'd chosen—the painting she'd chosen had been rich in autumnal colors—which had to mean that they'd not been refused access to the painter.

They'd not been refused.

Oh, the shock of it. Alice thought she might scream.

So she did just that. She fell back in the snow and she shouted for joy and she grabbed Oliver's arm and said, "This isn't the painting I picked—this isn't the one! The one I picked was in a meadow, and it was autumn, and there were leaves on the ground, and there were little homes everywhere, and, oh, Oliver," she said. "We made it!"

Oliver sat down beside her, looking solemn but kind, and wrapped his arm around her shoulders. "Yes," he said softly. "I daresay we have."

They hugged, he and she, for a very long time, just clinging to each other, happy to be alive; grateful to have survived yet another stage of Furthermore. It was starting to wear on them now, nearly dying all the time. Alice promised herself that if they made it back to Ferenwood she would never again complain about a lack of adventure. She would be perfectly happy with a walk to the town square and a peek at the boats in Penelope's garden. She tried to convince herself that it would be enough for her, that she could be happy with a simple, safe life tethered to Ferenwood, but even now, at the tail end of a crisis, she couldn't quite manage it. Because she knew that wasn't true. She wanted to go home, yes, and she wanted to spend more time with Father and she wanted to eat tulips and sit by the pond, but even after all the trials and tribulations of Furthermore—or perhaps because of them—she didn't think she could ever go back to an ordinary life. She knew she'd never say no to adventure.

Alice broke away from Oliver and beamed at him.

"Don't just park your hindquarters in the snow," someone barked at them. "Good grief, girl, you'll catch your death out there!"

Alice and Oliver looked up to discover a man scowling at them. He looked human enough, but the distance between his world and theirs seemed infinite. She realized then that a man in black and white seems impossibly gray, and even more impossible to reach; it was almost as though he existed in a different dimension.

Something was nagging at the back of Alice's mind.

A bit of conversation.

Something Tim had told her.

"Hey! I'm talking to you," the man shouted again, and Alice sprang to attention. The man was brandishing a cane at the two of them. Alice noticed that he had a scruffy black beard and wore a wool cap that pushed down over his eyes, and between his lips was an unlit pipe, and as he talked, it bobbed around in his mouth.

"Sitting in the snow in a silk gown," he grumbled. "Up, the lot of you," he said, poking Oliver with his cane. "Get inside."

She and Oliver stumbled to their feet and stared at the man.

"Are you—?" she started to say.

"Of course I am," he said. "Do you see anyone else here?

Now hurry up," he said. "I've put the kettle on, and it'll be whistling by now."

They did as they were told and followed the old man toward the half-globe home. The man stopped short a few feet and then began to disappear from his ankles up; it was only as she got closer that Alice realized he was walking down a set of stairs.

They quickly followed his lead.

It was him, then her, then Oliver, disappearing into the ground only to then climb their way back up; except when they finally faced a door, it opened from overhead.

Alice stomped the snow off her feet as they climbed and, as they crossed the threshold up and into the glass home, she did her best not to trail any dirt or wet onto the old man's floor.

Suddenly, she and Oliver were standing in the middle of a clear dome, and looking out at the snowy world from the comfort of a toasty, cozy sanctuary.

As promised, the kettle had already begun to whistle. The old man moved quickly and easily for someone who carried a cane, and she wondered for a moment why he carried it. She noticed then that there was no real kitchen, no living room or bedroom, but one big space where everything sat out in the open; there were no secrets here, no closed doors, no walls or windows.

All the furniture was minimal and spare: clean lines and simple frames, black seat cushions, gray pillows and a threadbare blanket that was neatly folded and placed atop a bed. Solid shades of gray dotted her vision; this home was a place where colors did not exist and patterns were not made. It was steady, sturdy, and extremely tidy. The rug underfoot was soft and gray and fluffy, and not bothered by a single spot.

Alice and Oliver weren't sure what to do with themselves.

It was a strange home for a painter, stranger still that there was no sign of his paintings anywhere. Alice cleared her throat, rocked back and forth on the balls of her feet, and waited for the old man to return.

He came forward with fast, heavy footfalls—now moving without the assistance of his cane—holding two cups of hot tea that spilled into their saucers with his every step, and set them down on a small table around which a large couch and a few chairs had gathered. No cream, no sugar, no please or thank you.

"Well, sit down, then," said the man, looking from her to Oliver, obviously irritated. He pulled the wool cap off his head to reveal a rather large tuft of dark hair that stuck straight up before falling into his face, and as she and Oliver tentatively took their seats, so did he.

He seemed much younger than Alice had originally thought he was. In fact, she was fairly certain he wasn't old at all. He was just crabby. She tried to get a better look at his face, but he'd ducked his chin into his chest, and his eyes were now partially obscured by his hair. Alice sat back, confused.

It was coming back to her now—her conversations with Tim—and she looked around, carefully cataloguing all the gray. There was not a spot of bright color anywhere, and Alice was growing more convinced by the moment:

This must be a prison village.

But how could it be? Could the painter also be an inmate? Alice wasn't sure. She didn't know Furthermore well enough to know whether this was possible.

Alice looked to Oliver and nearly told him what she was thinking (she was thinking that if this *was* a prison village, that perhaps this man might be able to tell her how to find Father), but fear had made her too afraid to hope, so she kept her theories to herself.

Oliver cleared his throat.

The painter crossed his legs and leaned back in his chair (she noticed then that he wore thick wool socks), and leveled them with a stare she couldn't quite match. Alice felt too open, too vulnerable and bright-eyed, so she looked away.

"So you've come about your arm, then?" he said to her.

Alice nodded.

"And how did you manage to lose it?" he said.

She blinked up at him, then looked down again, frowning.

"I—well, I made a mistake," she said, digging the toe of her shoe into the carpet.

"What kind of mistake?" he said.

"I followed a paper fox," Alice said quietly. "My right arm turned to paper." She hesitated. "And then the fox ripped my arm off." Alice didn't know why she was speaking so stiltedly or, more importantly, she didn't know why the painter made her so nervous, but her hand was sweating and her heart was pounding and her emotions were trying to tell her something she couldn't yet hear.

The painter laughed a loud, humorless laugh. "You followed a paper fox and got your arm ripped off." He sighed. "Yep. Sounds about right."

His voice was rough from lack of use, but there was something about it that made Alice feel like she was overheating. Something in it—somewhere in the rustiness—that reminded her of something, of someone she could not place—

"What's your name?" he said, tilting his head, and for just a moment, his hair shifted out of his eyes.

Alice thought she might collapse.

"Oliver," she cried. "Oliver—"

"Your name is Oliver? That's a strange name for a girl."

"*My* name is Oliver," said Oliver, who'd jumped up and was now looking anxiously at Alice. "What's wrong?" he said to her. "What's the matter?"

But Alice couldn't get the words out. She was seeing spots; she thought her throat might close up.

"Alice?" said Oliver, panicking. "Alice, what are you—"

"Her name is Alice?" said the painter, who was now on his feet.

"*Father*," she gasped. "*Father*."

And then she fainted.

I don't know how much time elapsed between when she fell and when she woke—Oliver says it was at least several minutes—but when Alice finally blinked open her eyes, they'd already filled to the brim with tears.

Alice Alexis Queensmeadow had finally found Father.

Accidentally, unintentionally (serendipitously), Alice had found Father and she was unsinkably happy.

Their reunion was long and joyous; tears were shed, laughter was shared, stories were recounted from all. Alice's and Oliver's stories are already familiar to you, so I won't bother relating them again, but Father's story was new, and certainly new to you, too, so I'll do my best to remember exactly what was said. However, before I do, I'd like to address one detail that must be bothering you:

Strange, you must think, that Father hadn't recognized Alice himself.

You are wise to wonder so. And when Alice first told me how it all happened, I thought it strange, too. But we must remember that Father had been locked away for three Ferenwood years in the heart of an impossible land. Father had never dreamed—never dared to think it possible—that his young daughter would, firstly, know a single thing about Furthermore and, secondly, have survived long enough to find him, when he, a grown man, had barely survived himself. He had never dreamed Alice might show up. In fact, when Father saw Alice and Oliver requesting permission to enter his village, he accepted their request solely because the young girl he saw—her white hair, her white skin—reminded him a great deal of his own daughter.

Alice, too, had no idea how much she'd changed since the last time she'd seen him. The girl who sat in front of Father now was a girl greatly changed from the nine-year-old Father remembered. This new Alice was confident and bold; she was articulate and passionate; she had become the kind of person who'd lived through hardship and survived with grace. Father hardly recognized her. Though it took very little encouragement for him to be reminded.

Now, let us return to their reunion.

As you might imagine, Alice and Oliver had thousands of questions for Father. What happened after he arrived in Furthermore? Why had he come? Why hadn't he told anyone?

What happened to get him stuck? Was he really a spy? And so forth. But as their conversations were exhaustive, rerouted by endless tangents, and punctuated by waves of tears and silent embraces, I will, in the interest of expediency, make an effort to summarize all that was said in a short set of paragraphs.

Father had indeed been arrested for wasting time, and Enslaved Imprisonment was indeed his punishment. He was sentenced to the prison village of Ink, which was where he'd been isolated ever since. It was a comfortable setup—he had his own home and he wasn't wearing shackles—but what was life without color? No friends, no family (not even a cellmate!), not a single thing to read. Father had been desperately depressed and lonely. He'd grown gruff and angry, and his bitterness made him reject nearly every job request he'd received. Being a painter, you see, was his enslavement. He was forced to do labor for Furthermore as a means of penance, and in this case, it was painting new limbs for those who'd lost them. Occasionally Father would paint someone a leg instead of an arm, or a finger instead of a toe, just to keep things interesting, but mostly it was a tedium of the same, boring work. "You'd be surprised," he said, "how many people lose limbs in Furthermore."

But Father's greater story began many moons back, beginning with his own Surrender and with the task he'd been tasked by the Ferenwood Elders. Father, as you know, had been sent to map the many magical lands and, after having lived and survived in Furthermore so long, he thought he'd have no trouble surviving again. "What I didn't realize," he said, "was that my brain was different when I was younger. I was successful because my mind was nimble and my ideas about the world were flexible. The tricks and twists of Furthermore were easier to navigate." He sighed. "But as I got older, I became more set in my ways. It was harder to think differently and it took me longer to figure everything out. I had so much more to lose this time around, and the fear crippled me. I was too nervous, too careful. I made too many mistakes." He shook his head. "I never should've come back. I wouldn't have dared if I didn't think it would be worth it."

Oliver, you see, had been right about why Father returned to Furthermore. He was no spy for Ferenwood.

His effort was entirely for Alice. Always for Alice.

This, dear reader, was the most difficult conversation for the group of them to get through, because there was so much emotion to contend with. Alice was devastated to have been the reason Father had put himself in danger. After all, Father had never *wanted* Alice to change—he'd only wanted her to be happy—and it broke her heart to think of all he'd risked for her. Thankfully, her hurts were healing quickly.

And Alice was learning to be happy.

Alice knew that being different would always be difficult;

she knew that there was no magic that would erase narrow-mindedness or iron out the inequities in life. But Alice was also beginning to learn that life was never lived in absolutes. People would both love her and rebuff her; they would show both kindness and prejudice. The simple truth was that Alice would always be different—but to be different was to be extraordinary, and to be extraordinary was an adventure. It no longer mattered how the world saw her; what mattered was how Alice saw herself.

Alice would choose to love herself, different and extraordinary, every day of the week.

Dear reader: I do hope you enjoy a happy ending.

We are coming upon the last bit of our story now—the bit where Father and Alice and Oliver finally return home—and I'm feeling bittersweet about it.

Father, as you might imagine, fixed Alice's arm in a pinch, and she was a fully limbed young lady once more. Alice, for her part, very deftly magicked the village of Ink into a land absolutely drenched in color, and Father was reimagined into an even more stunning iteration of his former self. Oliver, good sport that he was, tapped open his magical box with its little door, and they three clambered in, one after the other, and soon, very soon, they were right back where they started, back home in Ferenwood.

A great deal of time had passed while they journeyed through Furthermore, though Alice didn't know how much. All she knew was that it was winter in Ferenwood, which meant they'd been gone not quite a full year. Snow had descended upon the land in their absence, icing the many hills and valleys in a neat layer of white. Thousands of trees had attempted to shiver their branches free of frost, and when she squinted, Alice could see their green skeletons peeking through. Chimneys chugged atop warmly lit homes, and the town was still, and they three were silent, and Alice exhaled as she closed her eyes. She had never been more grateful for this town or for this life, and she never again wanted to take it for granted. She was happy to be home and happy to have a home. And she couldn't wait to see Mother's reaction, Mother who didn't know Father was here.

Alice and Oliver hugged each other tightly as they said their good-byes, and Oliver promised to come over the very next day to help her build an igloo and make plans for the spring. Oliver would be moving on to upper-level schooling now that he'd completed his Surrender, but Alice had no idea what she'd do next. Father was surprised to hear her say so.

"But, Alice," he said. "Didn't you say you received a black card? For failing your Surrender?"

"Yes," said Alice quietly. She ducked her head. "I did."

Father lifted Alice's chin and looked her in the eye. "That's nothing to be ashamed of. A black card just means you get another try the following year. Did you never unlock it?"

"What?" she said, hardly daring to breathe. "I get to try again? I get to do my Surrender over?"

"Of course you do," said Father, smiling. "What did you think would happen? Did you think the Elders would toss you out of Ferenwood?"

"Well, yes," said Alice. "I thought they might."

"I told you," Oliver said, beaming. "Didn't I? I told you to unlock it earlier—I told you you were supposed to unlock it but you didn't listen to me."

Alice went pink. "Alright," she said. "You were right."

"I'm glad I was right," said Oliver, who was grinning from ear to ear.

And then, finally, it was time for Oliver to go home. He hugged Alice once more, then hugged Father, too, and then he ran as best he could through the snow. "I'll see you tomorrow!" he called over his shoulder.

"I can't wait!" Alice called back.

And then she took Father's hand in hers, and Alice decided she would never, ever lose him again.

Alice and Father stood together quietly just outside their little home, each lost in their own thoughts. The house was just as Alice had left it (save the snow that iced the roof and blanketed the ground); and the chimney puffed gently in the soft evening light, and the windows were lit from the life within. It was a warm, welcoming sight.

But suddenly Alice was nervous.

Alice knew how Mother would react to seeing Father again, but she didn't know how Mother would react to seeing *her* again—and this new unknown frightened her. After all, Alice had run off without saying a single good-bye; she couldn't expect Mother to be forgiving. What about the ferenberries? What about the washing and the mending? What about the shame she'd brought upon her family by failing the Surrender? Mother was sure to be *livid*. Alice was certain that when the front door opened, she would be met with anger and punishment and crushing disappointment, and it almost made her wish she hadn't come.

For a moment Alice wondered whether she shouldn't run straight to Oliver's house and hide until Father could smooth things over—but she didn't think Father would allow it. In any case, Alice could no longer dawdle. Father was eager to go inside, and Alice couldn't deny him such a simple request. Not after everything he'd been through.

Father squeezed her hand and gave her an encouraging look and said, "Are you ready, darling? Shall we go in together?"

But Alice shook her head—she knew she should face Mother alone. (Though perhaps after Mother had her fill of yelling and screaming, Alice would call Father inside to save her.)

So Alice told Father her plan. Well, part of it.

"This way, it'll be a surprise," she said. "How Mother will cry when she sees you!"

Father laughed. "Very well," he said. "If that's what you prefer."

Alice nodded, Father hid, and the two of them shared a wink before Alice walked up to the front door. Then, after only a moment's hesitation, Alice knocked twice. Once for her and once for Father. (It was Furthermore tradition, after all.)

A moment later, the front door swung open.

Mother was exactly as Alice remembered her—beautiful and elegant and desperately sad. Her green corkscrew curls had sprung free of their ponytail, making her golden eyes seem somehow bigger and lonelier. Alice felt a sharp tug at her heart as she locked eyes with Mother, and both of them were suddenly still. Well, Alice was still. Mother appeared to be frozen.

"Alice?" she whispered.

"Hello Mother." Alice attempted a smile, but quickly dropped her head and shrank inward lest Mother should think she was being deliberately insolent. Alice swallowed hard and braced herself for the imminent onslaught of anger, determined to be brave for Father once more.

But then, dear friends, the strangest thing happened.

Mother fell to her knees.

She threw her arms around her daughter and pulled her tight to her chest and wept, long and loud. Mother's pain felt real and hot against Alice's small body, and Alice could almost *hear* Mother coming untethered, tears cracking open ribs to let the pain pass through. "I'm sorry," Mother cried. "I'm so sorry. Please don't ever run away again. Please forgive me."

"But, Mother—" Alice tried to say.

"I blamed you," she said. "I knew why Father left and I blamed you for it and I'm sorry. I'm so sorry."

"You knew?" said Alice, stunned. "You knew why he left?"

Mother looked up at Alice, eyes red-rimmed and puffy, and nodded. "He went to find color for you. He thought—he thought it would make you happy. But when he never came back, I blamed you for it." She shook her head. "I treated you horribly. Please forgive me, Alice. I can't bear to lose you both."

"But you haven't lost us, Mother," said Alice softly. "You never did."

Alice stepped backward to let Father step forward, and she wandered off in a daze, her head heavy and swimming with truths newly collected. For Alice, who'd only ever wanted to be loved and cared for, Mother's confession was a revelation. And a curious life lesson. She and Mother had both loved Father dearly; but though this love had carried Alice, it had crushed Mother, and this was a power she hadn't known a heart could possess.

Love, it turned out, could both hurt and heal.

Strange.

"I told you she loved you," said a familiar voice.

Alice was so startled she jumped nearly a foot in the air. "Why Oliver Newbanks!" she shout-whispered. "How dare you spy on me!" (But she was secretly pleased to see him.)

"I just wanted to make sure you were alright," he said, smiling. "I knew this would be a hard moment for you." The sun was setting overhead, making the sky look as if it'd been slit open to rush the sunshine out. Oliver appeared to be glowing in the halo.

"I am," said Alice, but she was quiet about it. Thoughtful.

"What is it?" Oliver said, studying her. "What are you thinking?"

"I'm going to redo my Surrender, you know." She sighed. "In the spring. And I'll finally have a task of my own."

"Of course you will," said Oliver, beaming. "And you'll do splendidly."

"Well," she said, examining her fingers. "I might be gone a very long time."

Oliver's smile slipped. He cleared his throat and said, "Right. Of course."

"So," said Alice, looking off into the distance. "I was wondering if you'd come with me."

Oliver blinked, surprised.

"I mean you don't have to," Alice said quickly. "Firstly it's illegal and secondly I know you'll be busy with other th—"

"I wouldn't miss it," he said. "Not for anything."

And Oliver smiled and Alice smiled back, and she looked up at the sky and wondered, as she closed her eyes, how this small, cluttered world had managed to make room for all her happiness. Father was home and Mother was kind and Alice and Oliver would be friends for a very long time and that, as they say, was that.

Or at least it is all I will say on the subject.

Until next time, dear reader.

THE END

Reader, you don't have to leave the world of FURTHERMORE quite yet. Turn the page for a peek into Tahereh Mafi's next darkly enchanting tale:

Infant snow drifted down in gentle whorls, flakes as large as pancakes glinting silver as they fell. Shaggy trees wore white leaves and moonlight glimmered across a glassy lake. The night was soft and all was slow and snow had hushed the earth into a deep, sound slumber and oh, winter was fast approaching.

For the town of Whichwood, winter was a welcome distraction; they thrived in the cold and delighted in the ice (the very first snowfall was terribly nice), and they were well equipped with food and festivities to keep toasty throughout the season. *Yalda,* the biggest celebration, was the winter solstice, and the land of Whichwood was electric with anticipation. Whichwood was a distinctly magical village, and Yalda—the town's most important holiday—was a very densely magical evening. Yalda was the last night of fall and the longest night of the year; it was a time of gift-giving and tea-drinking and endless feasting—and it was a great deal more than that, too. We're a bit pressed for minutes at the moment (something strange is soon to happen and I can't be distracted when it does), so we'll discuss the finer details at a later time. For now, know this: Every new snowfall arrived with a foot of fresh excitement, and with only two days left till winter, the people of Whichwood could scarcely contain their joy.

With a single notable exception.

There was only one person in Whichwood who never partook in the town merriment. Only one person who drew closed her curtains and cursed the song and dance of a magical evening. And she was a very strange person indeed.

Laylee hated the cold.

At thirteen years old, she'd long lost that precious, relentless optimism reserved almost exclusively for young people. She'd no sense of whimsy, no interest in decadence, no tolerance for niceties. No, Laylee hated the frost and she hated the fuss and she resented not only this holiday season, but even those who loved it. (To be fair, Laylee resented many things—not the least of which was her lot in life—but winter was the thing she resented perhaps most of all.)

Come sleet or snow, she alone was forced to work long hours in the cold, her kneecaps icing over as she dragged dead bodies into a large porcelain tub in her backyard. She'd scrub limp necks and broken legs and dirty fingernails until her own fingers froze solid, and then she'd hang those dead, dragging limbs up to dry—only to later return and break icicles off corpse chins and noses. Laylee had no holidays, no vacations, not even a set schedule. She worked when her customers came calling, which meant very soon she'd be worked to the bone. Winter in Whichwood, you see, was a very popular season for dying.

Tonight, Laylee was found frowning (her expression of choice), irritated (perhaps more than usual), bundled (to the point of asphyxiation), and stubbornly determined to catch a few snowflakes before dinner. Fresh flakes were the thickest and the crispest, and a rare treat if you were quick enough to catch a few.

If I may: I know it seems a strange idea, eating snowflakes for dinner, but you have to understand—Laylee Layla Fenjoon was a very strange girl, and despite (or perhaps because of) the oddness of her occupation, she was in desperate need of a treat. She'd had to wash nine very large, thoroughly rotted persons today—this was four more than usual—and it had been very hard on her. Indeed, she often caught herself dreaming of a life where her family didn't run a laundering business for the deceased.

Well, I say *family,* but it was really just Laylee doing all the washing. Maman had died two years prior (a cockroach had fallen in the samovar and Maman, unwittingly, drank the tea; it was all very tragic), but Laylee was not afforded the opportunity to grieve. Most ghosts moved on after a good scrubbing, you see, but Maman's had lingered, floating about the halls and criticizing Laylee's best work even when she was sleeping. Baba, too, was entirely absent, as he'd been gone just as long as Maman had been dead. Devastated by the loss of his wife, he'd set off on an impulsive journey not two days after Maman died, determined to find Death and give him a firm talking-to about his recent choices.

Sadly, Death was nowhere to be found.

Worse, grief had so thoroughly crippled Baba's mind that, despite his two-year absence, thus far he'd managed to travel only as far as the city center. In his heartbreak he'd lost not only his way, but his good sense, too. Baba's brain had rearranged, and in the madness and chaos of loss, no room remained for his only child. Laylee was collateral damage in a war on grief, and Baba, who had no hope of winning such a war, haplessly succumbed to this opiate of oblivion. Laylee would often pass her disoriented father on her sojourns into town, pat his shoulder in a show of support, and tuck a pomegranate into his pocket.

More on that later.

For now, let us focus: It was a cold, lonely night, and Laylee had just collected the last of her dinner when a sudden sound froze her still. Two loud thumps, a branch snap, a dull thud, the unmistakable intake of air and a sudden rush of angry whispers—

No, there was no denying it: There were trespassers here.

Now, this would have been an alarming revelation for any normal person, but as Laylee was a distinctly abnormal person, she remained unperturbed. She was, however, perplexed.

The thing was, no persons *ever* came here, and heaven help them if they did; stumbling upon a shed of swollen, rotting corpses had never done any person any good. It was for this reason that Laylee and her family lived in relative isolation. They had taken up residence in a small, drafty castle on a little peninsula on the outer edge of town in an informal sort of exile; it was an unkindness Laylee and her family had not earned, but then, no one wanted to live next door to the girl with such an unfortunate occupation.

In any case, Laylee was entirely unaccustomed to hearing human voices so close to home, and it made her suspicious. Her head high and alert, Laylee stacked her snowflakes into an ornate silver dinnerbox—an old family heirloom—and tiptoed out of sight.

Laylee wasn't a child oft bothered by the fuss and furor of fear; no, she dealt with death every day, and so the unknowns that startled most had little effect on a person who could talk to ghosts. (This last bit was a secret, of course—Laylee knew better than to tell her townspeople that she could see and speak with the spirits of their loved ones; she had no interest in being asked to do more work than was already stacked in her shed.) So as she trod cautiously back toward the modest castle that was her home, she felt not fear, but a tickle of curiosity, and as the feeling warmed itself inside her heart, she blinked, grateful and surprised to feel a smile spreading across her face.